DISARRHOEA

DISARRHOEA

KEVIN VODDEN

Published through Kindle Direct Publishing

© Kevin Vodden 2022

All rights reserved. No part of this publication may be reproduced or transmitted in any form or by any means without permission in writing from the author, except by a reviewer, who may quote brief passages in a review.

ISBN: 9798837233630

Cover design by Kevin Vodden

CONTENTS

Disarrhoea ... 7
Fearground ... 87
Terror Pericolosa ... 125
The Matryoshka Loop ... 213
Eat Thy Neighbour ... 261
Credit Where Credit's Due ... 289

DISARRHOEA

Disarrhoea, they call it. I've no idea where the name came from, any more than I know where the sickness came from. Three days on, the only certainty is that we're trapped in our home like everyone else – except for those helpless souls outside.

TV and radio programming are sporadic, and the internet is inundated with reports and images of tragedy and despair. Every news source raises more questions than it answers. There's little verifiable information and no practical advice, but the consensus across all media is that it's not safe to go out. If we set foot outside, there'll almost certainly be no way back.

It's been two days since Jess ventured out and involuntarily joined what's been dubbed the Legion of the Lost.

Meanwhile, I'm upstairs, cocooned in my room with my laptop, phone, chargers and other essentials for bunker survival, thanks to Keira and Coen, who don't seem to have been affected yet.

Other than searching for and sharing the latest news, there's little that I can do in my condition, so I'm devoting my Wednesday evening to recording the events that have unfolded in the last three days. Once that's up to date I'll keep a daily log, in case anyone wants to know in the aftermath what happened in this house – and in case I'm not around to tell the tale. I've decided to type this, rather than make audio or video recordings, as I don't want to alarm the children with anything that they might overhear and don't need to know about.

To my intense irritation as a journalist, my typing is frustratingly slow and I'm relying heavily on autocomplete. Nevertheless, I'm determined to persist with this, if only to give myself some sense of purpose, as I've been rendered redundant in virtually every other respect.

Stay at home, they say, and keep your doors and windows sealed – nothing about how to get medical attention or what to do if you run out of food. Fortunately, we have sufficient supplies to get us through another week; and the water, electricity and internet are so far unaffected. Let's hope we don't lose any of those between now and whenever this invisible menace releases us from our purgatory – if it ever does.

Day 1 (Sunday)

I'll designate Sunday as Day 1, since the first extraordinary occurrence was a car colliding head-on with a lamp post directly across the road.

'Just a drunk,' Jess quipped, even though it was four in the afternoon.

Ice couldn't have been a factor. The shivering puddles indicated that the temperature was still above freezing.

We hadn't been outside all day ourselves. The weekend's washing and shopping had been done, the bin didn't need emptying, and it was one of those Sundays when we were resolved to prevent the slightest wintry draft from invading our cosy habitat.

Jess and I stood and watched from the lounge room as the young driver clawed her way up the inside of her open car door and hooked both arms over the top. Failed by her buckling legs, she wedged herself nervously between the door and the frame.

In the background, faces flickered behind quivering curtains and blinds, while dusky outlines lurked in darkened doorways.

We hadn't even considered going out to offer assistance when Yasmin marched down next door's garden path and strode across the road, leaving Archie scurrying in her slipstream. On approaching the car, she tapped her chest and gestured towards her husband while uttering something to the young woman by way of an introduction. She then proceeded to carefully prise the driver out of her predicament before guiding her to the kerbside. The two of them sat down together, exchanged a few words, and then Yasmin pulled her phone out and made a call. Archie found a jacket on the back seat and draped it over the shoulders of the woman, who was visibly shaken and shivering – either from the cold or shock, or both.

Curtains and blinds flicked back into place, and doors swung shut as our fellow observers withdrew, apparently satisfied, as we were, that there had been no serious injury and Yasmin and Archie had the matter well in hand. Jess and I returned to the sofa, from where we only had to crane our necks slightly every now and then to see Yasmin and Archie still sitting on either side of the driver, presumably waiting for assistance.

It was a good thirty minutes before flashing blue lights prompted our return to the window, along with several of our neighbours.

After a superficial examination, the two attending paramedics sat down on either side of the woman.

Archie and Yasmin had shuffled to their respective sides to allow the pair access, and so found themselves perched at the ends of a somewhat tragicomical-looking row of five. We expected the medics to fetch a stretcher and transport their patient away, but instead they sat gazing at the ground in front of them, exactly as the other three had for the previous half hour.

Eventually the male medic stood up, strolled with no sense of urgency to the back of the ambulance, casually opened the rear door and stepped inside.

A minute later his colleague stretched her arms out horizontally in front of her, as if about to commence an aerobic exercise. She leaned forward, rose with imperfect balance and, without paying any further attention to the accident victim, made her way around the blind side of the vehicle, reappearing briefly at the back and then disappearing, leaving the rear door open.

There was no further activity for about twenty minutes, other than the twitching of curtains and blinds, and no sign of the ambulance crew as Yasmin, Archie and the driver remained seated, one space apart from each other, looking bewildered and seemingly discussing little as daylight faded.

Finally a decision was made. First Archie, then Yasmin straightened up and helped the young woman to her feet. Arms were linked as each appeared to be reliant on the others for support. Then, instead of turning in a line towards the ambulance, they closed in to form a wobbly six-footed tripod – or hexapod, I suppose – and zigzagged across the road towards Yasmin and Archie's open gate. Once at the gate posts, it was a full five minutes before they broke formation to pass through in single file and make their way up the footpath, holding hands but with an almost comedic lack of coordination.

Jess gave them a few minutes to settle into the house before phoning Yasmin to check that everything was OK. Yasmin told her that the driver didn't know why she'd veered into the lamp post. She said she felt as though she was steering straight down the road until the point of impact. The ambulance crew checked her over, as we saw, and found no injuries, so they didn't think it was necessary to take her to the hospital. Yasmin said that both the paramedics seemed rather vague, and she didn't know why the man got up and walked off without a word. His colleague said that she wondered where he'd gone, and she went to look for him. That was the last they saw of either of them. Meanwhile, Yasmin had called for roadside assistance, but it seemed that they were busier than usual and couldn't send anyone out before the next morning. Yasmin and Archie waited a while longer to see if anything was happening with the ambulance before deciding to go indoors to warm up and have a cup of tea. Yasmin also told Jess that she and Archie were feeling strange. It was obvious to us from the outset that the driver was unsteady, but it was odd that Yasmin and Archie should also be staggering on their way back to the house. Yasmin said that they were going to decide what else to do after they'd had some tea and biscuits, and Jess told her to let us know if we could do anything to help.

The ambulance didn't move for the rest of the evening, and we didn't see either of the paramedics again.

We learned from the local evening news that there

had been a spate of road accidents throughout the region all afternoon – vehicles colliding and pedestrians and cyclists being knocked down. How coincidental, we thought, that we'd had an incident in our street, too.

Dinner followed the end of the news at 6.30, then Jess and I watched a couple of sitcoms, while Keira and Coen amused themselves at the foot of the stairs with zoo animals, dinosaurs and the new set of building blocks that Grandma Emily had given Coen for his fifth birthday.

Distracted from the afternoon's occurrences by an hour of canned laughter, interspersed with cries of 'Stairquake!' accompanied by crashing, roaring and squealing, we didn't think of switching channels for a news update before going to bed ahead of another week of work and school. We were sure that the woman was being cared for next door, and her car didn't seem too badly damaged and would probably be towed away the next morning. Three days later, though, the car is still there, and so is the ambulance.

Day 2 (Monday)

I was woken before the 6.30 alarm by Jess's agitated voice downstairs. Remembering the previous day's drama, I slipped out of bed, went over to the window and peered through the curtains. I was surprised to see the ambulance still there, with its side and rear doors open, just as they were the night before – and there were two other vehicles adding to the congestion, also apparently abandoned with their doors open.

Across the road, the elderly couple at number 39

were standing on their doorstep, surveying the scene – she with her hands on her hips, and he scratching his head. They looked quizzically at each other, exchanged a word or two, and then he set off down the pathway. Two thirds of the way to the gate he hesitated, turned to look back at his wife, and then sat down cross-legged. She raised her hands to her cheeks and promptly made her way towards him. After stopping for a moment a few strides short of her husband, she managed five or six more small steps and sat down next to him, tucking her knees under her chin and wrapping her arms around her legs. It was the strangest sight – they just sat there looking at each other, then at the ground, then at each other, and at the ground again. Intrigued as I was, I was even more curious to know who Jess was talking to at that time in the morning, so I left the curtains slightly parted, donned my dressing gown and went downstairs.

She was speaking to her sister, Meaghan. I couldn't make much sense of Jess's side of the conversation: '… motion sickness … call a doctor … call me if you hear from her first, and I'll call you if I hear from her …,' so I popped two slices in the toaster, flicked the kettle on and went about my morning routine while waiting for the full story.

Halfway through my first slice of toast, Jess placed her phone on the table. She told me that she'd been up for over an hour and was worried about what she'd seen on the breakfast news. She'd tried to phone her mother to check that she was all right, but there was no answer, so she called Meaghan to ask if she'd heard from her. Meaghan hadn't, but she told Jess that she herself had symptoms similar to those that Jess had described to her, and as described on the news.

Meaghan said that she'd spent about half an hour around mid-afternoon on Sunday tidying up the garden, but had come in earlier than intended because she'd begun to feel unwell, as if she had a mild form of motion sickness. She watched TV for a while, but didn't feel any better, so she went to bed early, feeling strangely disorientated. Her partner, Sam, was away on Sunday, but was rostered on a returning overnight flight that was due to land early on Monday morning. Anyway, that was the gist of the call, and they agreed to let each other know as soon as either of them had managed to contact their mother.

I was a few minutes behind with my breakfast, even though I'd got up before the alarm, so I gulped down the last of my tea and toast and dashed upstairs to get dressed for work, leaving Jess to prepare the children's breakfast.

When I came back down just before seven, giving the kids a rousing shout as I passed their room, and skimming Jess's cheek en route to the garage, I couldn't have imagined how much our world was about to change.

With my seat belt fastened, I reached down for the remote control, opened the garage door, started the engine, shifted into reverse, checked the rear-view mirror, blinked to verify what I'd seen, turned round for another look, slipped back into neutral and turned the engine off. The end of our driveway was blocked by a large, white van parked askew with one front wheel on the footpath and its driver's door open. It wasn't there ten minutes earlier when I looked out of the bedroom window to check on the elderly couple still sitting on their footpath.

I stepped out of the car and walked down to the

end of the driveway, from where I could see several more vehicles parked haphazardly up and down the road in both directions. Some of them appeared to have run into others and were obstructing the entire street, which probably explained why the ambulance was still there. Meanwhile, the old man at number 39 was observing me between fists clenched around the bars of his gate.

Within a minute I began to feel light-headed, so instead of looking for the owner of the van to ask him or her to move it, I went back into the house to tell Jess what I'd seen. Clipping my knuckles on the back of the car on the way in and then scuffing my shoe against the shelving unit didn't seem significant at the time. With hindsight, though, leaving the garage shutter up and the internal door ajar was a mistake.

Once inside, I perched on the arm of the sofa, feeling decidedly queasy. I told Jess what was happening – not that I really knew – and she went out to have a look for herself. A minute later she stumbled in, slammed the door behind her and slumped down beside me on the sofa.

Suspecting that we'd been affected by something in the air outside, we agreed that we should close the garage, lock the connecting door and keep the rest of the doors and windows secured, upstairs and down, until we knew more.

When Keira and Coen came downstairs, our consternation must have been obvious, because Keira asked us what was up. I told them that they might not be going to school, as something was happening outside. With little more than a shrug and barely a glance through the window, they took their places at the dining table and set about their cereals as usual.

Jess tried again to phone her mother, but there was still no answer.

Meanwhile, I unmuted the TV to find out more about the chaotic images that I was seeing. There were accounts of widespread congestion on roads all along the east coast – north and south of us. Vehicles had been abandoned and people were wandering around aimlessly because they were incapable of driving or even walking straight. As to the cause, speculation at that stage centred on a suspected chemical leak – either an unreported accident or a deliberate act. However, it was thought unlikely that an accident on such a scale would not have been reported – unless it had and was being covered up. The general advice, albeit from no official source, was to stay at home and keep all doors and windows closed in case of airborne contamination.

After about fifteen minutes we muted the TV and turned our attention to social media to see what the reaction was to the morning's news. Stories, photos and videos had been posted of traffic at a standstill and drivers staggering out of their vehicles, but it wasn't yet clear how widespread the contamination was or what the cause was. Was it a chemical spill or a terrorist attack ... or the start of another pandemic?

I called my boss to say that I wasn't able to get the car out of the driveway, plus I wasn't feeling well. She said she couldn't get beyond the end of the street herself, so she reversed back home. She intended to stay put until she knew more, and we agreed that I should, too.

Jess tried to phone the school a few times between 7.30 and eight, but the out-of-hours message was still activated.

Meaghan called back shortly after eight. Sam should have been on her way home by then, but she'd just called to say that she wasn't feeling well and was resting in the airport lounge for a while before going to catch a bus. The symptoms that Sam described to Meaghan were similar to ours.

Jess and I spent the rest of the morning either online, in front of the TV or on the phone, updating and getting updates from relatives and friends. Some, like us, had been outside and described similar physical effects. Others hadn't and were so far unaffected.

Most of the morning's communication was with Meaghan, who, while having no news of Emily, gave us frequent updates from Sam, who was unable to find a way home, as there were no buses running, and the taxis parked outside were either unoccupied or the drivers had no intention of opening their doors. As the morning wore on, the airport became increasingly crowded with streams of long-haul passengers feeling unwell on arrival and having no means of onward transport, or no inclination to leave the building. There was also a shortage of staff, presumably due to illness or the unavailability of public transport.

I called my sister, Naomi, some time after nine to tell her what had been happening in our street since the previous afternoon and find out how she, Damon and Casey were. She said she'd seen a few 'funny' posts before going to bed on Sunday night, but she and Damon didn't generally watch the evening news, so they weren't aware of what had been going on until they woke up on Monday morning and turned the TV on. I asked her if they'd opened any doors or windows. Fortunately, Damon wasn't on the early shift, so he hadn't gone out and they hadn't opened anything. I advised them to keep everything shut, which they had anyway after seeing the morning's news, even though they're two hours' drive away from us and no-one knew at the time how localised this thing was.

It's hard to remember the exact sequence of events from two days ago, as so much was going on, but there were a few text messages from Naomi after our phone call, which give an idea of the timeline:

09.46: *All doors and windows locked but tiberius went out through the cat flap hope hell be ok.*

11.12: *Tiberius is back stumbling around in the garden sniffing and pawing the walls and door like he cant find the cat flap i wont risk going out to get him hell have to find his own way in.* Then: *Keeps meowing.*

11.35: *He kept rubbing himself against the door till the flap opened a bit i reached through and pulled him in the cat flaps locked now hope hes alright.*

12.10: *Looks like our neighbourhoods affected too chaos outside.* Then: *Staying trapped inside damos not gone to work.* Then: *Feeling a bit strange sort of light headed like seasickness damo too.*

By the time I'd replied to that one, Jess had gone. She'd been increasingly worried all morning that her mother might have had a fall and could be lying injured, alone and helpless at the foot of the stairs or on a slippery bathroom floor; and even though Jess wasn't feeling well herself and was aware that there were unknown risks outside, she was determined to go. I was against the idea, but she was adamant. She reasoned that, with a mask on, a scarf wrapped round her face, and her hood up, she'd be able to manage the twenty-minute walk to Emily's place.

Amid the morning's confusion, the children were as good as gold, taking turns playing games on the tablet, doing puzzles and colouring in their books. Jess told them that she had to go out to check on Grandma, as her phone didn't seem to be working, and that she'd be back soon.

That was the last we saw of her.

It wasn't the last we heard from her, though. Fifteen minutes after leaving, she phoned. It was a perplexing conversation. She sounded vague, saying that she wasn't able to cross the road near Mackeson's and couldn't walk in the direction that she wanted to. She felt as though she was going to fall over and needed to sit down – like we both did that morning after stepping outside, and like I still do two days later. She described people sitting on the footpath, in the road, in their garden or in their car. Some were trying to walk but were bumping into walls and lamp posts, or falling into hedges. Those attempting to drive were unable to avoid mounting the kerb or hitting other vehicles. She said she was having a short rest before trying again and would call back later. Mackeson's is about a third of the way, so allowing for another break to sit down, or even two, I expected her to be at her mother's within forty-five minutes.

An hour passed – nothing. I waited another five minutes and called her. There was no reply, other than her invitation to leave a message. I tried again, and again. It was at the fourth attempt that a young male voice answered. I asked for Jess, but the young man could only explain that he'd found the phone lying on the ground. I described Jess and what she was wearing and asked if he could see her. He could, across the road. I heard him call out, 'Jess!' He said she waved back and tried to walk towards him, but instead she turned and headed in a different direction, and then she fell over.

By a quirk of circumstance this young man had become Jess's lifeline. I desperately needed the help of this faceless stranger and didn't want him to give up. I asked him his name. He said it was Joel. I asked Joel if he could take the phone over to Jess. He said he'd try, and for a while all I heard was shuffling. Then Joel came back on and said that he tried to walk towards her but he kept veering away. He told me that Jess had stood up and was reaching out both arms to him from the other side of the road. There was a pause, and the next thing he told me was that she was walking, but not towards him – she was moving farther away, even though she was looking at him and still reaching out a hand. He said every time he tried to take a few steps towards her, he ended up somewhere off to the side, so he said he'd leave the phone on the ground where she could see it and come and get it herself. I heard him telling her in a raised voice what he was intending to do, and I was sure I heard a faint reply from across the road.

That was the last time I heard Jess's voice.

I sat there in the armchair, staring at the captions on the muted afternoon news, hoping that Jess would get to her phone and call me back. I thought about everything that I'd seen and heard in the last twenty-four hours and wondered if it was really happening, or if I was about to be woken up by the 6.30 alarm. Then Keira tiptoed over and discreetly pointed out that we hadn't had lunch yet.

I leaned forward with the intention of getting us all something to eat, but fell straight back as though a puppeteer had cut my strings. I told Keira that I wasn't feeling well and wondered if she could see if there were enough cheese slices in the fridge to make us all a sandwich. There were, so she gladly set about making cheese, lettuce and pickle sandwiches, with a tomato each on the side, which we ate like an apple, as I didn't want her to use a sharp knife, even though she's almost eight. I thought that we needed some ice cream after that, and the kids raised no objection, so we each had a generous scoop of Neapolitan.

I felt increasingly unsteady during the afternoon, so I gave up on my feeble attempts to leave the armchair, and instead half-watched the muted TV for about an hour while trying Jess's phone every few minutes.

Then Meaghan phoned. I didn't know that she didn't know that Jess had gone out. She'd been trying to contact her but couldn't get through. She was troubled by what I told her and was concerned about Jess's prolonged absence. She also told me that Sam's phone battery was getting low and that she hoped she could charge it somehow, so that she wouldn't lose touch with her as well. That made me wonder how much power Jess's phone had left.

Meaghan's call spurred me into action. I'd been putting off paying my first p.m. visit to the bathroom, but I couldn't delay it any longer. I leaned forward and stretched my arms out in front of me, as I'd seen the paramedic do the day before, tipped myself forward and teetered for an instant before my knees buckled and I collapsed in a heap on the floor. I was glad the children were upstairs at the time and didn't witness my moment of indignity. However, avoiding calling for their assistance meant that I had to fend for myself.

There was no way that I was going to get to my feet, so I crawled over to the foot of the stairs, hauled myself up at a rate of about four steps a minute, slumped onto the landing, rolled in the general direction of the bathroom, dragged myself through the doorway and clambered clumsily onto the toilet seat, where my legs established a reasonably stable tripod stance in partnership with the base of the toilet bowl. With one hand on the towel rail, I was able to complete the manoeuvres necessary to relieve the mounting pressure with alarmingly little time to spare.

After reflecting for a while on a mission accomplished, I glanced up to see Coen standing in the open doorway with a dribbly finger in his mouth. Expressionless and without a word, he closed the door, and I listened as his footsteps faded away.

That started me thinking about the children, and how they hadn't been affected so far – at least not to the extent that their mother and I had. Perhaps that was because they hadn't been outside, or because they were upstairs when the garage door was opened. Almost everyone else that we'd heard from described similar symptoms, with the exception of Naomi, Damon and Casey, who, as far as I knew, had kept their doors and windows closed. It crossed my mind, though, that their open cat flap might turn out to be a source of exposure. I mentioned that to Naomi as I exchanged a couple more messages with her there and then on the toilet, but she didn't seem particularly concerned.

I was still secure in the tripod posture when Meaghan phoned back. Neither of us had any news of Jess, but she'd heard from Sam again. Sam told her that no-one at the airport seemed to be going anywhere, so she had a decision to make: either walk the three and a half hours home, or stay at the airport for the night and see what options there were the next day – and possibly end up walking home anyway. She still hadn't been able to charge her phone, and so decided to buy a portable charger. Unfortunately, everyone must have had the same idea, as they were all sold out. Meaghan kept the call short to save power for another update.

Twenty minutes later I was back on the stairs, making a cautious descent, when Meaghan phoned again to say that Sam's phone had cut out during her latest call. The news from the airport was that the crowds seemed to be thinning, as there were no more arrivals and people were deciding to make their way to their onward destinations on foot. Sam told her that, although there was less jostling, people (herself included) were bumping into each other, colliding with walls and doors and tripping over inanimate objects, such as cordons and luggage. She said that her battery was on 4% shortly before contact was lost.

As we contemplated the fading afternoon light together, Meaghan and I wondered how Jess, Sam and Emily were going to get through the night. We considered notifying the police, but we didn't think that either Sam or Jess would be considered as missing persons yet. I wanted to go out and look for Jess, but even if I could get to my feet, I couldn't take a chance on being unable to find my way home and leaving Keira and Coen to fend for themselves. We agreed to sit tight and let each other know as soon as we heard anything new.

In the meantime I needed to complete my descent,

so that Keira, Coen and I could make preparations for dinner. They were both downstairs by then, having stepped over me while I was talking to their Auntie Meaghan.

We had pasties and baked beans with bread and butter that evening. I asked Keira to heat up the frozen pasties in the oven, as my fingers were finding it difficult to grasp what I was aiming for, and equally difficult to avoid what I didn't want to touch. I considered it relatively safe for my not quite eight-year-old daughter to use an oven for the first time, under my close supervision, of course, from my seat at the dining table – likewise with the microwave. I managed to open the tin of beans without cutting myself, and Keira followed my instructions to pour them safely into a bowl and heat them up. Meanwhile, I gave Coen the job of buttering the bread with a blunt knife.

The dinner-time conversation centred on when Mummy was coming back. I reassured the children that she was probably spending the night with Grandma Emily and would hopefully be home tomorrow. I was unable to reassure myself, however, that Jess wasn't sitting on the side of a road somewhere, thirsty, having not eaten since breakfast, and listening for a distant ring tone in the twilight, while facing the prospect of a night in the open, dressed only in her daytime clothes and with temperatures likely to drop below freezing.

After dinner I turned the volume up on the TV to catch the news of what they were now calling the mystery contaminant. The source was still unknown, as no chemical leak had been reported, and if it was a deliberate act, no-one had yet claimed responsibility. Accounts of disruption were coming in thick and fast.

Most flights had been cancelled that morning due to staff shortages and difficulties with refuelling and baggage handling. One airline had attempted a departure but the pilot taxied off the runway. Soon after that all aircraft were grounded nationwide. Roads were congested, trains were cancelled, and ships were unable to dock. Hospitals were in crisis with staff unable to get to work or operate equipment safely, and numerous emergency crews had been sent out but hadn't reported back. Hundreds, if not thousands of children who had walked or cycled to school, or who had set out to catch public transport, were missing. Their families had presumably been unaffected on Sunday and were still unaware on Monday morning of the scale of what was happening beyond what was visible from their windows.

Alarmed by all that I'd seen and heard, I decided to phone the police to report Jess missing. There was no reply in the twenty minutes that I spent listening to the automated message telling me that my call was being held in a queue, before I gave it up as a lost cause and tried Jess's number again – another seemingly lost cause.

Meaghan called once more that evening to say that Sam had managed to get to a public phone after queuing for over an hour. She'd decided to stay put for the night, where she at least had warmth and shelter, and then she'd think about what to do in the morning. Meaghan herself was feeling queasy, having spent most of the day sitting and lying on the sofa, while trying to get whatever news she could from any source.

After Meaghan's call, the children escorted me dutifully upstairs. They showered and brushed their teeth first, and we said goodnight before I took my turn, sitting down in the shower to avoid slipping. Once finished, I found that the towel rail was out of reach, so I crawled out wet, dried and partially dressed myself, then kneeled in front of the wash basin to brush my teeth. Having done everything that needed to be done in the bathroom, I sat down with my back pressed against the open door. From there I pushed myself up by straightening my legs as best I could and slid across to the wall, then along the wall as far as the open bedroom door, at which point I turned, braced myself in the door frame and launched myself towards the bed. Plunging face down onto the unmade bedding, I thought to myself how fortunate I was not to have missed the target.

I tried Jess's number half a dozen more times before going to sleep, aware that each call was lighting up her screen and running the battery down. I figured that a lit up screen at night would give her, or anyone, a better chance of finding her phone than it would in the light of day. I didn't dare think that the battery was already flat.

Day 3 (Tuesday)

Tuesday (yesterday) was the last time that I made contact with anyone via Jess's phone. In a way I was pleased to discover that the battery wasn't already dead as a result of my repeated calls on Monday night, but in the end it didn't matter anyway.

My heart skipped on hearing a female voice at the umpteenth attempt, but I realised instantly that it wasn't Jess.

I explained that I was trying to find my wife, and gave the woman a description, but Jess was nowhere to be seen; so I asked her where the phone was.

She told me that it was propped up against a fence.

I meant where, as in the location.

She said just outside number 15.

The woman seemed a bit slow on the uptake, so I asked her what road she was in.

She didn't know. She didn't live around here. She'd left her car the day before and was trying to get home. Her phone battery was flat and she had no idea where she was.

I asked her about the power level on Jess's phone. The woman said it was red, but she couldn't see the number clearly, as she didn't have her reading glasses.

I tried to elicit some information that might give me an idea of her location.

There was a newsagent's on the corner across the road, but she couldn't make out the name of the road.

Could she move a little closer, perhaps?

She could try.

For two heart-pounding minutes I heard nothing but breathing and shoes scuffing as I imagined the numbers next to the red battery symbol counting down. Then she said she could see Malahide Street and Venn Street.

Suddenly I knew exactly where she was – but that was three blocks away from where the phone was on Monday, and not in the direction of Emily's house.

The woman asked if I could tell her how to get back to the motorway.

I didn't want to waste any more of Jess's power on this conversation, so I quickly told her to follow Malahide Street and asked her to leave the phone somewhere conspicuous with the screen facing up, but not where it could be trodden on. I heard nothing else, and I don't know if the woman heard my directions or my request.

On impulse I tried to call back, but there was no ring tone. My last glimmer of hope of contacting Jess via her phone had been extinguished – despite her repeated assurance that she'd get back to me.

The finality of the disconnection left me deflated, and I was frustrated by the knowledge that Jess's phone was only six or seven minutes down the road. I imagined her becoming so disorientated so quickly on Monday that she couldn't get close enough after dropping it to pick it up; and I tormented myself with visions of her reaching her arms out to Joel from across the road while he was speaking to me on her phone, as if she were reaching out to me, pleading with me to go out and bring her back.

That was around 10.30 in the morning.

I'd woken up just before seven, feeling dizzier than I had at any time on Monday, so I sat on the edge of the bed for several minutes before venturing over to the window to see if anything had changed during the night. All the vehicles seemed to be just as they were before. The only activity was someone in a black hooded overcoat grappling with a loaded shopping trolley on the roadside between Yasmin and Archie's house and ours. He, or she (I couldn't tell), was having difficulty steering the load of toilet rolls, bottles and boxes away from the kerb, getting the trolley stuck between abandoned cars and not caring about scratching their paintwork on pulling it free.

Shopping before 7.15 in the morning, I pondered. More likely looting – unless these were legitimate purchases and this struggle had been going on since the previous day. I watched for ten minutes, and then, with a growing sense of futility, as there had been no messages or missed calls overnight and I expected that Jess's battery would be flat by the morning, I tried her number. To my surprise it rang, and I was strangely heartened to hear her voicemail greeting again.

There was no sign of Keira or Coen before 7.30, so I made my way unassisted to the bathroom by successfully retracing the previous night's route along the wall.

After showering on my knees, I knelt in front of the mirror with the intention of shaving, but soon gave up trying to establish any kind of razor-to-face coordination via my reflection while disorientated.

Once I'd mopped up in the bathroom, my next obstacle was the stairs. I shuffled out on my backside and crossed the landing, where I lowered my feet over the edge and contemplated the descent. I'd discovered on Monday that this was a manoeuvre best performed on my back, while gripping the banister with one hand, lowering myself one stair at a time with the other, and then spontaneously letting go at some point. I was pleased with my fairly controlled landing, but decided to move the shoe rack out of the way for future touchdowns.

Aware of the accumulation of bruises on my back, I resolved to drink as little as possible during the day to minimise the number of times I had to negotiate the stairs. As it turned out, I only needed to mount three expeditions yesterday – each ascent more arduous than the last, and each one followed by a freestyle luge personal best.

The kids must have heard me hit the bottom, because they appeared immediately at the top of the stairs and scurried down to rearrange the scattered shoes before checking that I was uninjured.

I asked them how they were feeling. They both said they felt OK, and then Keira asked, 'Is Mummy coming home today?'

All I could say was that I hadn't heard yet.

The children were content to take charge of breakfast, serving up cornflakes, rice bubbles and muesli with the last of the fresh milk.

After breakfast on the sofa, I leaned across to the window and saw that the trolley-pusher had progressed two houses down in the last hour, but was still battling against the camber in the road and was now wedged between the kerb and a van parked at about forty-five degrees. Although stuck, he or she was determined not to relinquish the trolley, which, in addition to containing vital supplies, appeared to be serving as a means of physical support.

I didn't put the news on during breakfast. I couldn't face it and didn't want to cast a shadow over our start to the day, so I waited until the table was cleared and the children had gone upstairs to brush their teeth before I switched the TV on.

Images were shown of disruption to traffic in several locations along the west coast, as well as here in the east. Vehicles were abandoned, and people were wandering aimlessly on roads. Evidence of more than one point of origin confirmed that the source was not localised, so the previous day's speculation regarding an unreported industrial accident could be discounted. The likelihood now was that this was either a deliberate act, a coordinated series of acts, or a natural phenomenon. Tests were being carried out to determine the nature of the contamination. A state of emergency had already been declared nationwide, and the official advice was to stay at home and keep all doors and windows secured, even in regions so far uncontaminated. Meanwhile, as far as could be ascertained, no other countries had been affected.

Transmissions became increasingly erratic during the day. Some channels were off the air completely, while others were broadcasting sound only, or vision with subtitles.

Googling the news locally, nationally and internationally added a little more information to what had been relayed on TV. The condition suffered by large swathes of the population was described by some as 'loss of direction syndrome'. People were losing their bearings completely on turning just a few degrees, not knowing which way they were facing, even when staring straight ahead. As a result, those afflicted had trouble finding their way to an open door. They could see it, but didn't know how to get there. Other stories told of people of all ages falling down stairs because they (or the stairs) were not where they were thought to be. Driving was impossible, even if a vehicle could be reached. There were reports of pedestrians walking into roads, slipping off railway platforms, falling down river banks, and other accounts of people unable to get to the toilet in time due to insurmountable furniture or a perceived shift in the orientation of the building. Many of those who were able to get to work before the onset of symptoms became victims of industrial accidents involving equipment or machinery that was in a slightly different place to where it seemed to be, or as a result of unsafe operation due to the unfamiliar configuration of the controls.

By the time another reporter came on, wearing a hazmat suit and talking about tests and studies, I'd had enough and switched off.

I tried to phone my mother-in-law, but there was no answer, so I sent a message to Naomi to ask how they all were and tell her that I hadn't heard from Jess or Emily. Her reply:

09.38: *Were still feeling weird but not like the people were seeing outside.* Then: *Tiberius has got it bad whenever he tries jumping up on a kitchen chair or our laps he half misses and slides off lol not funny but we see the funny side.*

So then I phoned Meaghan. She'd heard nothing from Sam and hoped that she'd started walking at sunrise and would make it directly home. I asked her how Sam would be able to find her way home if she was still disorientated, and with no access to the maps app if her phone battery was flat, but Meaghan just wanted to focus on the positives. If Sam set out at seven, she could be home by 10.30. I asked Meaghan how she was feeling. She said she felt unwell and was lying in bed, and she didn't want to talk any more.

I feel that I've been depriving Keira and Coen of attention since Jess left. I've been so self-absorbed since Monday, worrying about Jess and my own physical state, that I haven't had much of myself left for them. At least there are plenty of kids' programmes still being shown on the TV; and they have a shared tablet with several games apps to keep them amused – not to mention all their other toys and books. They only asked about their mother once yesterday. I guess, besides keeping themselves occupied for most of the day, they would have known by listening to my phone conversations with Naomi and Meaghan that I had no more news.

The children prepared yesterday's lunch – cheese, lettuce, peanut butter and pickle sandwiches with a small side salad. That finished off the bread and the lettuce. Between lunch and dinner they handed out some snacks – a tempting selection of fruit, nuts, chocolate and potato chips – and for dinner I opened two tins of spaghetti, which Keira heated on the stove, carefully following my safety guidelines.

I thought it would be useful to draw up a food inventory to give us an idea of how many days' supply we had left; so in the evening Keira enthusiastically set about listing all the items in the larder and fridge, while Coen counted them and pencilled in the numbers alongside the words that Keira read out to him. She insisted on doing it on paper, rather than on the tablet, as she likes to practise her handwriting. After they'd finished, I crossed out the chardonnay and pale ale and corrected a few spellings, despite having difficulty in controlling the direction of my pen. Then Keira, being the perfectionist that she is, rewrote the list neatly, this time drawing a picture next to each item. Coen thought that was a great idea, so he started one of his own, but he seemed discouraged on comparing his misshapen tins with Keira's cylindrical masterpieces, so he curtailed his effort by illustrating his entire page with spaghetti, which I nevertheless told him was wonderful, to Keira's disgust. By the time it was all done I didn't have the brain power to estimate how long everything would last, but there was no doubt that we'd be OK for a week at least, although our range of options would diminish daily.

While the children were absorbed in the inventory,

I phoned Naomi to compare our food supplies. She and Damon hadn't given it much thought up to then, but she said she'd placed an online order that morning for groceries and toiletries – twice as much as they actually needed, just in case there was any panic buying. Good idea, I thought. I'll try that. What chance of delivery, though, if people are staying at home because they can't drive or even walk in a straight line?

I almost forgot the other weird thing that happened yesterday afternoon. Around two o'clock, while I was upstairs for the second time, I heard the rattling of a gate latch. Our next-door neighbours – not Yasmin and Archie, but the young couple on the other side, who we haven't spoken to yet – were heading out. By the time I made it to the bedroom window, they were at the kerbside, attached to each other at the waist by a rope which trailed back up the driveway, and with their Jack Russell straining on its leash, frantically trying to get back to the house.

The man led the way across the road, carrying what looked like a bundle of shopping bags. The woman followed, with three or four metres of slack between the two, towing their obstinate dog along.

I wondered what their intention was. Why the shopping bags? And how far would their rope allow them to go? I thought perhaps they just went out to see if anyone was in need of assistance, while also giving their pet some exercise.

I watched with interest as they proceeded towards the back of the ambulance and then stepped through the open doors. I doubted that the paramedics would still be in there after two days, and there was nothing about our neighbours' reactions on peering inside, or their dog's, to suggest that they were.

The pair emerged a quarter of an hour later, noticeably less steady than they were earlier. She was now wearing a backpack, and he was labouring between two bulging bags which he was endeavouring to keep off the ground.

The woman picked up the rope at her feet and yanked half a dozen surplus metres down the driveway towards her. The Jack Russell promptly ran between the couple, winding its lead around the woman's legs and causing her to inadvertently step on its paws to avoid tripping.

Once extricated and back at the kerbside, the woman tugged on the taut rope to project herself confidently through the gateway at the first attempt. The man, however, still impeded by the recalcitrant canine, stumbled against one of the gate posts, spilling several packaged items from both bags. Taking advantage of the distraction, the dog ran loose towards the house as the couple scrambled to collect the various boxes and bottles.

With their spoils recovered, and now carrying one bag each, the pair jointly restored the tension on the rope. On an audible count of three, they thrust themselves forward, swinging laboriously from side to side as they heaved themselves back to the house, where they disappeared from view with their haul of medical supplies. Seconds later the remainder of the rope chased them in and the door slammed.

The plundering of the ambulance prompted me to phone Archie to see how he and Yasmin were and find out why the woman's car hadn't been towed away. With so much happening since Sunday afternoon, I hadn't given them much thought. I was also curious to know if they had any idea what was going on with the ambulance, or if they had any other news to share. There was no answer, though – just a voicemail message. I tried their land line, also to no avail, so I sent Archie a text message enquiring after them and asking him to call me. There's been no reply to that in the thirty-odd hours since, and I still haven't seen or heard from them since Jess spoke to Yasmin on Sunday night.

Before I went to bed I did some online shopping for food and toiletries – payment accepted and order confirmed, next day delivery. Hardly surprisingly, there was no delivery today.

Day 4 (Wednesday)

I've been trying Jess's number every hour or two since before dawn today, pinning my fraying thread of hope on a passing stranger picking up an abandoned phone that she or he happens to have a compatible charger for, taking it home, plugging it in and waiting for someone to make contact – and for absolutely no reason that would be of any benefit to the finder, who probably wouldn't be capable of getting home anyway. Nevertheless, I keep telling myself that false hope is better than no hope.

The rest of my morning didn't go well either. Once I'd done what needed to be done in the bathroom, including mopping up puddles with previously discarded clothes, I leaned back against the open door and slumped sideways onto the landing carpet. There was no sign of the children, so, with thoughts of breakfast, I slithered to the top of the stairs, swung my legs round and took the plunge, sliding down like a petrified starfish.

After gently massaging my bruises, I surprised myself by making it from the foot of the stairs to the kitchen on my knees in less than five minutes. So far, so good, I thought.

It was the first time I'd attempted to get myself any food since Monday. Out of practice, I clumsily scattered half a bowl of rice bubbles across the kitchen floor – but at least I managed to open our last carton of long-life milk successfully and pour enough into the bowl, while leaving plenty for the children.

The instant coffee was anything but that. I unhitched the jug kettle from its base and steered it across the kitchen bench towards the sink, humouring myself by whispering 'Exterminate!' as the Dalek lifted off and hovered under the tap to take on sufficient water for one cup.

Unfortunately, the change of direction for the return to base was too abrupt, and I tumbled backwards onto the ground, spilling half the contents of the kettle down my front. Undeterred, and determined not to be entirely dependent on Keira and Coen, I made a second, and this time successful attempt.

To cut a long story short, it took me twenty minutes to make a cup of coffee, during which time I fell onto my backside three times, first soaking myself in cold water, then splashing myself with hot water, and ultimately wasting at least three times as much coffee powder as I used.

I didn't imagine how much worse my morning would get when I first felt the need to relieve the pressure in my bladder. Reluctant to rush what remained of my precious beverage, and in no hurry to extract my backside from the puddle of coffee-soaked rice bubbles, I delayed my return to the stairs. It was only when I began to feel a sense of urgency, which quickly escalated into a state of alarm, that I slopped my bottom out of the sticky mixture, ditched the mug and made a frantic dash for the sofa on my hands and knees. In a blind panic I clambered over the arm, launched myself into a desperate dive and somersaulted over the back of the sofa at the other end, landing acrobatically on one foot. Surprised at being almost upright, and before I had time to fall over again, I attempted two unsupported strides towards the stairs, only to be wrestled to the ground by the coat stand. After freeing my sleeve from a tenacious hook, I steeled my abdominal muscles and lunged with all my might at the stairs. My momentum carried me a third of the way up, but I failed to hold on adequately and skidded back down on my belly, at which point I lost all control.

Embarrassed, but resigned to my helplessness, I shouted to the children to bring me my dressing gown and a bath towel. They must have been lurking just out of sight, no doubt having been disturbed by the commotion, because they both appeared overhead as soon as I called out. They duly obliged and I changed and cleaned up discreetly at the bottom of the stairs, while Keira took charge of their breakfast, serving up the last of the rice bubbles amid complaints from Coen that so many of his favourite cereals were on the floor.

We needed to wash some clothes and towels today, so, after clearing the table, the children guided me from the bottom of the stairs, where I'd remained during breakfast, back to the kitchen. From there I was able to show them how to load the washing machine, where to put the soap in, and what buttons to press.

All of that left me with no energy for anything other than watching the TV for the next few hours – not that there was much on offer. Almost all of the national and regional channels were either blank or showing recorded programmes. However, I did find one regional channel broadcasting live this afternoon. The presenter said that she and the news team had taken refuge in the studio for the entire three days since Sunday and were finding it increasingly difficult to obtain any verifiable news, with most of their information sourced personally from friends, relatives and colleagues in various states of distress or panic. She said that symptoms were becoming more advanced in the studio crew, who were finding it hard to operate equipment – hence the frequent and prolonged blackouts. Also, there was no food supply in the building, other than biscuits that were provided with tea and coffee during meetings, plus chocolate bars and savoury snacks in vending machines. They planned to reduce the frequency of their broadcasts to once every three hours, so I checked back at four o'clock for an update, which essentially consisted of stories of survival or tragedy garnered from social media, interspersed with random speculation from around the world as to what has happened here.

Having seen all I wanted to by 4.30, and as I was long overdue for a shower, I deemed it wise to make a more timely move to the bathroom than I did this morning. This time, though, I was lovingly shoved up the stairs by the children. Once at the top, I decided to stay put for the rest of the day. The kids fetched me whatever I needed, so I was content to remain in the bedroom and get started on the first four days of this journal.

While the washing was on this morning, I phoned Naomi to find out how they were and update her on all of our news – although I spared her some of the finer details. Even though she and Damon have kept the house sealed (apart from the cat flap being opened a couple of times), they've started noticing little things like knocking their elbows against doorways, reaching for a remote and needing a second attempt to get a grip, spilling liquids, and snagging their toes or tripping when getting dressed. There were a few photos accompanying text messages later in the day:

13.09: *Cant brush teeth in front of the mirror - i look like a clown with more toothpaste round my mouth than in it lmao.*

14.41: *No food delivery yet.*

17.01: *Damos board.*

I keep thinking how tough it is on Meaghan, going through this on her own, with her mother, sister and partner all missing. She says she's OK for food at least. They do their weekly shopping on Saturdays, so she has well over a week's supply of food for two – all to herself.

The kids are becoming restless. What else can I do to keep them occupied, other than teach them how to use electrical appliances? There's a limit to the amount of screen time you can subject a child to, and switching from TV to tablet and back again doesn't offer that much variety. As for myself, I'm resisting the temptation to crack open a beer. I'm unstable enough as it is, and I need to stay alert for the kids' sake, or in case we hear from Jess.

I'm wondering if the children are experiencing any effects at all. The house has been sealed for the last sixty hours, but I suspect that they would have inhaled some of what blew in when we had the door open briefly on Monday morning – or that they might have picked something up from me since then, if this bug is contagious. They both say they're OK, but Coen dropped and smashed a plate this evening while drying it. Hopefully it was no more than a five-year-old's clumsiness. While nothing is apparent physically, the emotional strain of missing their mother is obvious.

Lunch wasn't very exciting today. I decided that we'd use some perishable foods before opening any more tins, so we chomped on some crunchy raw broccoli, carrots and radishes, with a tomato sauce dip on the side. It was all rather hard work for Coen with his little teeth, but he enjoyed the last of the ice cream that we had for dessert. Dinner was better – microwaved pies, baked beans and defrosted garlic bread. Keira brought the beans and tin opener upstairs to me, as she wasn't able to get a firm enough grip herself, and I didn't want her to risk cutting her fingers. She assured me that she remembered how to use the microwave, so I only had to give her an idea of how many minutes each item needed. The meal wasn't perfectly cooked, but it was perfectly edible. Afterwards the three of us went through the inventory and crossed off the items that we'd finished during the day.

Our groceries and toiletries didn't arrive, so I've placed another order with a different company. Order confirmed, payment processed, 24-hour delivery. Perhaps both will arrive tomorrow.

I still haven't seen or heard anything of Yasmin and Archie. I tried phoning again this evening, but there was no reply. I can see from the glow out the front that their lights are on – not that that tells me whether they're OK or not, or even if they're at home.

I haven't seen a soul outside today, although I didn't look out of the window much after this morning's mishap, and I've been preoccupied for the entire evening with my first four days of journal entries. I did hear a woman or a young person crying this afternoon, and there were other voices from time to time, but otherwise it's been very quiet.

Meaghan has just shared this post: 'Missing. Have you seen Sam?' with a photo and details of roughly where Sam might be if she'd set out on foot from the airport early yesterday. No positive responses yet, but twenty-two shares already. That seems like a good idea, so I might create a similar post for Jess tomorrow morning.

I think that's about everything from the past four days. It's almost midnight now, and I started just after six. I'd have finished sooner if my fingers didn't keep missing the keys. It's as if the keyboard is slightly to the left of where it appears to be, so I have to make a conscious effort to adjust my aim to avoid the need for frequent corrections. Anyway, it's done now, and so am I.

I wonder what Day 5 has in store.

And I wonder where Jess is tonight.

Day 5 (Thursday)

It's been a depressing day, with no news of Jess, Sam or Emily, and there have been a couple of other worrying developments.

I went downstairs this morning, following my newly established bathroom and stairs routine, but came back up before lunchtime to spend the rest of the day in the bedroom. It's not that I'm sleeping badly, but I feel physically and mentally drained from morning to night. I don't even feel sick as such. I'm lucid and coherent, but my sense of direction and balance are severely impaired, which is extremely frustrating. I can't tell if it's getting gradually worse, as there's been no noticeable change in the last three days, but it certainly isn't getting better.

I didn't look out of the upstairs window before going down, or I'd have been aware of the woman sitting in our flower bed. The sight of her as I opened the lounge room curtains gave me such a start that I almost fell off my stool. She had her back against the fence and her fingers were pressed deep into the soil. She looked exhausted and dejected, and there was an air of resignation about her as she caught my eye momentarily before looking down and away. I looked away, too, to see if either of the children had followed me downstairs. They hadn't.

Setting the stool aside, so as to resume my observation from a less conspicuous kneeling position, I gasped on realising that the wretched woman was the driver of the car that had crashed on Sunday. She was so dishevelled four days later as to be barely recognisable, but I recalled the distinctive blue jacket that Archie had got out of the car for her. I began to speculate. Had she decided that the time had come to make her way home, or had she outstayed her welcome and been asked to leave? Yasmin and Archie would no doubt have considered the supplies that she was using up.

I wondered if she'd only just left the house, but she'd clearly been exposed to the elements for more than a few hours. Perhaps it took her a day or two to get out of next door's garden before finding her way, either inadvertently or intentionally, into ours.

When the children came down, I told them to stay away from the window and not to stare; and I reminded them that under no circumstances were they to open the front door. As much as we'd like to help, it's not safe.

I spent most of the afternoon seated near the bedroom window, discreetly looking down at the woman and watching her failed attempts to get back through the gate – stumbling, falling, rolling, crawling, it was as if she was trapped in an invisible maze. I thought of Jess and tried her number again. Could she be in a similar predicament to the woman in the garden?

Burning with curiosity to know what had happened between Sunday and today, and how the young woman came to be in our garden, I tried several times to contact Yasmin and Archie today, but there's still no answer.

We're five days into this nightmare and there's still no explanation of what's going on – no information about the cause, what's happening to us physically, how to alleviate the symptoms, whether or not we'll recover from this, or if we've suffered permanent brain damage.

It was futile searching for news on the TV this morning. The only three channels that weren't blank were devoted to entertainment. I flicked through them for a while, but none of them provided any updates. Even the regional channel that was broadcasting yesterday was off the air this morning, so I daren't imagine what's happened to them.

As of now we'll only use the TV to stream kids' programmes or watch DVDs. The last couple of days' news broadcasts have been too infrequent, unreliable and disturbing for the children. It troubled me to see how their facial expressions mirrored those of the people they saw on the screen. I, too, had mood hangovers for hours after watching some of the reports. We need the information, but at the same time we need to shield ourselves from an overload of emotional trauma. We have enough already with Jess missing.

Our best source of information now, albeit unofficial, is the internet, with professionals and amateurs all around the world speculating as to the cause of whatever this is, how long it will last and how likely it is to spread beyond our shores.

The term 'disarrhoea' is catching on, too. It's not that the condition does anything to loosen the bowels, but it makes the dash to the toilet all the more perilous when you have to crawl around furniture because your feet won't follow basic commands – even worse if you have to negotiate stairs and have well-meaning but equally disorientated family members shunting you into corners or collapsing on top of you until your bowels or bladder succumb and all is lost.

And then there's the food situation.

It's been a week since last Thursday evening's weekly supermarket shop. This morning we supplemented the last of the cornflakes with muesli, which didn't go down well, soaked in water instead of milk.

Before coming back upstairs, and with the idea of having rice and strawberry jam for lunch, I showed Keira how to use the rice cooker, and gave her specific instructions to let it cool down for ten minutes before serving. The meal turned out to be a great success, and better than ice cream, according to Coen.

With the children's safety being a priority, I decided that we'd have the last of the potatoes baked this evening to avoid the hazards of peeling and boiling. I'm confident now that Keira can manage the oven without my direct supervision, although I reminded her not to take anything out until the door had been open for ten minutes, and to always use the oven gloves. Coen's contribution to the catering was to bring the last tin of baked beans and the can opener up to me, along with a microwavable container with a secure lid.

For snacks between meals – eaten more out of boredom than necessity – we finished the potato chips and shared the last banana and apple, all of which we duly crossed off the inventory. We also used the last of the facial tissues today, so we'll start using dusters as handkerchiefs and save the remaining one and a half kitchen rolls for when we run out of toilet paper, which is certain to be this weekend. Unsurprisingly there's been no delivery of either of the previous two days' orders, so I think we can give up on the expectation of any additional supplies.

During dinner, which we had in here on the bed, Keira revealed that when she brought my tray upstairs she bumped the corner against the banister at the bottom of the stairs and almost dropped everything. She was concerned that she might be getting what the lady in the garden and I have, but I reassured her that it was just a little mishap and it probably won't happen again.

Coen keeps asking why we he can't go out and

look for Mummy. He's too young to understand the seriousness of what's happening outside, despite what we can see through the window. Keira, on the other hand, has more of a sense of the danger and is showing remarkable resilience, doing a lot of the work around the house that Jess would have done, and which Coen and I are unable to, for our different reasons.

There was a message from Naomi first thing this morning, which I didn't read until this afternoon:

07.52: *Casey cant sit up.*

I asked her what she meant. She replied:

14.07: *Shes been sitting up for weeks on her own but keeps toppling over now. Damo laughs but im like wtf.*

That could be a sign that their house has become contaminated, despite their efforts to keep it sealed. I still wonder about the cat flap.

There was also a message from Meaghan saying that her electricity went off overnight. They have gas heating, so she's OK for warmth and hot water, but she won't be able to charge any of her devices until the power is restored.

There's still no news of Sam, despite last night's post being shared over two hundred times. I was about to do a 'missing' post for Jess this afternoon, when I saw that Meaghan had done one last night, and also one for their mother, so I shared them both, as well as Sam's. The trouble is that, as far as I can tell, no-one that I've seen sharing and commenting lives anywhere near us. Still, we must try everything we can.

The other curious thing that I observed from the window today, coming into view late this afternoon, was three people roped together in single file, as if on a mountaineering expedition, but making little progress along the road with each one pulling in a different direction. As they approached, I heard the middle one, a teenage boy, shout something including the word 'Dad', so I assume that he's their son. In the five hours since they appeared, there have been numerous intense discussions and emotional outbursts.

As I sit here finishing off today's entry, I can still hear voices. I've just peeked out to see that the trio have made no progress up the street since I last looked an hour ago. It seems that they might be resigned to spending the night where they are, oblivious to the presence of the woman curled up on our flower bed on this side of the fence.

Meanwhile, it's time for me once again to endure the misery of an underpopulated bed, uncomfortable with the thought of Jess spending a fourth night who knows where – and with heavy rain forecast.

Day 6 (Friday)

I was woken this morning by Keira shouting that the electricity had gone off. My first reaction was to look at the alarm clock to see what time it was, but of course the display was blank. My phone showed that it was 10.25. We don't have gas, so we were facing the prospect of a day, possibly longer, without heating. It took a while for all the other implications to sink in: hot water, TV, modem, chargers ... and now, as I sit typing this in the glow of the laptop screen, lighting.

The battery levels on the laptop, tablet and phone

will be critical if the power isn't restored soon. Fortunately, after hearing of Meaghan's power outage yesterday, we kept all of our devices plugged in overnight, just in case – including Jess's laptop, which is the same make and a similar model to mine, so our batteries are interchangeable.

For such emergencies (not that we'd ever envisaged anything like this) we've had half a dozen candles, a box of matches and a lighter in the bottom kitchen drawer since before Keira was born. The children also have an LED night light each on their bedside tables, which they use instead of their bright lamps when they need to get up in the night. It remains to be seen how much power is left in their batteries and how long they and the four spares will last if used continuously.

Suddenly, survival planning seems imperative. We'll have to use the candles sparingly, one at a time, which means, in order to save the LED lights, we'll all have to stay in the same room from nightfall until bedtime. The candles will last for six days if we limit ourselves to one a day, but hopefully we can make them go a bit further. There's also a torch in the garage, but I'll think about whether or not to take a chance on getting it once the candles and night light batteries have been used.

There's nothing we can do about the cold, though, except wear our winter clothes all day as if we were outside, and get into bed early at night when the temperature drops.

So what happened this morning? Did terrorists launch missile strikes on our power plants by way of a second assault following Sunday's chemical attacks? Or is it that too many people have contracted a naturally occurring virus and are unable to get to work to operate the grid? Communications are so disrupted now that neither of those theories can be substantiated; so a third theory, needing no evidence whatsoever, is gaining currency on social media, with increasing numbers of individuals and groups claiming that this is part of some divine plan – and of course they all have their universal remedy.

The only certainty in this house is what we see with our own eyes – and what we witnessed outside today was tragic.

When I parted the bedroom curtains this morning, I saw the family of three sitting near the kerb, soaking wet from the overnight rain, only about five metres from where they were last night – but closer together, as their rope had become tangled. For the next couple of hours we heard intermittent yelling, but ignored it, as it was no different to yesterday's shouting. It was only when the commotion intensified and the screaming turned to crying that I dragged myself back to the window and saw the middle one lying motionless with the rope around his neck.

For the past eight or nine hours all we've been hearing is the parents wailing, sobbing and arguing. On the few occasions when I looked out before dusk, I saw them tugging at the rope, trying to move their son's body – but what can they do? They must be weak from hunger, and their son is obviously too heavy to move, especially with the additional weight of his saturated clothes – and I can only guess that the rain has expanded the fibres of the rope, making it impossible to untie. They're just stuck there, anchored in the darkness for another freezing night.

The other piece of news that Keira had for me this

morning was that the young woman was still in the front garden. She'd moved over to the side fence, closer to the house, and was therefore out of view from my upstairs window. Keira said that the poor woman was soaking wet and didn't look well, and that she wished she could put some food out for her. I, too, feel naturally inclined to disregard the risks involved in venturing downstairs and letting the woman in to give her food and shelter, but we just can't do that. We don't know if she'd infect us more than we've been infected already, or how much the opening of the door, even briefly, would increase the contamination in the house – depending on what it is that we're protecting ourselves from. Why isn't she still in Yasmin and Archie's house anyway?

It occurred to me this afternoon while gazing out of the window that I haven't seen a single bird since all of this began. I don't even know when I last heard a chirp or a squawk. It's as if the dawn chorus has been cancelled until further notice because there's nothing to sing about.

With the electricity off we'll have to eat whatever's in the fridge and freezer as soon as possible. Having adjusted our meal planning accordingly, we treated ourselves to the strawberry cheesecake for lunch. For dinner we ate the two defrosted pizza bases, topped with tomato sauce and butter, spread on lavishly by Coen, and the remaining three tomatoes, which I'd sliced rather haphazardly. Conscious also of the need to use up the remaining perishables, we shared the last two oranges this afternoon. Later on we indulged in the six squares of chocolate that we'd been saving for no particular reason. We'll try to eat whatever's left in the freezer in the next day or two, whether or not the power comes back on.

After lunch I heard a crash as Keira dropped my tray on the stairs – the first telling sign that the children aren't entirely unaffected, despite their assurances to the contrary.

With the electricity off, we've had to bring forward our evening bathroom routine, as we need to get that done in daylight now; so we showered immediately after lunch to take advantage of the light and enjoy the last precious drops of warm water.

I exchanged a few messages with Naomi this afternoon. She's worried about Casey being cold and all their frozen foods going off. To save battery power we've agreed to limit texting to one short message a day to let each other know that we're OK. I remember that she and Damon bought portable chargers for their last holiday before Casey was born, so hopefully they'll have some back-up power. We don't, so we'll definitely have to conserve our phone and tablet power in case Jess tries to get in touch.

I texted Meaghan afterwards to ask if there was any news of Sam, and to tell her that our power had been cut off as well. She still hadn't heard anything. My phone battery was around 94% by then, but hers was down to 65, so we've decided to limit our contact from now on to emergencies – or good news.

So now, with the modem off, we're entirely dependent on mobile technology for communication and information. As we need to save our data allowance for essentials, online games are no longer an option, so we got my dad's old compendium of games out this afternoon and played snakes and ladders – until Coen lost interest. Then Keira and I had a game of draughts while Coen amused himself with a colouring book.

Feeling peckish, and remembering that there were fifteen biscuits recorded on Tuesday's inventory, I asked Coen to fetch the biscuit jar up. He returned in no hurry, reluctant to reveal that there were only three left. All he said by way of an explanation was, 'We had some.' Meanwhile, Keira remained tight-lipped, intensifying her focus on the chequered board.

With the nutritional boost of a biscuit each, and with a score of one win each, I began teaching Kiera how to play chess, going over the basics and guiding her through a few opening moves before the fading daylight persuaded us to turn our attention to getting the ingredients upstairs for our first candlelit meal.

Coen said he didn't want to go downstairs, but wouldn't say why until I coaxed the reason out of him. He told us, 'The lady's at the window.' He must have seen her when he went down for the biscuits, but didn't mention it.

Keira was keen to see for herself and said that she'd bring up whatever we needed. I agreed and asked her to close the curtains straight away and not to stare.

She returned a few minutes later with a fully laden tray and a frown, saying that she waved goodnight to the lady, but she didn't wave back.

I didn't want the children's thoughts to dwell on the woman at the window, so I talked up dinner enthusiastically. As we prepared everything on a tablecloth on the bed, Coen remarked that we could cook our tomato and butter pizzas over the candle, but Keira pointed out that we needed to eat them today, not tomorrow.

I've put Keira in charge of the candles, as I'm too

unsteady and Coen is too young. We can't risk a fire. This evening I asked her to accompany Coen, and later me, as far as the bathroom door whenever we needed to go. She placed the candle carefully on the floor just inside the door before closing it, and then waited patiently in the darkness until the door was reopened. With hindsight, we could have used the LED lights.

After Coen's second candlelit visit, he announced that we were out of toilet paper, so we've started using the kitchen rolls, which we'd already placed on stand-by in the bathroom. They should last us a few days, then I don't know what we'll do.

It wasn't long before we began adding layers of clothing: pyjama bottoms beneath our trousers, two jumpers under our jackets, two pairs of socks, gloves, scarves and beanies.

As the candle neared its end while the three of us were absorbed in solitary reading, writing or colouring, I told the children that we should use the bathroom one more time before getting some extra layers of bedding out of the wardrobe and settling down for the night.

All's quiet now in the children's room, and I'm bringing my first entire day upstairs to a close in the dimmest possible glow of the laptop screen, keeping an eye on the battery level, which is at 71%.

The view outside is very different tonight with the street lights off and the moon illuminating the rooftops through frequent breaks in the clouds. Neighbours appear here and there at their windows, their faces either flickering yellow or starkly silhouetted against a cool white background, some in full view, others glimpsed between twitching curtains or partially opened blinds – all of them wrapped in warm clothing. Below, three desolate figures lie roped together in the middle of the road. In the background a motor is running. If I press my cheek against the pane I can see a fully lit upstairs window half a dozen doors along on the other side of the road – a household enjoying the luxury of light, heating and cooked meals for a while longer until their fuel runs out.

Day 7 (Saturday)

It's been another tragic day.

I was woken by the screams of Keira and Coen as they scrambled up the stairs and came crashing through the bedroom door side by side. Keira was crying, 'She's dead, Daddy! The lady's dead!' Coen implored me to come and look, saying that there were ants crawling on her face.

I hadn't been downstairs since Thursday morning, but I had to witness the horror that my children had been exposed to.

I slid out of bed, disregarding the cold, and Keira helped to direct me towards the doorway as I crawled on my hands and knees across the carpet. The children gathered a bundle of my clothes and guided me to the stairs, which I slid down in my now customary fashion on my back.

Taking no time to recover from the impact on my tailbone, I shuffled on my backside towards the window. Twisting my torso, I rose corkscrew-fashion to my knees, then held my balance momentarily before advancing slowly, supported by the children's arms beneath mine.

The young woman was also on her knees, but slumped forward. Her temple and the fingertips of one hand were pressed against the bottom of the pane. Her face was bluish-grey, and her matted, drizzle-soaked hair was trailing in a puddle on the ledge. Her half-open eyes were directed downwards. Ants had already established a trail into and out of her left nostril, while others were exploring her ear.

I asked Keira to close the curtains properly, and I told the children not to open them or look out of that window again. From now on if they want to see what's happening at the front of the house, they'll have to look out of my bedroom window, from where none of us will be able to see the woman below.

I hadn't considered until then what the children might have seen from their own bedroom this week. They haven't said anything. With the chest of drawers directly in front of the window, they'd have to stand on Coen's bed to see into anyone else's back yard, and they'd have to climb on top of the chest of drawers to look down into ours – not that they'd need to, as there's a clear view from our kitchen. Thankfully no strangers have strayed into the back yard, although it bothers me now that we don't have a padlock on the back gate.

I sent a short message to Naomi after we'd had some muesli to say that we were OK, but there was still no news of Jess, Emily or Sam. I didn't mention the woman in the garden, as I didn't want to alarm her or start a conversation that would drain our batteries. Her reply:

10.59: *Cold food and showers no fun casey screamed the house down yesterday damos like bugger showering im like you smelly sod lol - other than that were ok.*

Feeling starved of adult conversation, I phoned Meaghan, thinking that speaking would be a quicker way of communicating and would use less power than texting. She sounded irate and cut the call short, telling me that her phone's charge was down to 18% and not to contact her again. I wasn't thinking. Of course she's as anxious to save her battery for news of Sam as I am for news of Jess.

While I was still downstairs, I tried to take all our minds off the shocking start to our morning by involving Keira and Coen in the planning of the day's meals using food from the freezer that hadn't gone too soggy and didn't have to be cooked – not that we could afford to be fussy. So our evening meal consisted of the one remaining pie and pasty with mushy oven chips and peas. The defrosted peas were good, except that Coen doesn't like peas. I let the children share the uncooked pie and pasty between them and forced myself to swallow the chewy, wet, green substance in the box labelled 'Spinach Portions', rather than waste it. We'd skipped lunch earlier. No-one felt like eating, so we just had snacks during the afternoon – mostly nuts and dried fruit.

The children weren't in my bedroom this afternoon when the neighbours with the Jack Russell went out again attached to the rope that they'd used to get to and from the ambulance on Tuesday. I watched as they assisted the couple in the road by cutting the rope that had been pulled tight around their son's neck, and which they'd still made no progress in extricating themselves from.

It took only a few minutes. There was some conversation, which I couldn't hear, and the mother seemed to be pleading for something, but the neighbours didn't have anything to offer, other than that single serving of goodwill. With their mission accomplished, they hauled themselves and their scatty mascot back through their gateway, digging their heels in and swaying from side to side as if in a tug of war with the house.

The parents were left sitting in the road contemplating their loose rope ends – disentangled but disconsolate, as if the freedom they'd struggled so desperately to achieve twenty-four hours earlier was of no use to them now.

I no longer wanted to be one of the dozen or so onlookers with a box seat for the concluding scene of this family's tragedy, so I withdrew and proceeded to roll, pitch, and yaw my way along the floor to the bathroom.

I'm becoming more and more worried about Coen's mood. He keeps insisting that he wants to go and look for his mother, even though he knows we can't. There's no doubt that the fate of the woman in the garden has troubled him, as it has all of us, and perhaps he's wondering if his mother is also outside somewhere, cold, wet and hungry. I daren't imagine the worst. We're holding onto the hope that she made it to her mother's, and that they're sitting it out like we are until it's safe to go out again.

As I sit here at 8.30 p.m., monitoring the power levels on the phone and laptop, it occurs to me that I could charge my phone and the tablet in the car. But I wonder how high the risk of contamination would be in the garage. The garage shutter doesn't have a secure seal around it like the other doors in the house. If I assume that the air in the car is slightly less contaminated than the air in the garage, I'll only have to hold my breath between the house door and the car door, both of which I'll have to open and close as quickly as possible. It might be worth a try. I'll give it some more thought tomorrow morning when I'm less tired.

It was cold in bed last night – the first night without heating. It looks as though we're in for a similar one tonight.

I've just noticed that my phone is showing 'No service'. So what's happened now? Has some foreign power sabotaged our satellites, or have ground troops wearing respirators been deployed to blow up all our towers? Unless this comes back on, we'll be completely cut off from the outside world, and there'll be no way for Jess to contact us, and no way for Sam to contact Meaghan.

Day 8 (Sunday)

We're in serious trouble now. I didn't see this coming.

I was woken in darkness by a crash and a squeal and knew instantly that it was one of the children. I rolled off the bed onto my stomach and fumbled my way towards the open bedroom door, from where I could hear Coen sobbing downstairs.

I asked what had happened.

He groaned, 'I fell.'

I called to Keira.

She appeared almost immediately in the bedroom doorway on her hands and knees, silhouetted against the moonlight shining in from the back of the house. She stood up unsteadily, leaned to her left and fell over. Heaving a sigh, she tried again, took a step forward and stumbled, falling against the opposite wall. At her third attempt she used the wall for support, edged towards me a little, then turned her back to the wall, slid down and just sat there.

I asked her what was wrong.

She said, 'I feel dizzy.'

I called down to Coen, who was whimpering at the foot of the stairs, and asked him again what had happened.

'I fell,' was all he said.

I asked him how.

He answered, 'I'm dizzy.'

In my despair, I bombarded them with questions: 'Why are you dizzy, Coen? Why does Keira keep falling over? Did someone open a window, or a door? Did either of you go out?'

After a moment's silence Coen admitted to going downstairs and opening the back door before going to bed. He said, 'I thought I heard Mummy outside.'

I wasn't aware of anyone going downstairs last night.

He told me, 'You were in the bathroom.'

I asked if he was hurt.

He replied, 'I bumped my head.'

I asked if he shut the door when he saw that Mummy wasn't there.

He said, 'I think I left it open for her.'

It was obvious that the harm had been done, so it didn't seem to matter at that point whether the door was still open or closed. I had no intention of going downstairs to check, and I didn't want Coen wandering around any more. I told him to try to get back upstairs, and suggested that he and Keira spend the rest of the night with me.

Keira crawled into the room after me and I helped her onto the bed. We lay on our backs, listening for several minutes as Coen made his way up, crying intermittently. We offered him words of encouragement as he found his way to the foot of the bed, where we grabbed an arm each to pull him up.

There was little moonlight at the front of the house, so I turned my phone on and used the light to check him over for injuries. He had a bump on his forehead, but it wasn't bleeding. He said his elbow hurt, but he was able to move his wrist and fingers, so it seemed that he'd suffered nothing more than bruising ... aside from the sudden effects of full exposure to the contaminated air that we'd taken great care to protect ourselves from for a whole week.

I pulled the covers over us and we huddled together, Keira to my right and Coen to my left. We were cold, tired and confused, so there didn't seem to be any point in pursuing the matter. It was 2.24 when I turned the phone's light off, and we lay there until first Keira, then Coen, and then I fell asleep.

When I awoke, only Coen was in the bed, still sleeping. I heard the toilet flush and then water running. Recalling what had happened during the night, I wondered how Keira was feeling, and how she was coping in the bathroom.

I swung my legs out of the bed and shuffled on my knees to the window – not directly, but via an unintended detour to the ottoman in the corner.

After parting the curtains and sponging up an area of condensation a forearm square with my sleeve, I looked down at the body of the teenage boy lying in the same place as yesterday. There was no sign of the parents, and there was no other activity, human or otherwise – just a dog barking somewhere out of view. The road's shiny surface and the glistening grass signalled the sun's early advantage in its contest with the clouds.

I checked my phone. It was 8.43. The battery indicator showed 42%, and there was still no service.

Coen woke up to the click of the bathroom door, and we listened to Keira scuffing along the carpet for a full two minutes before her head and shoulders appeared low down in the doorway. She was already dressed, so she must have made it to the bathroom via their bedroom. She told us that she'd got Coen's clothes, too, and had left them on the edge of the bath for him.

After getting dressed myself, I crawled alongside Coen to the bathroom. It was no mean feat coordinating two bodies tending in different directions. Once in there, I lifted him onto the toilet and held him steady until he was finished, then we washed our faces and brushed our teeth, and I helped him on with his clothes.

In the hope that mobile communications would be restored sooner rather than later, I decided to go ahead with my plan to use the car's battery to charge the phone and tablet. The children would have to go downstairs with me, as I didn't want to leave them unsupervised so soon after they'd contracted diarrhoea, and I figured that this would be a good chance for us to get to the kitchen and bring the remaining food upstairs.

Clutching the tablet and leads that I'd asked Keira to fetch from the bedroom, and with my phone and car keys in my pocket, I led the way down. By going first, I'd be able to catch either of the children if they slipped, which fortunately they didn't, as they'd learned by observing me how effective the supine starfish pose was.

The wide-open back door confirmed the cause of the children's sudden onset of disorientation during the night. Clearly, whatever's contaminating the air outside is no less potent than it was a week ago – and now the house is full of it. Nevertheless, I closed and locked the proverbial stable door.

Kneeling on the kitchen floor, I crumbled our last four muesli bars into three bowls, added muesli, dried cranberries and sultanas, and moistened the mixture with water. I was thankful that the children had been washing the crockery and cutlery every day, or that would have been an unwelcome chore facing us this morning.

Breakfast was a messy affair, with Coen toppling over backwards several times, which he found amusing, judging by his constant giggling. For Keira the novelty of disorientation had already worn off. Her only concern was keeping herself vertical and her spoon horizontal.

Afterwards I set the children the task of packing anything edible into bags, along with a mug, bowl, fork and spoon each, and one knife, and taking everything to the foot of the stairs, where they were to wait for me to return from my expedition to the car, no matter how long it would take. I anticipated two hours of charging time.

On my way to the garage, while the children were occupied in the kitchen, I sneaked an angled peek through the side of the obscured front window. The young woman wasn't there – or at least the body wasn't upright any more. Regardless, I left the curtains closed.

Two thoughts crossed my mind briefly as I opened the door to the garage with my bag of devices and leads looped over my shoulder. First, it no longer mattered whether or not I held my breath on the way to the car to avoid further contamination from the air in the garage; and second, I was sure that the connecting door had been locked all week, but it wasn't this morning. I was too preoccupied with the details of my mission to figure out why.

It was just as well that I didn't have to hold my breath, because it took a full five minutes from the time that I closed the door and proceeded on my knees – all the while hanging on to the shelving unit and the car's mirror to maintain my balance and orientation – to the time that I executed the final manoeuvre of opening the car door and hauling myself round, up and in before slamming the door beside me.

I flicked the interior light on, inserted the key into the ignition and turned it. Seeing the dash light up gave me an unexpected buzz of excitement on rediscovering an untapped power source. The tablet had about 60% charge on it, so I plugged the phone in first.

I tried to find something on the radio to pass the time, and listened for about five minutes to a crackly conversation about conserving household energy, until I heard a clang at the back of the car, followed by scraping.

Glancing up at the rear view mirror, I was horrified to see the head and shoulders of two dusky figures emerging from the dark background of the garage door. I switched the car's lights on and turned round to see the glowing red outlines of a young man and woman, leaning forward on the back of the car with their arms linked. The diffused beams from the headlights illuminated and accentuated their dishevelled hair, sunken eyes and cracked lips, creating an image that could have been a still from an apocalyptic zombie movie.

I wondered how they could have got in, and then it dawned on me ... Coen!

I activated the central locking, muted the radio, extinguished the interior light and watched them in the mirror as they clawed at the window. They seemed to be asking for help. I thought I heard, 'We haven't eaten,' and 'Let us in.'

The pair began swaying from side to side, rocking the car. Then they slid towards the passenger's side and out of my rear vision. I turned my head and watched them floundering around the corner, keeping their arms linked. The man had considerable difficulty in coaxing his female companion along, but he wouldn't let her go.

My spine tingled with the realisation that I hadn't locked the internal door. What if they managed to get inside?

But of course, they'd already been inside. That was an unsettling thought. Who knows how long they'd been in the house during the night? Where were they while Coen was lying hurt at the bottom of the stairs? Were they already in the garage, or hiding in the shadows of the lounge room furniture, watching him and listening to our conversation? Maybe they weren't even in the house at that point. Perhaps they just happened to be in the back alley when our commotion caught their attention and enticed them in – in which case I should be kicking myself for not going downstairs and closing the door when I had the opportunity.

Regardless of any imagined scenario, the reality now was that the kids were vulnerable as long as I was sitting in the car.

I switched from headlights to sidelights to conserve power while contemplating the best moment to make a move, and hoping that the couple would continue round to the passenger side to give me the best chance of getting back into the house ahead of them. I'd been slow and unsteady for days, but I couldn't be sure about them. The woman wasn't in good shape, but I couldn't know if the man possessed a turn of speed that would get him from the far side of the car to the connecting door before I could cover half that distance – considering that my outbound journey took five minutes. I didn't like my chances, so, in addition to judging their maximum distance from the door, I figured that I'd have to pick a moment when their attention wasn't on me, and when both their heads were below the level of the window, so that I could slip out unnoticed and get a head start. Of course, I'd have to hope that neither of their heads would be on the ground, or they'd see my feet touching down on the other side.

I prepared myself as best I could for a quick escape by placing the tablet and lead back in the bag on my lap and waiting for the last possible moment to unplug the phone, which had only advanced from 42% to 46%.

3% later the couple had barely moved and were still clinging to the back corner of the car. I sat statuesque, occasionally flicking the phone display on to check the power level whenever I was sure that neither of them was peering in.

On 50% I heard a scuffle and a bump. I adjusted the passenger side mirror downward to see the woman lying on her side with the man kneeling beside her, trying to pull her up. I couldn't catch any of his words, but his tone was sympathetic and encouraging. By 51% she was sitting, and by 52% they were both on their knees leaning against the rear door, having made more progress through her falling over than during the previous fifteen minutes of puffing and grunting.

With the couple appearing to be taking a break from their exertions, I estimated how much time I'd need for the phone to charge fully. The car's charger was slow, having only added 11% in little under half an hour. At that rate I'd need two more hours.

Another ten minutes passed with no significant movement outside, so I decided that, if the couple didn't take the one or two more steps towards the optimal position, I'd make a break for it anyway.

On and off I monitored the clock on the garage wall. It occurred to me that it was the only timepiece in the house that could confirm what my phone and the car's clock were telling me – that I'd been in the garage for about three quarters of an hour and it was time to make a move. I reflected that Jess had ... has a solar-powered watch, but we have nothing mechanical and nothing else battery powered. I would have liked to have taken the clock inside, but under the circumstances it wasn't an option.

By 60% I felt a pressing need to go to the toilet. I started thinking about astronauts' suits, and my mind transported me from a zombie apocalypse to outer space – specifically the scene from the movie, 'Alien', in which Ripley opens an airlock to rid herself of the pursuing alien, while narrowly avoiding being sucked into space herself. My airlock was the short distance between the car door and the doorway back into the house, but my dizziness could 'suck' me in the opposite direction towards the back of the car, allowing the aliens free access to my unguarded escape pod. I couldn't think with any sense of reality. I had to get inside and trap the invaders in the garage. It was them or me. If they were to prevail, they could lock me out and the children would be at their mercy.

But they weren't aliens, were they? They were human beings. How would they survive in the garage without food or water?

Nothing was happening, so I had time to think. What would I do once safely inside? Would compassion override my instinct for self-preservation to the extent that I'd risk unlocking the door again to throw a bottle of water into the garage and offer the intruders a last chance of escape that their lives might depend on? They were obviously weak, and sharing our food with them was out of the question, but to deny them water would be to sentence them without hope of reprieve to a death incarcerated in darkness, and condemn one of them to witness the dying moments of his or her loved one, just as the parents of the boy outside were condemned to watch their son die. Most likely she'd go first, I thought, as she was undoubtedly weaker, and then he'd suffer his own slow demise beside her decaying body. Meanwhile, the three of us would be upstairs listening to them pleading and scraping and hammering on the door at all hours, day after day. Horrible thought!

There was no more time to consider the pros and cons. I had a full bladder. The couple were still at the rear passenger door, but they were as far away from my escape route as I could now hope for. I disconnected the phone, which was only on 63%, slipped it into my left trouser pocket, put the lead in the bag with the tablet, then took the keys out of the ignition and pushed them deep into my other pocket. Sliding the bag straps up my arm and over my shoulder, I pulled gently on the door handle, hoping for an inconspicuous exit.

The click resonated like a pistol shot as the car's interior light flashed on. Annoyed with myself on both counts, and noticing the tops of two heads turning, I baled out, landing awkwardly and hitting the back of my head on the floor. With no time to check for injuries, I kicked the car door shut, while somehow using my leg's momentum and flailing arms to spin and rotate me 180 degrees, so that I was now face down with my head pointing towards the internal door. I pulled on the base of the shelving unit and hauled myself forward, cursing at myself for not turning off the car's lights. With my right cheek pressed to the ground, I could see two pairs of legs in a kneeling position on the other side. One of them launched into a failed leap towards the front passenger door, and a body slumped to the ground. The couple's arms must have been firmly linked, as the second was on top of the first in an instant. I couldn't tell which was which, as my view of their heads was obstructed by the front wheels.

Alarmed at the progress that the intruders were making by repeatedly falling over in the right direction, I pulled on the shelving unit again with all my might, at which point the straps slid off my shoulder, allowing the tablet to spill out. Not wanting to lose precious seconds, I freed my arm to enable me to shove myself away from the car wheel and towards the door.

Judging that I was close enough, I pulled myself up onto my knees, while at the same time dragging the tablet along with my trailing foot, and swung an arm in the general direction of the door handle. I missed and fell flat on my face. As I lay there, I heard male and female groans and the slapping of hands on concrete. The aliens were in pursuit! Not daring to look round, I pushed myself upright, took another swipe at the handle and missed again, but this time I kept my balance, having edged a little closer.

Distracted by something metallic clanking on the ground behind me, I turned to see two figures illuminated at the front of the car. The man was kneeling upright, supporting himself against the work bench, having knocked a spanner on the floor, while the woman was on all fours. The angle of the shadows across their faces gave their features a sinister slant which told me that they knew they could reach me by falling in my direction one more time.

Suddenly desperate, I lunged at the door and managed to clamp my fingers onto the handle. I turned it and fell to the side, but hung on. The door opened and I wriggled through the gap on my side, arms inside, but legs still in the garage. Keira grabbed an arm and pulled. I rolled onto my back and raised my legs clear of the door. Keira slammed it shut and turned the key.

As she and I lay sprawled on the floor, I felt a huge sense of relief, in spite of my limited success. To my annoyance I'd left the tablet in the garage, and the car lights were on, so I expected that the battery would be flat by tomorrow – unless someone in there turns the lights off.

I was relieved to find that my phone was still in my pocket, but it occurred to me that I'd left the garage remote control in the car. I can't recall now if the small compartment where we keep the remote was closed when I made my escape. It's not obvious that it's a storage compartment when it's closed, but if it's discovered and the electricity is eventually restored, the couple will be able to get out. That would be a good thing insofar as they'll have a better chance of survival outside; but if they leave the garage open, we'll be exposed to other intruders.

My reflections were interrupted by Coen, who was sitting on the bottom stair holding the handles of three bulging shopping bags and saying, 'Daddy, I want to go to the toilet.'

So did I. We had to get back upstairs.

This time the children led the way, while I moved the three bags up one step at a time ahead of me: bag, bag, bag, left hand, right knee, right hand, left knee, bag, bag, bag ...

Unfortunately, Coen didn't make it to the bathroom in time. On reaching the top just ahead of Keira, he became overexcited, lunged forward and wet himself.

As soon as I caught up with him, I guided him into the bathroom, where I helped him to shower and change his clothes.

It wasn't long before we heard banging and scraping on the door downstairs, along with pleas to be let out of the garage. I'm not prepared to risk it. The safety of the children is paramount.

After consoling ourselves with lunch, while trying to ignore the disturbance below, I washed Coen's trousers and underpants in the bath using shampoo, as we hadn't brought the soap powder up.

We're all staying upstairs from now on, stranded, with our back-up power supply cut off from us, at least until we can be sure that the couple in the garage are no longer a threat. I guess what I mean by that is ... until I'm sure they're both dead.

What's happened to my humanity? Despite a lifetime of civilisation, we humans are capable of quickly reverting to our primal instincts as soon as our social structures and infrastructures collapse. We'll kill in order to survive and protect our young, just like any other creature.

I'm concerned now more than ever about the children's emotional well-being. Coen's morning fits of laughter gave way to afternoon and evening temper tantrums – presumably his way of venting his frustration at the loss of control of his motor skills. Keira is more inclined to simply get on with whatever needs to be done than complain. As for me, I'm wearing my stoic mask and keeping a tight lid on my anger at what has transpired in the last twenty-four hours, as blowing my top won't do anybody any good.

There was no specific planning for the day's other meals. We just put together whatever cold ingredients seemed to go together. We shared two tins of soup with rice crackers for lunch, and had tinned tomatoes in a cheesy pasta sauce for dinner. We should have cooked the eggs when we had electricity. Now it looks as though they'll go to waste, unless we're desperate enough in the coming days to eat them raw.

I took a chance on lighting our third candle tonight, as Keira was too unsteady. I carefully fixed it onto a tray with a little molten wax, but was prepared to douse any accidental fire, which was just as well, because I knocked it over immediately. It fell harmlessly onto the tray and the flame went out, but I decided not to try it again. Instead, I used the dim glow of the laptop screen for light. Meanwhile the children occupied themselves in their own room for an hour or so with one of their LED lights on, while also making the most of the waxing moon. We'll hope for a little more moonlight in the coming days and might even spend our evenings in the back room, depending on the moon's phase and visibility.

When the children came back in – Coen carrying the night light and Keira holding up her superhero rabbit book – I took a break from typing and read three chapters to them before seeing that they made it safely to the bathroom to get ready for bed.

We're staying together again tonight for warmth, light and comfort. Exhausted, the kids fell asleep in an instant, seemingly undisturbed by the resumption of banging, scraping, shouting and pleading, which had ceased shortly after I began reading. Perhaps the prisoners in the dungeon could hear my voice and found some comfort in listening to a story.

Although I'm mentally drained myself, I'll finish off today's journal entry, as I need to reflect on the events of the day.

I'm constantly thinking about Jess and wondering if she's trapped in someone's garden or garage, and what I'd want those residents to do if they knew. Of course I'd want them to open their door and give Jess food, water, dry clothing and a warm blanket – but would I want them to do that if they were afraid that opening the door might increase the contamination in their home? In all honesty, I couldn't expect anyone to abandon whatever protective measures they'd maintained rigorously for the past week and place a higher priority on the welfare of a single stranger than on the security of their own family – especially if they feared that there were others waiting outside to take advantage of them lowering their guard. Would I want any parents to witness the effects of contamination on their children that I've seen in mine today? The answer has to be no – and that's my justification for imprisoning those two people in our garage. Besides, two more hungry adults would consume our dwindling food supplies twice as quickly. I can't take responsibility for circumstances beyond my control, or decisions made by trespassers. They'll have to stay there without food or water, in unhygienic conditions and in cold, damp clothing until the electricity comes back on.

I've just looked outside for the first time tonight. The boy's body is still in the road, but there's no sign of anyone else, except for a scattering of flickering figures framed in their windows and mounted on our street's moonlit frieze.

The generator's off tonight. They're either conserving fuel or are out of fuel – or they've turned it off so that they and everyone else can hear the commotion coming from our garage.

As I finish off here, I'm wondering what we're going to do tomorrow.

I'll put ear plugs in before I go to sleep tonight, in the hope that I'll be less troubled by the yelling and sobbing downstairs.

I've almost drained my laptop battery, despite trying to type as fast as possible and resist the temptation to correct typos. It's in the red zone at 9%, so I'll swap it with Jess's in the morning. Hopefully tomorrow will be less eventful and there won't be so much to record – although somehow I doubt it.

Day 9 (Monday)

I opened my eyes this morning to the sounds of rustling and rummaging and the chink of cutlery on crockery. Having no inclination to move, I lay on my back, scrutinising the ceiling, listening to Keira and Coen through my ear plugs discussing what to have for breakfast, lunch and dinner. I didn't catch every detail, but I heard Keira shush her brother a couple of times when he raised his voice, so as not to wake me up. I had no idea what time it was, and I didn't care. I knew what day it was, though ... Jess had been gone a week.

I remained motionless for several minutes, worrying and wondering about everyone and everything. There was no sound from downstairs, so I thought maybe it would be safe to open the garage door very briefly, just wide enough to toss a bottle of water through. Surely by now the couple would be too weak to push their way past me. I dismissed the idea on remembering the progress that they made yesterday simply by falling over, and convinced myself that they'd only need to trip over me in the doorway to get in. Then it occurred to me that perhaps they weren't a couple at all. They might be complete strangers whose pathways simply happened to converge at our back gate.

When it seemed that the day's menu had been more or less finalised, I stirred myself with a feigned yawn and a stretch, plucked out the ear plugs, raised my head so that I could see the children sitting on the floor at the foot of the bed, greeted them cordially, slid effortlessly from the mattress to the carpet, freestyled towards the window and hoisted myself up to perch precariously on the chair. Paying little attention to the children as they proceeded to outline the day's meal plans, I scrunched up the bottom of one of the curtains to wipe away the overnight accumulation of our liquefied breath, and gazed out on a cloudy but dry day.

Surveying the grey desolation, I noticed that the boy's body had been rolled onto its side, but nothing else appeared to have changed. A curtain flapped here, and a blind fluttered there as the voices behind me fell silent, but there was no sign of life in the street. I guessed it was morning, but as there were no shadows I couldn't be sure until I checked my phone.

With no other source of information or means of communication, this triple-glazed spyhole is our only link to the outside world. I spent much of today seated near the window, as many of our neighbours did; but there was nothing to observe – not a single passer-by. Everyone must have accepted the futility of trying to go anywhere.

The children's silence persisted as I looked round at them. Their eyes widened, as if in expectation of a response.

All was quiet below until I turned and toppled off the chair, hitting the floor with a thump. That was the cue for the percussion duo to launch into a performance which lasted a full half-hour. Improvised chords were struck with vigour on the wooden door, and then on a range of metallic surfaces – probably the car panels. We have a panoply of potential percussion instruments in the garage, including spanners, pliers, saws and several garden tools. I hoped that the couple wouldn't find or be able to wield anything heavier than the shears. Fortunately, we don't own a crowbar or a sledgehammer. However, there is a claw hammer, a mallet and a chisel along with the car jack and tyre levers in the car boot, which can be accessed via the release button below the steering wheel. The hammer could certainly do some damage to the connecting door, especially in conjunction with the chisel. As for the garden tools, we don't have an axe, but we have a mattock, which would make short work of any door panel. I hoped it was in the back yard, but couldn't be sure. In any case, it would take considerable strength to swing it accurately, and I doubted that either of our captives was capable. With perseverance, though, the garden fork or shovel, if they were in the garage, might have proved effective.

The fading crescendo and slowing tempo signalled that the couple's efforts hadn't been sufficiently coordinated or targeted. Most likely they were unable, as I would be, to hit the same spot repeatedly for a sustained period of time – assuming that they could even see what they were doing. It seemed that their only option was to make the loudest possible racket with the implements available, and they certainly gave it their all. The three of us listened on the landing until the din died down and we were confident that the door had withstood the battering – but the pair didn't give up entirely.

Half an hour of silence was broken by an enormous thud – a single blow far greater than anything that could have been struck with a hand tool. From the bedroom we felt the shuddering of the garage shutter. My initial thought was that a vehicle had been driven into it, but our driveway was still blocked by the white van. Having no further clues as to what had happened, I can only guess that our car was put in neutral and the couple somehow managed to roll it a few centimetres backwards. Despite the loudness of the impact, the force would have been minimal and certainly not enough to compromise such a sturdy structure. If nothing else, the attempt served as a reminder to us that the siege was far from over.

A period of calm ensued, maybe twenty minutes, during which I wondered if our captives had achieved any significant success in weakening either the internal door or the shutter, and then we heard a high-pitched buzzing. They'd found the cordless drill!

I hadn't considered the drill to be a tool that they could use to penetrate the connecting door, and I had no idea how much charge the battery had, as it hadn't been used for months. We could only sit and listen to the same repeating pattern: drilling ... breakthrough ... power off ... power on ... drilling ... breakthrough ... power off ... power on ... probably a hundred times before the buzzing slowed to a whirr, and then to a low hum, before finally fading to a stop.

Seconds later the hammering resumed. By this time I was imagining our door in shreds, merely requiring a few remaining splinters to be twisted off to enable the zombie aliens to climb through. However, as the afternoon wore on and the sun went down, the banging lost its intensity and the man's cries became weaker and increasingly desperate. We didn't hear the woman's voice at all.

Of course, they didn't get in, or I wouldn't be sitting here typing this now. Either there would have been a bloody battle with unthinkable consequences, or we'd be in the middle of a stand-off for control of the stairs and ultimately the food supplies. Or perhaps they'd have fled through the front door, leaving it wide open.

Throughout the day I agonised over the decision that I'd made, and tried to find an alternative solution, but the same two options remained – leave two human beings to die, or free them and jeopardise our own survival.

Our meals are the only distraction we have from what's happening below – if you can call them meals now. The inventory has thinned alarmingly in the last week, and we're down to the foods that have been low on our list of preferences, plus ingredients that we can't cook without power, such as rice, lentils and spaghetti.

Today's menu, designed first thing this morning by K & C Catering and edited by yours truly, consisted of the following:

Breakfast
Home-made muesli and peanut butter dumplings

Lunch
Corn kernels in French onion dip with mixed nuts in strawberry jam

Dinner
Crunchy potatoes and buttered carrots with chick peas in lime chutney, seasoned with mixed herbs

and curry powder

Unfortunately for me, I wasn't able to enjoy a single guilt-free mouthful, making every meal so unpalatable that I might as well have had the raw eggs and onions.

This morning we ran out of paper towels – the ones that we'd brought up from the kitchen to use in the bathroom – so this afternoon the three of us had a discussion about which of their books we should use instead. I pointed out that the texture of the black and white pages in their colouring books would feel softer and be slightly more absorbent than glossy full-colour pages. For their part, each of the children thought that the other's books would be more suitable.

Eventually we reached a not entirely amicable compromise which involved Peter Pan, playful puppies and four quarterly financial planning statements. On seeing my contribution emerge from the desk drawer, Keira suggested, 'What about the paper in the printer?' Inspirational! I didn't know why I hadn't thought of that before. After such an earnest discussion, we all looked at each other and burst out laughing. So now we have about 300 sheets of recycled A4 in the bathroom, which the children are determined to use sustainably in order to postpone the sacrifice of their colouring books.

It was good to see their faces brighten up again, if only for a minute. They've certainly had nothing to smile about in the last week. For me, too, that moment of shared laughter eased the chronic pain of Jess's absence and distracted me from the constant dizziness and the frustration and uncertainty of this whole miserable situation – just for one precious minute.

None of us can walk straight now, or even stand unsupported for more than a few seconds, so I have to be in the bathroom every time to make sure that the children don't slip and hurt themselves, and also to ensure that they wash properly. We'll continue showering in the afternoons, when the water is at its least cold, and make it as quick as possible to minimise the squealing.

Actually, Coen was the only one who showered yesterday, following his mishap. He mistimed his dash to the toilet twice more today – the result of a five-year-old's reasoning that he won't wet himself if he doesn't need to go to the toilet. By the time he realises that denial only delays the inevitable, it's too late. Keira's been OK in that respect, unless she hasn't and has been keeping it to herself.

I didn't start up the laptop until after our evening meal, intending to conserve power by making use of the display to illuminate the bedroom while working on today's journal entry. The battery started on 8% and I let it run down completely before switching to Jess's, which was fully charged after the last night of electricity. As I save this and shut down now, it's on 53%.

Day 10 (Tuesday)

Soon after sunrise, while I was watching the neighbours opposite watching the neighbours opposite, there was an almighty roar from the garage – more like that of a wounded wild animal than a human. It was followed by an anguished, elongated, 'No!' bellowed several times by a male voice. The ensuing heart-rending sobs confirmed the inevitable.

I'd carried out my first execution.

The children were plainly distressed by the wave of emotion surging up from below. None of us uttered a word as Keira's quivering fingers meted out the last of the nuts for breakfast and we spooned out our peanut butter and jam toppings. I wondered if the children understood what had happened downstairs and if they had any idea how callous and calculating their father had been – and why.

With our mood subdued by the sobbing, we ate half-heartedly, and were still scraping and licking our plates when we heard the shattering of glass. The three of us stared at each other in wide-eyed silence as we listened for more – but there was no more.

Sitting here tonight, with the children asleep, my mind is tormented by speculation as to how the tools in the garage might have been put to a grisly alternative use.

This morning's upset disrupted the day's routine. I'd intended to organise afternoon showers again, but lacked the motivation. Unsurprisingly, there were no objections. We're all running out of clean clothes, especially Coen, and the towels were damp and smelly, so we did some washing in the bath, not sparing the shampoo. It'll take days for everything to dry on hangers in temperatures not rising much above zero, and with so much moisture in the enclosed air.

With three days' laundry hanging in the wardrobes and draped over the backs of chairs and open ottoman lids, I endeavoured to alleviate Keira and Coen's boredom this evening by asking them to update our food inventory, including illustrations, but neither of them can direct a pen in any way that produces anything legible now. Instead, Keira helped me to list here what we have left:

muesli (enough for breakfast tomorrow)
the last scrapings of strawberry jam
half a jar of lime chutney
an almost full jar of hot English mustard
a few squirts of tomato sauce
20+ dried apricots
2 carrots
2 onions
6 eggs
rice, spaghetti and lentils (enough to feed us for several days, if we could cook them)
mixed herbs
curry powder

We finished the last two tins of soup and the last tin of baked beans today – minestrone with beans for lunch, and farmhouse vegetable with beans for dinner.

After breakfast tomorrow we'll face the prospect of a meagre lunch consisting of the only remaining edible ingredients: two rubbery carrots, Jess's dried apricots (which we three wouldn't normally go near) and half a jar of lime chutney.

Earlier this evening, planning ahead, I soaked the rice, spaghetti and lentils by filling all three containers with water to see if any of them will soften up, however long it takes. If none of them are chewable by tomorrow night, we'll have to consider whisking the eggs and mixing in some of the herbs and curry powder to make them a little more appetising.

That will leave chopped onions and mustard for

breakfast on Thursday. I don't know how long we'll be able to survive beyond that. Once everything's gone, we'll have no choice but to venture out and forage, as there'll no longer be any risk outside greater than the risk of starving indoors.

It occurs to me now that it might be safe to go back into the garage to see if there's enough power in the car's battery to charge the phone and tablet – assuming the tablet hasn't been smashed. If there is, and it hasn't, I'll be able to continue my journal on the tablet, while keeping the phone fully charged for when communications are restored. Of course, if the car lights were left on, it won't be an option. There's only one way to find out, but I dread to think of what I'll be confronted with down there. How much of the door will be intact, and how close were the prisoners to breaking through?

I was haunted last night by visions of the woman lying on the back seat of the car, her face shrivelled and reptilian, eye sockets empty, and dried crimson fissures zigzagging outwards from her imploring orifice. I visualised the man half-kneeling on the front passenger seat with his head and shoulders slumped over a myriad of scattered rubies and diamonds; on the driver's seat beside him, a hammer and a blood-splattered saw.

It's so cold tonight!

I'm not bothering to put this in any particular order now – just getting down what I think of as I think of it. When I continued with this evening's log after doing the inventory, the laptop battery was on 34%. It's on 21% now. Knowing that it's going to run out of power at some point tonight, I had a go at starting today's entry on paper, but my first attempt at a letter streaked off the edge of the sheet and the pen skidded onto the floor. I left it where it landed.

I've resisted switching to voice or video recordings because I don't want the children to be privy to my innermost thoughts and fears – and besides, I don't look or sound good. Also, typed errors can be more easily rectified than blundering speech, so I'll continue to type. In any case, I'm a journalist. This is what I do.

I've just crawled back in from the bathroom after a longer break than intended. The water pressure doesn't seem quite right, and I think the water's a bit off colour. I couldn't be sure using the LED light. We'll see what it's like in the morning.

15%.

I wasn't going to have any beer tonight, but I've succumbed, feeling stunned, admittedly teary-eyed, thinking of Jess. Is she lying somewhere at this very moment, cold, wet, starving, dehydrated, thinking of me, Keira and Coen ... her mother ... Meaghan ... helpless, desperately hanging onto any hope of ever seeing us again? Or did she meet her fate days ago, alone, with nobody there to hold her, comfort her, stroke her hair or say goodbye? I have to believe that she's still alive, out there somewhere, making her way home little by little, drinking rainwater and eating whatever food scraps she can find, and that any moment now we'll hear her calling out to us from the front gate, and we'll rush to the door to let her in. To hell with further contamination! We're already as contaminated as we could possibly be. And wouldn't it be wonderful if the electricity were restored at that very moment? We'll put the heating on again and have warm showers and cook Jess a welcome-home meal of rice, spaghetti and lentils, and during the night there'll be a force 8 gale which will blow away all the contaminants and purge our lives of this misery. The dizziness will pass, and everyone who went missing a week ago will find their way home, and we'll all be able to get to work in the morning, and the news will be broadcast that this was a freakish, but fleeting phenomenon, and the nightmare is finally over, and everyone will be able to charge their devices and let their loved ones know they're OK, and Jess's mum will phone, and we'll get a text message from Meaghan saying that Sam went back to the airport last week and has been safe and sound there ever since with plenty of airline food supplies, and there'll be a message from Naomi telling us that Casey can sit upright again, Damo's had a shower and Tiberius has stopped falling over (lol).

6%.

In reality, though, I wonder how many of our relatives and friends are even S

FEARGROUND

'Step right up! ... This way, ladies and gentlemen, boys and girls, for the experience of a lifetime in the most extreme funfair in the universe!

'Yes, madam, this way to purchase your tickets, sign your disclaimer and deposit your phone.

'That's right, sir, tickets are only issued in exchange for one device per adult to ensure that nothing detracts from the ultimate fairground adventure. All devices will be returned at the end.

'I see you've brought the little ones with you today. How sweet! You won't be disappointed.

'Yes, sir, as the sign says, "Perpetual Extreme Fairground Fun!" You're in for the time of your life!

'Join the queue, everybody! No need to jostle! We'll get you all in. Two dozen at a time. If you're not among this two dozen, you'll be in line for the next.

'Make way for the stretcher bearers!

'No, sir, nothing to worry about. It's just another satisfied customer – all smiles under the oxygen mask.

'Your money's worth, do I hear you ask, madam? I'll say you'll get your money's worth! Wait till you see what we have in store for you ... Yes, ma'am, a merry-go-round, a crooked house, a hall of mirrors, a ghost train, a coconut shy and a roller coaster, all in one stupendously stupefying super-value thrill package.

'What's that you say, sir?

'Retro?

'You were expecting something new? ... More hi-tech?

'I can assure you, sir, that you'll find these amusements quite out of the ordinary.

'Stand aside over there to let the nice people from the mobile burns unit pass!

'Is that twenty-four now? Let's see ... a family of four ... No, two families of four.

'And who are you with, madam?

'On your own.

'Are you gentlemen together? ... You are?

'A group of three young gentlemen over there ... a delightful young couple ... a lovely elderly couple ... and another young couple ... and is that a family of three ... with a little boy?

'What's that, sonny? ... You're ten! ... Oh, my, you're in for some fun this afternoon.

'And who's that over there? ... Two little ones! How old are they, madam?

'Six and four! How enchanting!

'What's that, madam? ... You want to know if they'll be safe.

'I can assure you, madam, they couldn't be safer if they were snuggled up inside the belly of an anaconda.

'I think we might be ready to go in now, if you all have your tickets. I can see that our assistants are itching to usher you in. Let me introduce them to you.

'Right behind you, with the oversized head, anaemic complexion, bruised and bloodshot eyes and cynical ear-to-ear grin, sporting a striped tailcoat and drainpipes splattered with red stains, is ... Diabolico the Clown!

'Thank you, ladies and gentlemen, for your warm

applause.

'And to my left, draped in a black, full-length hessian robe with a cavernous hood that I dare anyone to peer into, and wielding a surgically sharp scythe, which I assure you is mostly only used for coaxing purposes, allow me to present to you ... nobody.

'Muted gasps from the audience ... Thank you all nonetheless for that.

'These two and a horde of sub-human servants, mechanical devices and organic-synthetic hybrids will escort you from one thrilling experience to the next.

'Don't be alarmed, ladies and gentlemen! That agonised wailing was the hinges of the closing gate, bemoaning its inability to release you from fate's ubiquitous embrace.

'So now let Diabolico show you the way to your first attraction – a merry-go-round consisting of twenty-four living, freshly deceased, decomposing or fossilised equine beasts. Yes, ladies and gentlemen, boys and girls, one for each of you!

'Step right up and select your mount! You'll find that some are still warm – possibly even feverish – but most are stone cold and generally dry, although one or two might feel a little sticky or slimy. Don't worry about the smell – it's natural putrefaction.

'I suggest that the parents lift their little ones up first.

'Up we go, everybody! ... Settle into the saddle!

'If you can't manage to secure the stirrups yourselves, nobody will help you.

'Yes, that horse is rather slippery, madam, having given up the ghost only two days ago.

'Make haste! Make haste, all of you! ... Up, up,

up!

'Hold on tight. You're in for the ride of your lives! If everybody's ready, let the ominous organ music begin.

'Scythe raised ... and they're off!

'Ice Maiden, the 40,000-year-old fossilised filly makes a good start to lead by a nose as we round the right-hand bend that never ends, hotly pursued by Ready Steady Neddy, feverish but still breathing, despite having been impaled on its pole three days ago. Take care, that jockey! Ready Steady Neddy's sweaty!

'Gaining ground on the inside is the decomposing figure of Wormhole – neck and neck with The Headless Carcass. The pace is hotting up as Tripod, unhindered by his obvious handicap, slots in behind the front-runners.

'As the race gathers pace, wrap the reins around your wrists, riders. The centrifugal force will intensify. You can already feel yourselves being pulled to the left as we continue around the bend. Wedge your feet into the stirrups and grip the horse's torso between your legs. Don't worry about the rib cage collapsing beneath you or anything vile dropping out. Squeeze tight with all your might, or you might fly off!

'What a sight to behold! The riders' hair and the remains of manes are sucked sideways as the field enters the final furlong of this sharp right-handed sprint.

'A jockey has been unseated! It looks as though Hanging On – one of three that started the race alive – hasn't hung on. Both horse and rider have tumbled under the hooves of their pursuers as they rush towards the finish line.

'Into the home curve, the screams of the pallid jockeys drown the sound of the organ as Perpetually Second crosses the line just behind something that has decayed so much as to be no longer recognisable.

'Cut the power! The race is over!

'What a spectacle! Enjoy the deceleration, ladies and gentlemen, boys and girls, but don't step out of the stirrups yet. The centrifugal force has separated your blood cells from your platelets and plasma – but the effect is temporary. Nobody will tell you when the colour has returned to your cheeks, and Diabolico will ensure that you suffer only minor bruising as you dismount.

'Don't try to pick up your friend, gentlemen. He's best left where he is. Someone will be along in a while to attend to ... whatever that is.

'My dear guests, whether or not you're able to stand unaided, I'd like you to make your way immediately to the travelator, installed for your convenience to convey you directly from the winning post to the Crooked House.

'Don't let your dizziness deter you from dragging yourself along the ground. The spinning sensation and the double vision will pass.

'Oh, my dear lady, you didn't digest that very well, did you!

'Yes, that's a good idea, lean on each other for support – but make sure you step around that. We don't want any accidents not of our doing, do we?

'Just slide off the merry-go-round if you can't get up.

'Come along, little girl! Don't dilly-dally, or we'll have to leave you behind and you'll be stranded here all night with owls hooting and things that you can't see in the dark touching you.

'Begging your pardon, madam, I'm only joking. We wouldn't want your precious miss to miss any of the fun, would we?

'All aboard the travelator, then! ... All twenty-three of you!

'What do you mean, you want to leave? You haven't begun to get your money's worth yet. Besides, the gate that we came through will only open from the other side, so we are, in effect, heading for the exit anyway.

'Is that the last one on the conveyor belt?

'Just drag his legs on, would you, somebody?

'There's no need to walk – or even stand – you'll glide effortlessly towards the Crooked House no matter what state you're in.

'That's it ... Is everyone on now?

'Away we go, then.

'If you're still feeling giddy, hang on to the rail, or someone's ankles. Hopefully we'll be there before any of you has time to throw up again.

'But look!

'What's that up there?

'Could it be?

'It is!

'Ladies and gentlemen, boys and girls, observe the centre of that pretty flower towering overhead.

'Diabolico, pull the lever, if you please!

'Ha ha ha ha ha! ... A refreshing shower from an oversized flower! ... But don't be alarmed, it's not water ... it's vegetable oil! ... We can't have you visiting a crooked house without being thoroughly coated in oil, can we? ... That would be no fun at all! Oh, no, no, no!

'Don't fuss, little boy! You'll appreciate the Crooked House all the more in slippery shoes!

'We're almost there now. It's just on the other side of this waterfall.

'I'm joking again, of course. It's not water ... It's more oil!

'Do I hear squeals of delight? You really are enjoying yourselves, aren't you?

'Fanfare, maestro, please, to herald our arrival at our destination.

'It's time to stand up now, whether you feel like it or not.

'Make sure you move clear of the walkway as you step or slide off the end. We don't want you all piling up in a heap, do we?

'You really must try standing now, sir.

'That's it ... almost.

'Nah, try again.

'Come along now, everyone ... Shuffle up ... Side by side, so that you can all see.

'Behold!

'It's OK, madam, just leave him there. He'll get up when he's ready.

'Welcome, ladies and gentlemen, boys and girls, to the Crooked House!

'Did you ever see a less impressive structure? Three wonky storeys, each with who knows how many rooms and an interconnecting whatever.

'You'll notice that the house has been constructed at an angle of fifteen and a half degrees from the perpendicular, which means that, whenever you're heading from left to right as we view the house from here, you'll be skating downhill. When you're going from right to left, you'll feel as though you're huffing and puffing up a treadmill. And when you're moving this way or that, you'll be risking twisting an ankle on the slanting floorboards. So take care!

'You'll find that some rooms and corridors have no windows, and there's a spiral staircase that ... well ... spirals, and leads to goodness knows where, so one way or another you should find yourselves deliciously disorientated ... Oh, and I should mention that there are a number of other interesting features that you'll delight in discovering for yourselves.

'But enough chatter from me! ... I'm such a windbag! ... Onward we go!

'Once you're off the travelator, follow the zigzag pathway to the front door.

'Sir, would you like to go on ahead and ring the bell? See if anyone's at home?

'Good man!

'The handle's on the right ... That's it, pull it down.

'Ha ha ha ha ha! ... Shocking! ... That must have given you a real buzz!

'What's sizzling?

'Oh, surely not your fingers! ... It's probably just the vegetable oil.

'Oh, my! Look at that, boys and girls. The door's opening. I wonder who could be at home.

'That's right, sir, step inside.

'Everyone else follow, one by one. Feel free to explore. It's so much fun inside a crooked house, isn't it? The children especially will love it. Why not climb the spiral staircase and see where it leads to, or wander down the corridors and in and out of all the rooms ... and you really must step out onto the balcony at the back of the house for a most unexpected view.

There are so many unimaginable surprises in store for you. It's so exciting! But time is short. We have a bus to catch in ten minutes, so make haste!

'In we go, every last one! Don't worry about dripping oil in the house – it's good for the wood. And don't be alarmed if you hear any creaking or shrieking – the house is designed to echo the emotions of its occupants.

'It appears that one of the young gentlemen whose friend came a cropper on the carousel has already discovered the red room on the ground floor.

'You'll notice, my good man, that the room has no windows ... just an entrance ... and no exit.

'You look perplexed. Are you wondering where the door that you came through has gone? How puzzling!

'Look around you. It's like being inside a red box, with just one small opening at the base of the wall in front of you.

'It looks like a fireplace, doesn't it? Perhaps that's your only way out now, since the door behind you has disappeared.

'There's no hearth, and it's just about shoulder width, so if you lie on your back you'll be able to look up the chimney. You might as well. There doesn't seem to be any other option.

'That's it, down you go, on your back ... Now push with your feet to slide in until you can see up inside.

'There! ... Can you see it? ... What on Earth could that be?

'Yes, I do believe you're right ... It's a guillotine!

'Ladies and gentlemen, did you feel the building twist and jerk then? I think the house is happy. It's almost as if it can feel you all moving around inside and is savouring every moment of your visit as much as you are.

'I see that a rather curious little girl has strayed from her family and wandered into a room furnished with just a wardrobe.

'Wouldn't you love to see what's inside the wardrobe, little one? It might be the passageway to Narnia ... You've heard of Narnia, haven't you?

'Do you like Turkish delight? ... Wouldn't you love to see if there's all the Turkish delight you could possibly eat in the wardrobe? You could take some back for your little brother.

'Why not open the door and see what's inside?

'That's right, turn the key. I'm sure the door will open by itself then.

'There you are! ... Look, it's magic! ... Can you see inside?

'It's rather dark, isn't it? Perhaps you'd like to step inside, so that you can see better.

'That's it, in you go.

'The passageway to Narnia must be very long.

'Can you see anything now?

'Not yet?

'A few more steps, maybe.

'Perhaps you should go back and close the wardrobe door behind you, or the rest of the magic might not work.

'Ooh, the structure buckled sharply then, didn't it? Someone's having a good time somewhere in the house!

'Now what's occurring on the first floor?

'It looks as though that sweet old lady has become separated from her husband.

'Where could your husband have gone, my dear?

'I think it's very likely that he stepped out onto the balcony at the back of the house to admire the view. I'm told that the vista is not to be mista.

'Would you like to see it? Your husband might be out there already.

'Yes, that way, through the glass doors. Mind you don't slip in your oily shoes.

'How strange that it's dark outside.

'Is there a switch somewhere?

'No?

'There seems to be no exterior light at all ... just a faint glow from the room ... not enough to illuminate the balcony. But why is it pitch black at the back of the house in the middle of the afternoon?

'That's curious, too ... nails scattered on the floor. What could they be for?

'Watch your footing, my dear. That might be a bottomless pit on the other side of the balustrade. You wouldn't want to slip and tumble over, spinning head over heels into nothingness, would you?

'Can you see anything yet?

'No?

'Is this really the time to begin a figure skating routine, my dear?

'Hold on to the railing. You mustn't let go, or you'll plunge into the eternal abyss, dehydrating and shrivelling up more every day, never to see your husband again – and he'll never know what happened to you.

'You're curious, nevertheless, aren't you? You'd like to have a look over the edge.

'I'm sure you'll be OK as long as you hold on tight. You only need to lean over a little to satisfy your curiosity.

'A little more.

'So dark and so deep.

'What was that? ... Something cracked ... What's happening?

'The balustrade's giving way! ... The nails on the floor! ... So that's where they came from!

'Ladies and gentlemen, isn't it wonderful when the foundations shudder like that?

'I know you'd love to stay longer, but our time in the Crooked House is almost over, so I must ask you to make your way to the front door, where you'll find the Whirlwind Bus outside, waiting to take you to the Hall of Mirrors.

'Madam, you seem distressed.

'Who? ... Your daughter?

'How old did you say? ... Six.

'Would she be partial to Turkish delight, by any chance?

'I wouldn't worry, madam. We know that she's in the house somewhere. If you'll just board the bus, we'll make sure that she rejoins us at the Hall of Mirrors as soon as she comes out. We'll send the bus straight back for her after we've dropped everybody off.

'Come along now, everyone! The sooner we arrive, the more time we'll have when we get there.

'Eighteen, nineteen, twenty ... That's odd. I'm sure I counted twenty-three people entering the house. There must be others still inside.

'Your wife, sir?

'And your friend, too.

'Never mind. They're probably having a lovely tea party together with this lady's little girl.

'We won't send a search party in yet and spoil their fun. In any case, we need to board the Whirlwind

Bus, which is about to depart for the Hall of Mirrors.

'Don't worry, sir ... madam ... sir ... nobody will stay here to greet them when they come out, and Diabolico will return with the bus instantly after dropping us all off.

'All aboard, then, for a cyclonic ride to the Hall of Mirrors!

'Crank up the engine, Diabolico!'

'And here we are at the Hall of Mirrors ... All change!

'Yes, young lady, it's not called the Whirlwind Bus for nothing.

'Off we get now! ... Make your way round to the other side of the bus and step very carefully across Crocodile Creek, then follow the Psycho Path up to the entrance to the Hall of Mirrors.

'Yes, madam, it's clearly signposted.

'That's it, sir, just two stepping stones ... three giant strides.

'Make sure nothing's dangling, or it'll be snap, snap, snap, and you'll think you've been slicing onions.

'Over we go!

'I was just joking about the crocodiles ... they're alligators.

'What if ...? ... What if what, madam?

'Don't think about it, my dear. Nobody's looking for the three missing people in the Crooked House right now, and Diabolico has just left in the bus, so if you lose your footing and fall into the creek, or if you slip on the psychopathic pathway and slide all the way back down into the jaws of an alligator, you'll have to fend for yourself.

'Simple advice ... Stay out of the jaws of an alligator.

'That's it, everybody ... one by one.

'Are we all safely across the creek now?

'Yes, madam, I know that four of you aren't, but the show must go on!

'I know, madam.

'If you've quite finished ...

'Allow me to bid you welcome, ladies and gentlemen, boys and girls, as you enter the Hall of Mirrors.

'Shuffle along now, so everyone can see.

'Are we all in?

'Yes, madam, I meant all twenty.

'Now, as you look around the hall you'll see twenty-four mirrors of all shapes and sizes – one for each of you.

'Yes, and four spare ... Thank you, young man, for your perspicacity and wit.

'What's that, sir? ... Boring, you say?

'Indeed! I can assure you that this is no ordinary hall of mirrors. What you'll see reflected is an image of yourself in the future as you take your dying breath ... a snapshot of your last living lungful.

'A hoax, is it, madam? ... I'll let you be the judge of that, if you'll just make your way to any mirror of your choice. Might I suggest the full-length mirror over there, framed with petrified gargoyles?

'An excellent choice, madam!

'So, ladies and gentlemen, who dares to look beyond the looking glass?

'Select and reflect!

'You came for a thrill, now prepare for a chill!

'That's right. Just choose any mirror.

'Who's that laughing?

'How funny, sonny! You're an old man! Look at that long, grey beard! And how lucky you are that you're destined to live to a ripe old age with a nose like a beetroot full of buckshot!

'Who else can see how they will appear as they disembark at the end of life's journey?

'Ah, this gentleman over here ... a little thinner on top, if I may say so, sir, and a few more lines, but otherwise you're a picture of health ... under the circumstances.

'I beg your pardon, madam?

'Well I never! You look exactly the same as you do today? ... And you're wearing the very same clothes and jewellery ... Hmm, similar hairstyle, too, although somewhat ruffled ... I can't account for the startled expression, though ... Perhaps the mirror's not working properly ... You might like to try another.

'Ah, here's the elderly gentleman whose wife stayed behind in the Crooked House for a tea party ... A portrait of serenity, if I might say so, sir ... eyes closed ... sleeping ... not much older ...

'Hmm ... who else do we have?

'Ah, now here's a lovely young couple holding hands and sharing a mirror ... but they don't seem at all amused by the reflection of a frail old woman holding hands with an overweight, middle-aged man who looks young enough to be her grandson.

'What's that you say, madam? ... That one's not working either? ... Nor that one, even though it was working for the young man over there.

'I'll make a note of that: "Mirrors working for everyone except one lady". Nobody will look into it.

'What's that, sir? ... No head?

'Hmm.

'I think we've seen all we needed to see now. Diabolico has made a whirlwind return, so we can make our way to Ghost Train Central Station. The platform is directly behind the Hall of Mirrors, so we'll exit via the elegant velvet drapery at the back.

'It appears that nobody but nobody returned on the bus with Diabolico. Nevertheless, please let me assure you, ladies and gentlemen, that any guests who have, for whatever reason, been unable to keep up with the main party will be reunited with their friends and loved ones at the end of the tour ... if possible.

'Now what's the commotion over there?

'Is that lady all right? ... Why is she sprawled on the floor like a stranded starfish?

'What? Not breathing? ... But that's no joking matter ... She seemed so full of life a moment ago – quite determined to find a mirror that worked.

'Is she with anyone?

'No?

'It seems she's on her own ... How unfortunate.

'Never mind, just leave her as she is. Nobody will get help and contact her next of kin.

'Meanwhile, dear guests, we must move on! We cannot allow these small distractions to delay us. The train departs in exactly three minutes.

'Come along, everyone! Through the theatrical curtains, up the steps and onto the platform.

'Yes, sir, just the one platform, and one track going in one direction. As the sign says, "Coconut Shy via The Haunted Tunnel".

'Here comes the train now.

'It looks perfectly normal, doesn't it? You wouldn't think it was a ghost train at all – apart from the semiopaque driver.

'Everyone stand clear as the train approaches. We don't want to add to the number of ghosts that we have already, do we?

'You might want to put your fingers in your ears now.

'Have patience, little one. Wait until the teeth-grinding screeching stops.

'There ... That's it.

'Now step across the gap, squeeze through the doorway and take a seat.

'Shall we let the small ones and the elderly board first? There's no rush. There are twenty-four seats, but we'll only need nineteen.

'Come along, sir!

'What's that, sir? ... Not without your daughter?

'But I've already assured you that you'll be reunited at the exit. Diabolico has just conducted a thorough search of the Crooked House. There wasn't a soul to be found, so the tea party must have finished. The chances are that your little girl is already on her way to the exit with the others via some terribly dull route. There's no point in you, your wife and son waiting here, or even going back to the house yourselves. We don't want to keep your daughter waiting alone at the exit while nobody's looking for you, do we?

'That's right. You know it makes sense. Come aboard. Find yourselves a seat. There are three close together at the back.

'Look ... Diabolico is still smiling, so all must be well. Only when Diabolico changes its face do we need to worry.

'What's that, madam?

'*Its* face?

Yes, madam, *it*. Diabolico is of indeterminate gender ... Indeterminate in many other respects, too.

'And you, young lady. Come along now! You're the last one holding us all up. Can't you see that nobody's waiting to blow the whistle?

'Is that it now? ... Everybody seated?

'No, madam, there's no more need for seat belts than there is for doors or a roof. We don't want our travellers to feel unnecessarily secure, do we?

'There's the whistle ... and away we go, accelerating like a snail through syrup ... straight into the tunnel.

'Oh, my, it's dark!

'What's that panting sound?

'Is that the puffing of the engine or the collective gasps of our guests anticipating the worst?

'It's too dark to make anything out at the moment, but our eyes will soon adjust.

'What was that?

'Did anyone see that? ... Just then, when the light flashed.

'A skellington, you say, sonny? ... You mean a skeleton ... What a clever little boy you are!

'You're not frightened of skeletons, are you? Skeletons aren't alive.

'You think that one was? What a vivid imagination you have!

'Listen!

'Who screamed?

'Was that one of you? ... Or was it something otherworldly with sinister intent?

'Do I detect a faint glow ahead?

'Did you see something move over there?

'A shadow!

'Another skeleton, you think?
'A pirate skeleton!
'But skeletons don't move ... and there be no pirates in this here grotto, Jim, lad.
'Oh, I beg your pardon ... Quentin ... and what makes you think that it's a pirate skeleton?
'You saw a sword?
'A cutlass, was it?
'You certainly know a lot about pirates.
'Yes, and skeletons.
'Well, let's hope you're not right about this one, because if there is a pirate skeleton lying in wait, grinning at us with malicious intent, we might have to abandon ship, me hearties.
'What's happening? Can't see a thing now.
'Footsteps!
'Has someone or something come aboard?
'You might be right about the pirate skeleton, matey.
'Who screamed?
'Light the emergency candle, driver!
'Has anyone seen the driver?
'We're still moving very slowly, so the driver must still be on board, otherwise the dead man's handle would have dropped the anchor, so to speak.
'What was that?
'I could have sworn I saw a glint of steel and the sparkle of a diamond-studded eye patch, just for a moment there ... but there's nothing now.
'If only we could see.
'What's that you say, miss?
'Your boyfriend's gone?
'How can you tell?
'You can feel a puddle on the seat?

'Warm and sticky?

'I'd say that's a natural reaction brought on by terror.

'Yes, my dear, and so is disappearing.

'No doubt he'll turn up later feeling extremely embarrassed. I wouldn't worry about it. As soon as we're out of this tunnel, you'll be able to wash your hands and Diabolico will come back in and look for him.

'At least we're still moving.

'Lightning!

'Oh, that was a gruesome sight! ... Did you see that?

'What did you say, miss?

'It's red? ... What's red?

'The puddle?

'It's probably just a trick of the light ... That ghoul in the coffin that we just passed looked orange in the lightning flash, but everyone knows that ghouls are green.

'Sounds like bats overhead now ... Can't see a thing, though.

'Oh!

'Did you feel that on your face? ... Like a spider's web ... Clingy.

'Now what's happening?

'Driver, why has the train stopped?

'The strands are tickling, like gossamer ... and there seems to be so much of it.

'Driver!

'Still no response ... No emergency candle ... Nothing.

'Madam, I can't stop it sticking to your face. Don't try to brush it away, though, or it'll be all over your hands as well; and try not pull on it or make it vibrate in any way. You don't know who or what will sense the vibrations.

'Don't worry, dear friends. We're sure to start moving again soon.

'Please, madam. Panicking won't help.

'Yes, I know it's impossible to see anything, so we should probably just sit still ... and be silent.

'Shh!

'What's that muffled tapping sound?

'It's getting louder ... rhythmical ... like four people dancing in bare feet, or wearing long, black hairy socks ... coming this way!

'I think they're running alongside the train now.

'Make sure you don't tug on those strands.

'They're getting closer, whatever they are ... shuffling ... grinding and squelching.

'Keep very still, everyone ... hold your breath.

'They seem to be moving away now. It sounds as though they're climbing up the side of the tunnel.

'Overhead now.

'Candle light at last. Thank you, driver!

'Madam? ... Where are you?

'Oh, my! ... How did you get up there? ... It is you, isn't it? ... I can hardly tell ... Your face is almost completely covered.

'And who are those four dancers in long, black hairy socks twirling you around?

'I did warn you about tugging on the strands.

'Driver! ... We must move on!

'I'm sorry, madam ... Nobody will come back for you.

'Please don't scream ... You'll frighten the little ones.

'Are we moving?

'Yes, we're on our way again ... Such a relief!

'It's OK, children. The nasty dancers won't come after us now. That nice lady will keep them occupied for days – possibly weeks.

'Let us reflect for a moment and shed a tear for her brave soul. May she eventually rest in peace.

'Look, it's getting lighter in the distance. We can't have far to go.

'What's that up ahead?

'It appears that we're about to pass under some kind of slashing mechanism attached to wires and pulleys ... with a compacted mass of something unsavoury suspended above it ... dripping.

'Don't slow down, driver!

'Duck, everyone!

'That was close! ... Those blades are razor sharp!

'I beg your pardon, sir?

'Yes, those are indeed real people hanging up there. You see that one is still alive – got caught in a noose yesterday and whisked up ... Couldn't catch another train anyway without a valid ticket for today, even if she could get down from there.

'Thank goodness the driver's not stopping here.

'Look! There's the opening of the tunnel! We've almost reached our destination.

'Ladies and gentlemen, boys and girls, as we approach the station, please ensure that you don't leave any possessions or parts of your anatomy on the train; and don't worry about whatever else is stuck to you – like that yellow matter sliding down the side of your head, madam. There will be hundreds of biomechanical parasites on the platform swarming to suck and lick everything off you as soon as you disembark.

'We hope you enjoyed the ride. If there's anyone in

your party who boarded the train but has, for whatever reason, not completed the journey, please notify the staff at the information desk when we reach the exit.

'No, we're not far from the exit, madam. It'll be immediately after the roller coaster ride.

'Now, as the train slows to a halt, and before we alight, I'd like you to check beneath your seat, because tucked under each of the Ghost Train's twenty-four seats is a sealed envelope.

'I'd like you to remove the envelope and secure it somewhere about your person, so that it doesn't get consumed with all the debris. Please don't open the envelope until we get to the Coconut Shy, which is in the large, doomed tent that you can see on the other side of the track.

'Did I say doomed?

'Please remain seated until the screeching stops.

'Not your screeching, young lady. I meant the brakes.

'That's it ... Off we get.

'Hold on tightly to your valuables – and the envelope.

'Here they come! It'll be quick.

'Don't scream, sir, or they won't get everything off you.

'Yes, sonny, they are very noisy, aren't they?

'Nearly done now.

'That's it ... All finished?

'You see, I told you it would be quick.

'What's that, young man? ... You're in more of a mess now than you were before you got off the train?

'That's unfortunate. Some of them do have a tendency to regurgitate immediately.

'I'm still not sure what that is on the side of your

head, madam. They didn't seem to want that.

'Anyway, let's move on.

'Cross the track and enter the tent via that inviting flap. Once inside you can enjoy a complimentary coconut drink, served to you by the survivors of our failed attempts to fuse organic matter with various machines and electrical appliances.

'Most of them are perfectly harmless, although I wouldn't get too close to the vacuum cleaner, if I were you.

'The inviting flap is flapping.

'When the flap flaps, dash inside.

'In you go!

'And the next one ... Wait for the flap to flap ...

'Go!

'That's it, children ... clap to the beat of the flap.

'One by one, or even in twos, in we go.

'Once you're inside, make sure you get your drink ... You'll feel delightfully refreshed.

'Is everybody in now?

'Two, four, six, eight, ten, twelve, fourteen, sixteen ... seventeen.

'You can stop clapping now, children ... There's no more flapping.

'So, ladies and gentlemen, boys and girls, here we are in the Coconut Shy.

'Where are what, sir?

'The coconuts?

'The gentleman would like to know where the coconuts are.

'Wait for it ... Drum roll ... The coconuts ... are shy!

'Boom, boom! Couldn't resist that one.

'Come right in, all of you.

'Move forward.

'Don't be nervous, little one. Lawnmowers don't bite. Not even this one, even though it still has most of its teeth. It's only snarling because it wants you to take the cup ... That's its way of smiling.

'Does everyone have a drink?

'Very good! ... Enjoy!

'Now let's open the envelopes!

'That's it, my sweet, rip it open!

'What do you have, sir?

'A card with a picture of a hard hat on it? ... Well, you're in luck, because that headwear is a piece of sturdy industrial hardware – and it's your prize!

'Take the card over to Diabolico and exchange it for one of those protective helmets.

'You, sir, over there ... and you, madam ... the same! ... Then go and claim your prize!

'What's that, young lady?

'Yours has a picture of a coconut on it? ... Really?

'You'd rather have a coconut than a helmet? ... Well, that's most fortunate, because there isn't enough protective headwear for everybody.

'And you, sir ... another coconut!

'More helmets over there.

'Aah, the little boy has a helmet, but his sister has a coconut.

'Everyone with a picture of protective headwear, go over to Diabolico and collect a helmet. All those with a picture of a coconut, hold on to your card.

'I can assure you that there will be more than enough coconuts for all those with a coconut card.

'In the meantime, please finish your delicious drink and hand your empty cup to the dishwasher.

'Now, let's see ... How many people do we have

without a hard hat?

'One, two, three ... four.

'Thirteen with and four without.

'I must say, you're all beginning to look very relaxed. Such happy smiles on all your faces!

'Look up, everyone!

'Behold! ... High up in the dome ... a net bulging with coconuts!

'Diabolico, let the fruit fly!

'Oh, here they come! Coconuts galore for everyone!

'You're all so calm and carefree that the coconuts appear to be floating – drifting downwards like balloons inflated with not quite enough helium – not at all like the hard-shelled projectiles that they are, hurtling towards you with all the force that gravity can muster.

'Spare a thought for the trembling coconut in bygone times, facing a firing squad, lined up alongside its brothers without arms, not knowing if this shot or the next would be the one to shatter its kernel and splatter the sweet contents all over its comrades, to the triumphant, milk-curdling cries of its executioner.

'No doubt your parents taught you to treat others as you would wish to be treated yourselves; but was such charity only reserved for those of your own kind? Did it not extend beyond your own species, or beyond the animal kingdom?

'Ladies and gentlemen, boys and girls, you are about to experience the coconut shy from the eye of the victim. This is the coconuts' retribution on behalf of all those assaulted in the past and those who continue to suffer bombardment in the name of entertainment today.

'But it seems you don't have a care as you marvel wide-eyed and open-mouthed at the fibrous husks hovering overhead, rotating slowly, seemingly suspended in time and space, when in reality those missiles are locked onto their human targets and homing in with a vengeance.'

'Well, you certainly have had a refreshing sleep, haven't you, little lady?
'The last yawn I saw like that was in a hippo enclosure.
'What's that, sir?
'I'm sorry, you'll have to repeat that.
'Hmm?
'I'm afraid I can't make sense of your muffled mumbling.
'It's no use struggling, sir. You won't be able to get out of that seat. The harness has been locked remotely to ensure your safety and won't be released until we reach the exit.
'Yes, I can see that you're concerned about your collarbone. We'll make sure that nobody treats that when we get to the other end.
'Madam, that's a nasty-looking gash on your nose. How fortunate that you're clutching a first-class ticket and are ready to roll.
'Hmm?
'What's that?
'I'm sorry, madam. I don't know what you're saying.
'Well, hello, sonny! ... Look at you, all bleary-eyed after your nap.
'No, don't try talking. You won't be able to yet.
'Now, we're just waiting for the last of our guests

to wake up, and then we'll have a pre-launch briefing prior to departure.

'I think you might be the last one to wake up, my dear ... Everyone else seems to be ready to go, judging by all the fidgeting and murmuring.

'Diabolico will check that everybody's eyes are open. We wouldn't want anyone to miss a spectacle such as this.

'One or two of you are still looking a little vague.

'Thank you, Diabolico.

'Don't worry, my pasty-faced friend, I'm sure the little boy didn't mind you using the zappy stick.

'Isn't it marvellous how Diabolico is always smiling? ... The wonders of do-it-yourself surgery!

'Now, if I might have your undivided attention, ladies and gentlemen, boys and girls – and if you could all stop humming for a moment and breathe naturally – I'd like to welcome you aboard ...

'Fanfare, Diabolico, please!

'Don't you love that tiny toy trumpet, children?

'Ladies and gentlemen, boys and girls, welcome aboard the Deoxyribonucleic Roller Coaster!

'We're almost set for departure on the highly anticipated final leg of our epic journey from the entrance to the exit, where most of you will be reunited with your loved ones and you'll be able to have your bumps, bruises, burns and broken bones attended to.

'Oops! I shouldn't have mentioned the burns yet.

'If you find that you're not sitting next to your friends or family members, it's because you were dragged here hastily in a semi-conscious state by a motley mob of composite creatures with intrusive appendages, and seated wherever and however it suited them.

'Yes, madam, the back of the seat and the headrests are high and wide, so don't worry if you can't see anyone you know. There's a very good chance that they're somewhere on board.

'You'll also notice that, although you're gradually coming to your senses, your tongue feels numb and inflated. That's a lingering effect of the delicious coconut drink that you were treated to earlier.

'So I'm afraid, sonny, that you won't be able to call out to your mommy to find out which seat she's in and tell her about Diabolico using the zappy stick ... and it's no use looking at me with those mournful manga eyes.

'Of course, it also means that there'll be no screaming on this ride.

'You look worried, young lady.

'There's no need to worry. What's about to happen will happen whether you worry about it or not.

'Look ahead now, everyone, and you'll see the track rising steeply towards the sky and disappearing into the clouds.

'Don't cry, little girl, it's not that bad ... yet.

'Diabolico, release the handle and set in motion a sequence of events that will defy all logic and reason as we head skyward on the world's only scream-free roller coaster.

'Crank it up, my comical accomplice!

'Here we go!

'The ascent will be swifter and smoother than on any conventional roller coaster, but it will take longer because we have farther to travel. Have patience. The higher we go, the faster we'll descend.

'I hope none of you are afraid of heights or have a heart condition. We'll be going higher than you'd ever imagine possible.

'Hold on to your harness!

'If you look over to the side, you'll see that we're already higher than any roller coaster you've ever been on before.

'Are your ears popping, poppet?

'As we reach the lowest clouds, prepare yourselves for a brief period of zero visibility.

'In we go.

'It's a white out!

'Suck that stratocumulus into your lungs!

'You must be wondering, as you sit there in white-knuckled, wide-eyed blindness, how it was possible to build something so tall and yet ensure its stability. Perhaps it isn't possible, you might think, as you feel the structure swaying.

'That's it ... We're emerging! ... Brace yourselves for a view like no other as you shrug off the last of those white wisps.

'Behold! ... Blue sky!

'And still we maintain our steep trajectory!

'Look down to the side, ladies and gentlemen, boys and girls, if you have the nerve.

'The temperature has certainly dropped, hasn't it? It's far too chilly for your summer attire up here.

'If there were mountains around us, we'd be just above the snow line.

'Although we've left the lower layer below us, there's one more cloud ahead. Do you see where the roller coaster track appears to disappear?

'Judging by the little clouds you're all creating now, the temperature must be around zero Celsius ... and their increasing frequency indicates that breathing is becoming laborious for some of you at this altitude.

'Still we continue to climb ... approaching the solitary altostratus that shrouds the summit and surely signals the start of our descent.

'Yet there appears to be no downward track on the other side.

'It's no use grimacing, little girl. If you'd listened to Mummy this morning when she told you to put your muffs and mittens on, your ears wouldn't be stinging now and your fingers wouldn't be blue, would they?

'It is cold, though ... very cold ... and getting colder.

'Minus 1 ... minus 2 ... minus 3 ...

'There's no need for that aggressive scowl, mister. It was your choice to buy a ticket.

'Minus 4 ... minus 5 ... minus 6 ...

'And still we climb!

'Minus 7 ... minus 8 ... minus 9 ...

'Don't cry, little boy. We've almost reached the freezing point of tears. Can you imagine what would happen to your eyes if your tears suddenly froze?

'Minus 10 ... minus 11 ... minus 12 ...

'Ice crystals appear to be forming around the weeping wound on your nose, madam. If they're uncomfortable, just pick them off and flick them over the side ... if you can manage that without snapping off your frozen fingers.

'Oh, dear, I shouldn't have made you laugh. Now you'll have red icicles hanging from your lips.

'This is an unusual cloud, don't you think? ... Not changing shape at all ... denser ... almost solid, like an ice plateau carved into the upper troposphere.

'The track is beginning to bend onto it, and we seem to be slowing down.

'Can you feel your spine realigning and your liver

levelling out?

'I sense your collective anticipation ... You could cut the stratosphere with a knife.

'What do you think we'll see up here, boys and girls? Could this be where Jack Frost lives?

'I must say, dear guests, you all look a picture of ill health with your frostbitten flesh and crystallised hair ... oh, and that steaming pool of what looks like minestrone between your feet, sir, quickly solidifying.

'If you'll disregard the altitude sickness for a moment and keep your eyelids from freezing together, you might see two liquid angels resembling your grandparents seeping through the hastily stitched seams of an octahedral cathedral and trickling through a pearly portal to accept an invitation from Odin, Hera, Allah and Hathor to a game of two-dimensional one-upmanship ... or whatever your oxygen-deprived grey matter can dream up.

'At last ... the mechanism has disengaged and we've begun coasting.

'Time to snap out of your reverie and see what's really there to see, and not what your mind would like there to be.

'Don't despair, madam. Worse things happen at sea ... although probably not. Ha, ha, ha!

'Look, there is a downward track after all ... It's a double helix!

'Going down!

'Ooh, your intestines are revolting ... rising up to overthrow the contents of your stomach.

'Your wide-mouthed silence shows how thrilling you find the sensation of freefall – especially with a hurricane-force wind blasting your eyeballs.

'Am I mistaken, or has the temperature begun soaring?

'Rapid defrosting is something that very few humans get to experience.

'We've plummeted so far so quickly that we should be decelerating by now – but we're not. The ground is expanding alarmingly as we spiral downward. We can't possibly stop in time. Our only hope is that black hole.

'If only you could all scream ... Screaming might save us.

'Close your eyes!

'In we go ... plunged into darkness as the roller coaster's breakneck deceleration moulds everyone's torso into the harness.

'Slower ... and slower.

'Relief at last as the pressure on your ribs is gradually eased.

'Levelling out now.

'If you open your eyes you'll see nothing. We must be passing through an underground tunnel ... or a wormhole.

'Almost horizontal now ... and still warming up.

'The steam that you're inhaling is a heady blend of evaporating cloud crystals, terror-induced sweat and a range of other bodily fluids and secretions, all mixing with methane to form an intoxicating concoction in the overwhelming heat.

'We could be in the lava tube of an active volcano ... or a subterranean shisha bar.

'What's that sound – rumbling and roaring all around?

'Is an eruption imminent, or are the demons of the underworld clamouring to feast on their latest express delivery of fear?

'Flames!
'We're rolling towards an inferno!
'At last I can see your faces ... red and flickering with rage.
'What's that, sonny?
You can speak! ... The effects of the coconut drink are finally wearing off.
'I didn't quite catch what you said, though.
'You've had enough and want to go home?
'Too much enjoyment all at once for such a small boy.
'Was that a flare shooting across the track, or a fiery demon performing a ritualistic dance?
'Look, everyone ... Diabolico's face paint is melting, and nobody's robe is beginning to smoulder.
'Would you mind repeating that, madam?
'Try to hold your tongue in when you speak. It's still rather puffy and your words are muffled.
'You need to thleep?
'You can't go on?
'But we must proceed to the exit. It can't be far now.
'What's that, sir?
'Well, perhaps you *have* done something to deserve this. Perhaps fate has driven you into this hell hole for a reason.
'More flares! ... Shield your eyes!
'Did they miss everyone?
'No, not everyone ... Something's sizzling in the front row.
'Put that beard out, sir!
'Ooh, the smell of singed hair!
'What was that jolt?
'Did you feel that, ladies and gentlemen? ... I do

believe we're starting to climb.

'If we can just get past those flame-throwing horned demons without being abducted or reduced to ashes, we might make it out of here.

'Never mind the burns, little girl ... Just think of all the fun you're having.

'Gently does it ... If we can pass this vent before the next flare shoots out, we should be out of danger – unless there's something more malevolent down here and it spots us and gives chase, shouting obscenities at us backwards in an extinct language, in which case we must hope that we pick up enough speed to shake it off.

'There's the vent to our right ... Completely dark inside ... Not one pair of glowing eyes.

'It seems that our fears were unfounded ... Fortune favours the foolish.

'We're safely through, yet we could easily have been incinerated.

'Now for the climb that will hopefully take us up to the exit.

'Do you see that shaft of light ahead, ladies and gentlemen?

'Just outside the tunnel are mechanised mummies holding torches aloft to guide us safely back and repel any invisible evil that might have found its way on board ... and might be in possession of any one of you.

'Who's that sobbing?

'You, sir. Why are you sobbing?

'The burns feel real and you're certain that your collarbone is broken ... and you think nobody cares?

'You're absolutely right, sir. Nobody cares.

'And you, madam ... I see in the encroaching

glimmer of daylight that you've painted a fresh fissure on your forehead. Such skilful application of theatrical make-up under challenging conditions! It adds so much to the authenticity of the adventure. I applaud your efforts, madam – although I must say that the illusion of oozing blood would be more effective if it didn't look so much like barbecue sauce.

'It actually hurts, you say.

'I suspect that the heat might have caused some distress, too, especially among the elderly.

'Here's one.

'Are you still with us, sir?

'I said are you still with us?

'Give him a poke, Diabolico.

'Nothing?

'Try the zappy stick.

'Still no response?

'Never mind. We might be able to revive him outside.

'Meanwhile, nobody will hand out sanitised towels to freshen you up before we exit the tunnel.

'As the Deoxyribonucleic Roller Coaster eases gently to a halt and the safety harnesses are released, I'll ask you to ensure that you have all of your belongings with you before leaving your seat to rejoin your family and friends.

'Ladies and gentlemen, boys and girls, I hope you've enjoyed the ultimate fairground experience. Diabolico would like to ...

'Joey? ... Who's Joey?

'Madam ... You keep saying, "Where's Joey?"

'Who's Joey?

'I see ...

'Are you sure he was with you in the Coconut Shy?

'Hmm ...
'Did he have protective headwear?
'He didn't.
'Well, that's not necessarily a reason for him not to be aboard the roller coaster. Perhaps he wasn't secured properly. The little ones have a tendency to slip through the gap in the harness.

'Did anyone see something small fly off the roller coaster?
'No?
'Well, that's positive ... although it was dark a lot of the time, and the backrests are very high. If he'd been flung over the side, the chances are that nobody would have seen him go.

'Not to worry, madam, people go missing inexplicably on funfair rides all the time. Generally they either turn up later, sometimes on the evening news, or they don't turn up at all.

'What's done is done. There's no point in crying over spilt milk, or any other liquid for that matter.

'Here's a smiley sticker.

'As I was saying ... Diabolico would like to express its unbridled sadistic joy in ensuring that you all reached the pinnacle of perverse pleasure more times than was good for your mental health ... and nobody hopes that you don't have recurring nightmares for the rest of your lives.

'Please don't go rushing in a blind panic to the exit. As soon as you've received whatever medical treatment you need, you can collect your phones ... and I'd like to remind you that you signed a disclaimer on entering, in effect acknowledging that if you leave here minus a leg you won't have the other one to stand on.

'Hu! Hu! Hu!'

'Step right up! ... This way, ladies and gentlemen, boys and girls, for the experience of a lifetime in the most extreme funfair in the universe!'

TERROR PERICOLOSA

'This is Monarch of the UK Ark, Lifeboat 1. Do you copy, UK Ark?

'Is that still a negative, UK Ark?

'Is any other ark receiving?

'If anyone in the fleet can hear this, please acknowledge. We've had zero response to our transmissions since landing on Proxima Centauri b three weeks ago. This will be my final attempt at communication. I'm the last remaining crew member on board, and am preparing for disembarkation and abandonment of Lifeboat 1.

'In case this transmission fails or is not received, I'm recording it so that the crews of any other lifeboats, whether British, American, Russian, Indian or Korean, will have access to information regarding our discoveries and the conditions on and beneath the planet's surface – including the mystery craft, our access point into the canyon, the subterranean route taken, and encounters with the life forms below.

'At the end of this recorded transmission I'll switch the lifeboat systems to standby and go in search of Trebuchet, who was investigating the other craft when the stellar flare occurred three hours ago. The flare interrupted our communications and I've heard nothing from him since, although his channel is still open. If he's survived the surge in temperature and is mobile, we'll make our way directly to the canyon to pick up the trail marked by the advance party, and hopefully rejoin the survivors within twenty-four hours. If I don't find him immediately, or his status is terminal, I'll have no choice but to make the descent alone. I can't afford to waste oxygen on a futile search or a vain rescue attempt – even though he's my assigned breeding partner.

'Following the departure of the second group ten days ago, Trebuchet and I remained on board to monitor subsurface-to-surface communications, and have been endeavouring to establish surface-to-orbit contact to relay information to the fleet – seemingly without success.

'So, assuming that none of our previous transmissions have been received, I'll take it from the start, referring to the lifeboat's log so as not to omit any vital details of our mission. I'll also play the most relevant recordings of reports and observations from the first members of our fleet to set foot on Proxima b.

'Before I begin, though, I have the unhappy duty of reporting the loss of six of our landing party. Zephyr, Shard, Kerid, Mirage, Crete and Druid did not survive the descent into the planet's crust. The other six were still alive underground when Galleon last made contact almost nineteen hours ago, shortly before all subsurface-to-surface communications ceased.

'In memory of those whose lives have been lost, both here on the planet and during our multigenerational interstellar odyssey, I'd like to acknowledge the momentousness of our achievement.

'1,268 Earth years after our ancestors set out for the Alpha Centauri system from our pollution-ravaged home world in a fleet of twenty-two arks, we can celebrate the landing of the fleet's first fourteen colonists on what we hope will be a new home for us and all of the species that have survived the journey with us. I emphasise *the fleet's* first fourteen colonists, as we've discovered that we're not the first human arrivals on this planet. I'll say more about that later.

'Our touchdown was hair-raising, to say the least. Full thrust on landing barely countered the pull of Proxima b's gravity. Our propulsion system cut out a second too soon and we came down hard. But considering that Druid and Crete's only practice at controlling this boat was undocking, hovering, turning and redocking with minimal thrust in the restricted space and zero gravity of the lifeboat bay, they did a pretty good job. No casualties, but we suspected that there was some damage to our communications equipment externally, which we still haven't been able to identify. The main transmitter and receiver, as well as the back-ups, are all functioning as far as surface-to-surface communications go, but there's been no indication that any of our signals have been picked up by the fleet. Trebuchet suggested that the extreme levels of electromagnetic radiation might be interfering with surface-to-orbit communications, but I'm not so sure. The fact that contact was maintained during our entire transit surely invalidates that theory – unless distance is also a factor and the arks' subsequent relative positioning in orbit has pushed us out of range.

'Out of range of every ark for three weeks, though? I don't think so. I'm sticking with the unidentified damage theory. Either way, hopefully the fact that we haven't detected another lifeboat in three weeks means that the UK Ark at least has received our warnings and is assessing the situation before sending any more colonists down.

'In spite of our faster than ideal descent, Druid managed to get us close to the centre of the plateau, about 600 paces from the canyon, and 1.2 kilopaces from the hitherto unidentifiable structure, which we now know to be a spacecraft. We spent the first twenty-four hours aboard the lifeboat analysing the environment, scanning the mystery vessel and drawing up a plan of action before anyone ventured out.

'Our first impression of Proxima Centauri from the surface of Proxima b was one of a fiery orb toasting the horizon at a distance of a mere 7.5 million kilometres. From our location close to the planet's terminator line, and with the bow of the lifeboat facing the red dwarf, we've been able to observe the star safely through maximum tinting as it perpetually rises above and dips below the horizon, never in full view, but never completely out of sight, all the while shooting shadows at us via millions of scattered rocks of every imaginable shape and size.

'Away from the shimmering background glow of Proxima Centauri's flickering corona, the sky is dark and crystal clear all the time, giving us a striking view of Alpha Centauri A and B – a pair of gems visible to us for half of the Proxima b year, emerging from the orange to bejewel the black as they arc across the canopy every 11.2 Earth days.

'On approach, the terrain around the plateau appeared to be perfectly flat, and strewn with reddish brown boulders and rocks that match the colour of the stones and dust on the tableland beneath us. The plateau itself is mostly surrounded by escarpments, but with a gradual slope averaging around 20% on our port side, leading down to what appeared from orbit to be a vast, dry lake bed fading into the blackness beyond the terminator. We can only speculate as to whether the lakes on the dark side have been sufficiently shielded from the destructive force of the stellar storms that would have stripped away all conditions for life on the bright side. The prospect of frozen lakes storing a substance that might be drinkable in its liquid form is something that future landing parties will have to explore – if the challenge of accessibility can be overcome.

'Our observation from orbit of the lack of diversity in the overall surface shades of reddish-brown, or of any variation that might have promised vegetation, are confirmed as far as we can see.

'An unexpected feature that wasn't visible from the ark is the steam which is constantly rising from the canyon and from countless other vents of various sizes on and around the plateau. The vapour immediately suggested to us the presence of subterranean moisture of some kind, but only outside exploration would determine the composition and source of these gases, and whether or not the moisture, if collectable, would be drinkable.

'We've been here for almost two Proxima b years now in our twenty-one Earth days, so we've experienced all of the planet's seasons twice – if you can call them seasons. With no atmosphere and no visible vegetation, the only evidence of seasonal change is the apparent expansion and contraction of Proxima Centauri – and of course the outside temperature, which climbs to about 18° Celsius at the height of summer, and drops to minus fifteen in mid-winter, 134 Earth hours later. You can calculate for yourselves what the seasonal temperatures are likely to be in the middle of the scorched side and on the permanently frozen dark side. As we've known all along, if any part of this world is habitable, it has to be somewhere along the terminator line.

'While we can choose landing locations along the band where the temperature is tolerable, there's no way of avoiding the radiation on the surface. On a tidally locked planet with no magnetosphere, our chances of survival are slim in stellar winds two thousand times more powerful than Earth's solar wind. Decades of monitoring the frequency of flares on our approach to the star system have at best enabled us to estimate times of low probability of a stellar storm in order to deploy a lifeboat crew as safely as possible – aside from exposing us to electromagnetic radiation far beyond what the human body has evolved to withstand, even inside these suits with their hydrogenated boron nitride nanotubes.

'The other great unknown when the fleet set out, of course, was the atmosphere – or rather the lack of it, as it has turned out. We can adapt physically to the lower temperatures; and we've trained for years to take on ten per cent more weight than in the ark's simulated gravity; and now we're hopeful of being able to source a non-toxic water supply; but unless we can breathe on this rock, we won't survive. We boarded this boat knowing that if the atmospheric pressure was too high or too low, or if there was insufficient oxygen, either on the surface or below, the journey of fifty generations would have been in vain.

'Although the composition of the planet's gases, including the presence of oxygen, can't be determined from inside a lifeboat any more than it can from orbit, the barometer tells us that the atmospheric pressure is too low for us to survive on the surface without these suits, whether there's oxygen present or not. Ultimately, for the fourteen of us transported down here in our microbiome, the only true test of breathability would be on a living being.

'After thirty-six hours of observation, Galleon and Zephyr agreed that the external sensors and gauges had provided us with all the information we could possibly gain from inside. Kerid, given the green light by our co-commanders, wasted no time in suiting up and carrying the pressurised sustainer containing M1 into the airlock. Galleon secured the internal hatch as Kerid placed the small, transparent life support capsule on the ground in clear view of both cameras before unlocking the lifeboat's external hatch. As it slowly opened, she paused, peered into one of the cameras, then stooped to open the sustainer's vents. The rest of us watched in silence on the monitors as the mouse twitched, bucked, convulsed, and collapsed onto its side with its abdomen pumping furiously. It jerked its head once, thrust its legs out and then lay motionless – all within ten seconds. Kerid immediately closed the outer hatch, then repressurised and oxygenated the airlock in the expectation that the mouse would recover. It didn't. The barometer had already indicated that it wouldn't be able to breathe for long, but we'd hoped that the brief period of exposure would enable us to revive it. Much depended on the presence of oxygen and the toxicity of any other gases entering the airlock.

'The mouse's instant demise told us what we would have preferred not to know. The experiment shook us with the sobering realisation that we had to use the remaining four mice sparingly, because the "guinea-pig" for the sixth attempt would be one of us.

'The video recordings from the two cameras are here for anyone who'd like to see M1 busting its lungs.

'I guess we're fortunate that mice were able to survive on our ark, otherwise we'd have had to transport chicks or larger animals down here. Of course, if we're going to establish a sustainable colony, chicks will have to be brought down at some point – and lambs, too, although it'll be a hell of a job hauling lamb-size sustainers through the planet's labyrinthine crust.

'Having established beyond any doubt that it wouldn't be possible to breathe unassisted on the surface, the next step would normally have been to ascertain the nature of the gases emanating from the canyon. However, we were all far more curious about the craft that had beaten us to this star system, and so Zephyr's proposal that we investigate that first was supported unanimously.

'According to the external gauge, the average temperature in the thirty-six hours prior to the disembarkation of the first reconnaissance party was 8° Celsius, rising to eleven when Proxima Centauri was predominantly above the horizon, and not falling below five – so conditions were ideal for a team to set out.

'The anomalous structure that we'd puzzled over from orbit, which was so obviously inconsistent in shade and shape with the rest of the landscape, and appeared to have either landed on the plateau or been built there, did indeed turn out to be a spacecraft, about half a kilopace in length. Other non-natural objects nearby were identifiable through the telescope as a double-rear-wheeled vehicle with front caterpillar tracks, an array of photovoltaic panels, numerous boxes and a tripod. Markings were visible on the hull, but we couldn't tell from here what they were.

'The existence of this other vessel has given us plenty to consider. First, it's either from Earth or it's not. If not, it either originated here on Proxima b or it came from some other planet. Its size and the familiarity of the other objects around it lead us to believe that it's from Earth, in which case it left Earth after the departure of our fleet, since history tells us that our fleet was the first. The ship's very presence here, whether it left decades or centuries after our fleet, confirms Proxima b as the most favourable destination for colonisation in the absence of any habitable planets or moons in Earth's solar system. There's also little doubt that the crew were of the same opinion as us regarding the optimal location for early exploration and potential settlement, and presumably chose this barren, rocky plateau as a vantage point which would also provide access to the canyon. We expected to find the answers to some of our questions on deployment of the first reconnaissance party.

'Galleon, our co-commander and mechanical engineer, assigned Swift, our electrical engineer, and Europa, our historian, to accompany him on the first expedition to investigate the unidentified craft. In doing so, they became the first members of our fleet — though probably not the first humans — to set foot on Proxima b. The three were tethered in single file by two six-pace lengths of rope hooked onto their utility belts — Galleon ahead of Swift, Swift ahead of Europa — in case of any unforeseeable hazards, such as a concealed crevice.

'Their early exchange of comments concerned the suits, which we'd only trialled on the ark in conditions that were simulated to approximate those on the surface. Here's the recording of what Swift had to say about her suit during the 1.2-kilopace walk to the mystery vessel.'

'The suit feels heavier than it did in training on the ark. We expected that, due to the planet's gravity being 1.1 times the ark's simulated gravity. Nevertheless, joint mobility is adequate ... Still a bit tight around the shoulders, though ... I'm having to make a conscious effort to lift my feet so as not to drag them through the dust, which is ankle deep ... The adjustable oxygen flow, dehumidifier, cooling and communications are all functioning as tested before disembarkation – quite remarkable considering the suits were constructed almost thirteen centuries ago ... I'm looking forward to trying out the feeding tubes before we head back ... Not so the waste management system, even though it's imperative that we check that the suction pump, deodorising unit and receptacles are securely fitted and working effectively before we venture any farther afield ... Imagine being trapped inside a suit with a malfunctioning waste management system.'

'That precipitated a wave of mirth around the lifeboat.

'As the team approached the craft, Galleon gave us a verbal inventory of the items abandoned outside, which included an all-terrain vehicle designed for two humanoid operators with two passengers seated at the rear, dozens of disconnected PV panels, numerous reels of cable, and boxes containing various tools and instruments. He described a large hatch on the starboard side of the ship – the side of their approach. It was hinged at the top, and raised, with a ramp deployed. Galleon and Swift boarded, while Europa remained outside to survey the exterior.

'We have no video capability outside the lifeboat, just audio. I'll play the recording of Galleon's initial observations on entering.'

'It looks like a storage or loading bay ... used to house the hardware that's outside ... There's more of the same in here: panels, instruments, tools ... and a hoist ... There are numbers on the instruments, with symbols similar to those on the hull ... and the same symbols and script on signs mounted all around the bay ... but there's nothing resembling our alphabet ... Maybe Europa can make sense of it.

'Try some of those switches and buttons, Swift.

'We're trying some switches and buttons on the instruments and tools, and some on the wall, but nothing's happening. Whatever their power source was, it's been dead for a long time.

'There's a smaller internal hatch at the forward end of the bay, which looks like the access point to an airlock ... It's open on this side, but the hatch on the inside to the left is closed ... We're going in to see if it can be opened manually.'

'There was a pause of several minutes while Galleon and Swift figured out how to open it, so I'll skip forward.'

'... left turn leading into a corridor.

'Stepping into the corridor now ... There's no lighting as far as we can see ... I mean, no actual lights ... We can't see to the end either way, left or right.

'Yeah, lights on.

'We're turning our helmet and cuff lights on now ... Still can't see clearly all the way down, but this will have to do for now ... We'll need to bring the auxiliary lighting next time, unless Swift can get the photovoltaics outside working and hook them up to something

in here.
'Yeah, that way.
'We're going right ... towards the bow of the ship ... We could have turned left, but I think we're more likely to find the bridge up front.
'Now approaching a doorway to our left ... No door ... just a doorway ... Can't see any light from the loading bay now ... Just relying on our lights ... Stepping through ...'
'Galleon was silent again for a while as he and Swift took in what they were seeing.'
'It looks like it might be a control centre ... Could be the bridge ... There are ... eight ... twelve seats and consoles ... It looks as though they're designed for human or humanoid operation ... but no occupants ... no bodies ... no skeletons.'
'He went on to describe what appeared to be the ship's helm. He said its layout was undoubtedly designed for human or humanoid operation, but most of the components of the console were unlike anything that he or Swift had seen before, with markings in a language that neither of them recognised. They found no material records of any kind. Presumably the ship's log was stored digitally and would require power for access – and probably an authorisation code. Without power they couldn't determine anything about the ship's means of propulsion. That would necessitate a different approach via a physical access point that we still haven't located three weeks on. Searching for it during the first sortie would have taken more time than had been allocated, so Swift and Galleon made use of the remaining time to explore whatever rooms, cabins and storage compartments were accessible. They found no signs of life, but there were items of

clothing in most of the compartments, including two space suits. The suits were not dissimilar to ours, which suggested that they were constructed around the same time; so, unless they'd been in storage for decades or centuries before launch and there had been no further improvements in suit technology in the interim, this ship would have left Earth soon after the departure of our fleet.

'There was a protracted silence before Galleon summed up.'

'The ship appears to have been evacuated with no trace of disturbance or panic ... Everything suggests an orderly exit ... It's all so clean ... very little dust inside ... and nothing to indicate how long this thing has been here and how long ago it was abandoned ... or why.'

'Back in the lifeboat, the rest of us continued our speculation as to the ship's origin and departure date. While there appeared to have been very few advances in suit technology between the time of our fleet's readiness and the launch of the later craft, there must have been a significant breakthrough in terms of propulsion. Yet, according to all of the scenarios modelled thirteen centuries ago, the exponential rate of environmental destruction and social decay allowed barely sufficient time for the completion of our multinational fleet of nuclear-powered arks based on existing designs. There are no records of any revolutionary advances in propulsion prior to our ancestors' departure – and certainly none were approved for incorporation into any of the arks.

'Unless there's more to those two suits than was immediately apparent to Galleon and Swift, this ship would have left within decades of our fleet rather than centuries. On the other hand, the method of propulsion required for it to have left after us and arrived before us would suggest a century of progress rather than decades. Based on our knowledge of the time, alternatives to nuclear fusion, such as the Alcubierre drive or wormholes, were at best untested theory; the Bussard ramjet was in the early stages of development; and plans for a ram-augmented interstellar rocket were still on the drawing board.

'To find answers to all of these questions, we needed more time to access the ship's data and examine the propulsion system itself – neither of which we've managed to achieve in the last three weeks. Our last chance was Trebuchet's lone sortie – and now he's missing.

'We hoped that Europa's historical knowledge and investigative skills might provide us with some answers. Here's what she had to say after Galleon and Swift emerged from the loading bay.'

'It's from Earth. The seating and controls in the vehicle tell us that ... But there's more. There's a flag engraved and imprinted on both sides of the hull. I'd say that the chances of an extraterrestrial civilisation using flags similar in dimension and design to ancient Earth flags to represent its origin are infinitesimal. Come and have a look.

'You see how the colours have faded, but the outlines are still clear ... Three equal horizontal divisions, with an emblem in the centre – a typically terrestrial tricolour ... Now, look closely ... The top and bottom sections have retained some of their colour, indicating that they may have been darker than the middle third ... so that was probably white, or yellow. The emblem is the same colour as the bottom ... They

both seem to me to have a hint of red – but then everything we see on this planet has a red tinge ... The top less so, though – maybe green, blue or even black.

'Another interesting feature is the two dividing lines between the three segments. They're not actually lines ... See? ... It's either a decorative pattern or some kind of script, repeated along the bottom of the top colour, and along the top of the bottom colour.

'The emblem's interesting, too – four thin crescents in a quasi-spherical arrangement. The two inner crescents meet at the bottom and appear to be supporting a strong vertical line at the core. The two outer crescents could be symbolic of a protective embrace. I'm wondering if the design might be a centuries-old representation of the Reactor ... The only other component – small but no doubt significant – is placed overhead. Its position might depict intelligence or control. If the emblem does indeed represent the Reactor, the feature above the core might be a stylised coil.'

'Europa broke off, and the three of them discussed their collective findings, while, in the lifeboat, we listened intently and tried to visualise what they'd described to us.

'After a lengthy pause, Europa resumed.'

'I'm unable to identify the flag, but I know for sure that it isn't a flag of any of the twenty-two nations of our fleet. As for the script, I don't recognise that either. It's definitely not Roman or Cyrillic, and I'm familiar with Chinese, Japanese and Korean, so we can rule those out. That leaves regions known at the time of departure as the Middle East and Central Asia, where there was a wide diversity of written forms. I'll have to see if there's anything like it in the lifeboat's

database when we get back.'

'As it turned out, there were no matches for the script or the flag in the lifeboat's database. However, Europa recalled that there were two Middle Eastern arks among the original twenty-two. We all know the story of the Saudi Arabian ark losing power soon after its final round of orbital embarkations, and crashing into the Pacific Ocean to become the fleet's first major casualty. Few of us were aware, though, of the fate of the Jordanian ark thirty-eight years later, when it inexplicably blocked all contact with the rest of the fleet, and was tracked for another fifteen years on a divergent heading, three degrees off course, until all trace was lost. We wondered if it could have been one of those nations making a second attempt, or another country that hadn't been included in the departure plans ... like Pakistan, or Thailand. Europa didn't know which countries in that region had the potential to develop interstellar technology that would ultimately surpass ours.

'As if we didn't have enough to contemplate, Matrix, our astrophysicist, chipped in from another angle. All along we'd assumed that this was an interstellar spaceship with a propulsion system more advanced than ours; but what if it were just a landing craft, with little more thrust than our lifeboat, despite its size? If so, what happened to the mother ship?

'Although many questions were raised during that first excursion, a great deal was achieved. After confirming the functionality of their feeding tubes and waste management systems, Galleon, Swift and Europa headed back with a selection of artefacts from the ship, and samples of rocks and dust for Mirage, our geologist, to examine.

'Mirage found no organic matter in the samples and concluded that the pyroxenes present in the rocks and the perchlorates in the regolith, while indicating the existence of oxygen on the planet, would be toxic to humans and would not support plant life native to Earth. He communicated his findings directly to the UK Ark, but neglected to make an audio recording of the transmission, so the only detailed record is in the data file "Mirage001".

'The other aims of the first mission were to measure our oxygen consumption and the durability of the various power packs under real conditions. At the end of the trio's three-hour sortie, their oxygen gauges showed consumption at 24%, 26% and 27%. All three had regulated their flows manually, so their individual consumption varied, but we were satisfied with an estimate of ten to twelve hours' supply on a full tank – in effect, a ten-hour one-way descent into the canyon in search of water, food and a breathable atmosphere. Once departed, there would be no point in returning to the lifeboat and depleting the on-board supplies of oxygen, food, water and power reserves, which were projected to last three weeks. Now, twenty-one days later, there's only enough oxygen for me and M5 to survive for another twenty-four hours.

'The integrated systems powering the suits' deodorising and dehumidifying units, as well as communications, all came back above 90%, as did Europa's lighting batteries. However, Galleon and Swift's helmet and cuff light batteries were below 80% – a figure that impressed upon us the need to use our lights sparingly when recharged for the final time.

'As for the physical effects, all three reported aching and swollen ankles, as well as a slight backache.

The increased gravity is something that we've been dealing with in the lifeboat by frequently reclining our backrests and elevating our legs. There's no compression anywhere in the suits, so once outside, the swelling – or peripheral oedema, as our medics called it – has to be managed by periodic rest. If our great-great-grandparents had known what we know now, they might have initiated the one per cent a decade increase in the rotation of the ark's mid-section a hundred and fifty years ago instead of just a century ago. Either that, or the last five or six generations could have been rostered on to spend eight working and recreational hours a day in the mid-section instead of six. In that respect the livestock and vegetation will be better suited to conditions on the planet than we humans, having never been exposed to anything but simulated gravity.

'Perhaps my criticism of our progenitors is harsh. After all, they got us here, which is more than can be said of the commanders of the seventeen arks that didn't make it. Unlike most of the others, our civilisation has thrived and our ecosystems have flourished. We've avoided catastrophic collisions with cosmic dust, loss of power-generating capability, structural disintegration, spontaneous combustion, propulsion failure, navigational errors, starvation due to extinction of flora and fauna, depopulation resulting from gender imbalance or disease, civil conflict, societal collapse, and wilful self-destruction.

'Who knows what's really been happening on board the other four arks?

'For anyone on the Russian, Indian, Korean and US arks who can understand what I'm saying, or for the benefit of anyone else who discovers this soon-to-be abandoned craft, I should explain that we've been maintaining our 24-Earth-hour day-night cycle here on the planet, just as we and our ancestors have done for the last millennium and a quarter on the UK Ark. The original idea was to ensure continued use of the Gregorian calendar and consistency of dating methods across arks, while also helping to replicate the native environmental conditions of all the plant and animal species that have accompanied us on our odyssey. However, we'd be wrong to assume that every other interstellar community has followed the same pattern for such a long time.'

'Our second sortie followed one of our scheduled rest periods, during which the interior of the lifeboat was darkened and silenced for the equivalent of one third of an Earth day – or roughly three per cent of a Proxima b year.

'As the canyon is 600 paces away at its nearest point, only a two-hour outing was envisaged for a preliminary exploration of the terrain along the rim. Zephyr, our other co-commander and biologist, was accompanied by Mirage, our geologist, and Shard, our dietitian, who took M2 along in its sustainer. The two main objectives were to ascertain the composition of the steam emanating from the canyon and surrounding vents, and to see if there was any possibility of descending into the canyon far enough to find a natural shield from exposure to electromagnetic radiation once we'd relinquished the security of our suits – assuming that we could find sources of oxygen, water and food in sufficient accessible quantities to sustain us for long enough to need a radiation-resistant rock layer.

'Well, the good news is that we do need protection from the radiation, but it's too soon to tell if the six surviving crew members below ground are deep enough for adequate long-term protection.

'This, from Zephyr, once the team had found a spot overlooking a ledge just inside the canyon, where the vapour was rising all around them.'

'This will do ... There's plenty of steam here ... And there's a ledge, no more than a pace and a half below the rim. One of us can climb down with the oxygen sensor and hopefully get a clear reading ... M2 can go down as well.'

'I'll stop Zephyr's recording there and switch to Shard, as he volunteered to climb down.'

'Pass M2 down first ...

'Yep ...

'OK ... Got it ...

'Yep ... OK ...

'Uh, Lifeboat 1, I'm standing shoulder deep inside the edge of the canyon ... The ledge is about a pace wide where I'm standing, and fairly level ... It slopes down and narrows, then gets quite steep before levelling off again and widening ... I can't see clearly beyond a dozen paces or so because of the vapour rising from below and the build-up of moisture on my visor ... M2 is on the ledge beside me ... I'm going to take a reading first to see if there's any oxygen in this mist.'

'For a while all we heard was Zephyr and Mirage offering guidance.'

'... have to keep wiping the damned visor ... There's something, though ... It's reading something ... I'll get you to look at this, Mirage.'

'With that, the dietitian handed the sensor up to the geologist, explaining later that he passed it to Mirage because of the poor visibility through his visor and the steam. There were spontaneous cheers on board when Mirage announced, "Oxygen content 3%". Zephyr then instructed Shard to move the sustainer lower down the ledge – as far into the steam as the six paces of rope connecting them would allow – and then open the vents.'

'OK ... Yep ... Got the sustainer ...

'Moving along ...

'Uh ... I can only go about two more paces ... but there's a good vent within reach ...

'Nearly there ...

'Setting the sustainer down now ... right over the steam ... I can see M2 OK ... Can you see M2, Zeph?'

'She couldn't.'

'Opening the vents now ... Get ready to time this ...

'Vents open ...

'Mmm ...

'M2's gone into a panic already ... jumping about ... trying to climb the walls of the sustainer ... doing somersaults ... seems to be having trouble breathing now ...

'It's lying down ... gagging ... I'm going to close the vents ...'

'We waited.'

'The vents are closed ...

'M2's not moving.

'How long was that?'

'Trebuchet on comms shouted nineteen seconds as Mirage came through the speaker with the same number.'

'That's longer than M1 ... twice as long!'

'Yes, it was twice as long, but still under twenty seconds – and the mouse was just as dead. 3% oxygen in low pressure was far from enough for it to survive, but it was probably the presence of a poisonous gas that finished it off so quickly.

'M2's demise aside, we were all elated by the discovery of oxygen. It strengthened our resolve to explore the canyon, and raised our hopes of finding a higher concentration of oxygen in an environment with zero toxicity and higher atmospheric pressure.

'Three more suits were confirmed to be functioning exactly as they were when tested on the ark; but again the going was heavy, and Zephyr, Shard and Mirage all complained of aching feet and ankles.

'Our calculations following that second sortie provided us with confirmation that a single portable oxygen supply would last ten to twelve hours, depending on the level of exertion, if used continuously. So our mission was clear. We had to gamble on finding greater quantities of steam containing higher concentrations of oxygen and no toxic gases – within ten hours. We theorised that if we could achieve some measure of breathability, with atmospheric pressure greater than on the surface, our oxygen could be alternated with the steam while descending, thereby extending our supplies until we'd acclimatised or were able to breathe unaided.

'Just like the lifeboat landing, the journey underground is a one-way trip. If the subterranean environment doesn't provide the conditions to sustain a human body, there's nowhere else for us to go. All we can do is report our findings to the fleet and leave these recordings, so that the arks' commanders can make their decisions about future landings.'

'Zephyr led the advance party of six for the initial

descent into the canyon. Kerid, one of our two medics, and Crete, our co-pilot on landing, were the only ones of the six who hadn't trialled their suits since our arrival, so they suited up ahead of the rest and stepped outside to check their systems in surface conditions before departure.

'It had already been decided that Europa would join the first group, despite her potential value as a historian in the event of subsequent discoveries being made at the site of the mystery craft. The ark's commanders had decreed that breeding pairs should remain together in the search for a location for settlement. Europa's pairing with Mirage, who was indispensable to the advance party as a geologist, took precedence over her function as a historian.

'The team set out in single file, with Zephyr at the front, roped at a distance of six paces to Mirage, who was in turn attached to Kerid, followed by Crete, and then Europa, with Shard at the rear. Crete and Mirage transported M3 and M4 in sustainers, while Zephyr took the microscope and half the seeds and seedlings that we'd brought down to the surface. Everyone's ex-pack – their survival kit – contained a smock, blanket, cup, knife, flint, solid food supplements and an extra canteen of water for when all of the internal supplies were depleted and the suits could be discarded. Various tools were distributed among the group, including a spade, hacksaw, hammer, chisel, pliers and two oxygen sensors; and Kerid took care of the medical kit consisting of bandages, scissors, splints, herbs and balms. For added safety, everyone was equipped with a lightweight ice axe strapped around the wrist opposite the one on which the cuff light was worn.

'The first stage of the descent was straightforward

and hazard-free. Less than half an hour in, Shard gave us some feedback on the soles of the boots, saying that the soft, deep-tread overlays gave the soles adequate grip and liquid displacement on the moist, rocky surface.

'Despite the effectiveness of the overlays, the axes soon proved to be indispensable, as Kerid slipped off a narrow, sloping ledge into a crevice. Fortunately, she managed to wedge her axe into a fissure on falling, which left her dangling from the wrist strap. Mirage and Crete, having stood firm a couple of paces either side of her, took up the slack on their ropes and pulled her up with little difficulty. Listening from the lifeboat, we feared for a few alarming moments that we'd lost one.

'Along the way, Mirage described his first impressions of the subterranean environment.'

'We're just over an hour into our descent. The daylight that illuminated our way beneath the rim of the canyon has gradually faded with each twist and turn, and now we're relying entirely on our helmet and cuff lights – remembering that we have to use them sparingly. Zephyr at the front and Shard at the back are the only ones with helmet lights on. Europa and I are using cuff lights, so that we can see the finer detail in our surroundings.

'Nothing is clear, though, as our visors are constantly steaming up and require frequent wiping. There's more vapour here than there was at the entrance to the canyon. It's drifting slowly upward from the passageway ahead, and from ravines around us; but there's also steam hissing and whistling through narrow vents, suggesting a build-up of pressure somewhere below.

'There are numerous passageways to our left and right ... openings of all shapes and sizes, most leading downward, but some going up ... It's possible to descend in almost any direction.

'The planet's crust appears to be very irregular in structure – at least here beneath the plateau ... It's highly porous, forming tunnels, ledges, bridges and crevices ... reddish-brown igneous rock walls, with dust and small stones under foot, similar to those on the surface ... then shiny black tunnels, possibly volcanic, like lava tubes.

'A few insurmountable obstacles and precarious pathways have forced us to backtrack twice to find an alternative route. We're taking care to choose the most secure surfaces and the least hazardous gradients – but always descending.

'We've been able to scratch arrows into the softer rock walls, so look out for them when you're down here. They're around chest height.'

'Five hours after setting out, and with oxygen supplies below 60%, the group stopped to test the atmosphere on M3, while also taking the opportunity to sit down with their feet raised.

'Mirage announced that the oxygen content, which had been increasing in the higher density steam, was now up to 12%.

'All eight of us in the lifeboat listened intently as Crete described how he set down the sustainer in the thick of the mist, sat down beside it and opened the vents.

'The results of the test were encouraging. M3 showed no immediate sign of distress, unlike the first two mice. It was only after ten or fifteen seconds that it started scampering around and gasping. Crete kept the vents open for a total of forty seconds before re-sealing and reoxygenating the sustainer. It's not possible to restore the pressure once released outside the lifeboat, so M3 was never going to survive. Yet, remarkably, it was a further four minutes before its eyelids stopped flickering.

'After an exhausting first five hours, and insufficient rest to ease the discomfort in their lower legs, our pioneers resumed their race against time. With only enough oxygen in their tanks for another six to seven hours, they needed to find out very soon if a human could breathe deeper down. The oxygen readings and the fate of the mice indicated that it might be possible to survive underground – but they had to keep moving, despite having no certainty that all the passageways ahead would be clear. They'd been fortunate so far in that respect.

'The incoming signal from all six communication channels remained strong. We didn't know whether to expect interference, intermittent loss or a total blackout. Trebuchet and I surmised that the unexpected clarity was due to the porous nature of the planet's crust.

'We heard very little conversation for the next three hours as our crewmates continued their journey, unimpeded and with no further incidents. Information regarding the steadily rising oxygen content alternated with discussion about which route to take, and groans and comments about aching ankles. Visibility was at times poor, necessitating the use of a third helmet light and an extra cuff light.

'Just before the eight-hour mark, Zephyr declared that it was time for a brief rest before the final trek, which would culminate in the raising, one by one, of all visors as the gauge on each tank crept towards the inevitable.

'However, with an external oxygen reading of 17% in their current location, and with M4 to be saved until their ultimate destination, Crete volunteered to undergo a brief test of breathability. Zephyr consented, knowing that sooner or later someone had to – but it had to be very brief, and with the internal collar sealed to minimise the loss of pressure in the suit. Crete agreed and talked us through it.'

'Turning the oxygen supply off temporarily ... I don't want to skew the result by contaminating the atmosphere with pure oxygen ...

'About to raise the visor ...

'I'll just take one breath and close it immediately ... We've no idea what gases are in the 83% that isn't oxygen, but it didn't do the mice any good ...

'I'll just get a lungful and see what happens ...

'OK ... here goes ...'

'There was a sense of everyone in the lifeboat holding their breath. Two seconds of silence were followed by a spluttering cough and a sneeze. We assumed that Crete's visor was down by the time Zephyr asked him if he was OK and urged him to turn his oxygen back on – and there was an anxious wait while he cleared his airways and regained his composure sufficiently to comment.'

'That was ... like nothing I've experienced before ...

'The taste ... acrid ...

'It's stinging my eyes and my nasal passage ...

'I can feel a slight irritation in my lungs, too ...

'Hard to inhale ... just one breath.'

'That was all he said for a while, until, in response

to Zephyr's next question, he affirmed that he was OK to go on. His health and fitness would be closely monitored from that point on.

'Zephyr's subsequent motivational speech was essentially a reminder that this was to be their final push, and that they'd keep going until, one by one, their gauges read zero and they had to breathe unaided or perish.'

'We're continuing our descent in the hope that the oxygen content in this ... Do we call it air? ... I'll call it air ... What else can we call it? ... Anyway, we're hoping that the oxygen content will continue to increase, while the toxic components will diminish sufficiently for us to survive.'

'It seemed that Crete had suffered minimal ill effects from his single inhalation, and there was no further mention of any irritation in his respiratory system. He had little trouble keeping pace with the others as they negotiated a succession of sloping tunnels and near-vertical passageways that necessitated the use of ropes and axes as climbing equipment for the first time.

'Following an intentional but uncontrolled slide down a tubular chute, ending in a splashdown in a shallow pool at the entrance to an egg-shaped chamber not much bigger than the lifeboat, the team found themselves in dramatically different surroundings. The surfaces were jagged and more porous, and there was steam hissing and whistling through vents and fissures all around with a force unlike anything previously encountered.

'Zephyr described a wetter environment with increasing amounts of moisture trickling down the walls and into a stream that flowed through one of two narrow openings on the far side. They chose to squeeze through the smaller one and follow the stream, stepping over and wading through it as it criss-crossed their path and merged with other inflows along the way.

'Two and a half hours into what we hoped wouldn't be the final leg, Zephyr's commentary cut off abruptly. There was an unsettling pause on all channels before Zephyr responded to our expressions of concern.'

'We've reached a cavern ... It's huge ... I mean ... nothing like the pockets that we passed through before ... This is vast ... We can't even see the ceiling ... just a mass of cloud above the veils of mist that are swirling around us as we move.

'Underfoot there's a layer of fine, wet ... What is it, Mirage? ...

'Silt? ...

'Silt, Mirage calls it ...

'We're leaving deeper, wetter footprints here.

'Not so fast, Shard. There might be something beneath the silt. Sweep around with your axe handle – or use the shovel.'

'Mirage cut in to say that they had an oxygen reading of 19%, and an ambient temperature of 15° Celsius.

'Back in the lifeboat, Matrix speculated that if the cavern was somehow pressurised, and the remaining 81% of the atmosphere was less toxic than it was closer to the planet's surface, it might be possible to breathe – and if not there, maybe deeper down.

'We listened as the advance party followed Zephyr's instructions to spread out while taking care not to step on any hidden hazards.

'Then Kerid yelled, "It's a lake!"'

'For a while we heard only incoherent murmurings in tones of astonishment, until the resumption of Zephyr's audio enabled us to visualise the addition to the landscape.'

'Lifeboat 1, we've discovered a steaming lake in an enormous, misty cavern. Our lights are illuminating the fog, which has a greenish yellow tinge in here, unlike its wispier whitish appearance up to now.

'We're standing a few paces from the shore, as far apart as our ropes will allow. Visibility along the shoreline to my right is thirty or forty paces. It's impossible to see the full expanse of the lake in front of us through the fog, which must be denser over the water than on the shore, presumably due to a higher degree of evaporation.

'I wonder ...

'Let's try something ...

'Put your helmet lights on, everyone.

'Aim your beams in the same direction as me ...

'Mirage, over here ... Get your light on ... Yeah, cuff lights, too. Why not?

'Europa, this way ...

'Now converge ...

'Look at that ...

'Nothing ...

'OK, turn slightly to the right now ...

'That's it ... just there ...

'It's incredible ... We can't see far across the lake at all ... maybe fifteen paces with our combined lights concentrated on the same spot. Our beams are penetrating up to a point, but then the fog becomes so dense that it just creates a wall of absorbed light.

'Now, everyone, switch all your lights off.'

'A brief pause was the prelude to a jumble of garbled utterances, interspersed with gasps of incredulity.'

'We can see in here!

'All our lights are off, but we can see each other.

'The mist is glowing ... all around us ... It appears all the more greenish yellow now that we've turned our lights off ... except in the distance across the lake, which is black as far as we can see.

'The light source seems to be on the rock walls – or the rocks themselves. Looking behind, I can just make out an illuminated arch around our point of entry. The illumination wasn't obvious when we came in, as our lights are much brighter ... and there are more dark patches around the cavern, high and low, which must be other holes in the walls. Whatever's causing the glow must be on the ceiling, too, because the clouds above us appear to be backlit.

'Let's go and have a closer look.'

'We listened for several minutes to the observations of the advance party as they examined the rocks and explored the cavern further. Zephyr described a luminous green substance – like lichen, she said – covering the cave walls. She guessed that it was on the ceiling, too. There was none to be seen on the ground, though, unless it was concealed beneath the thick layer of silt. She wondered if it was organic, and if they were the first humans to encounter extraterrestrial life.

'Mirage described the walls as being irregularly perforated with vents of various shapes and sizes. There was no doubt that many of them led to the surface, as the now-familiar hissing could also be heard overhead. Jets of steam were shooting up through small holes and cracks in the lower walls of the cavern, while elsewhere the fog was drifting in via larger openings from passageways that led deeper underground. All around, liquid was dripping from the ceiling and running down the shimmering, luminescent walls.

'It wasn't long before everyone's eyes had adjusted to the new light and they could see adequately through the mist to enable them to keep their suit lights off and save power. Crete pointed out pertinently that the one vital thing they weren't saving was oxygen – and right now they were going nowhere.

'They hadn't intended to rest, but took the opportunity anyway to elevate their aching legs.

'Meanwhile, Kerid suggested that this might be a good time to test the atmosphere on their last mouse.

'Zephyr agreed, Mirage opened the vents, and we waited.

'To everyone's amazement, M4 suffered no immediate adverse reaction. As a minute passed, and then two, astonishment turned to relief, and then elation, as it became evident that the combination of higher oxygen content, lower toxicity and greater atmospheric pressure made breathing possible –at least for a rodent.

'Then we heard Kerid shout, "Europa!" It was a while before we in the lifeboat discovered why.

'On impulse, ten and a half hours into the descent, with oxygen reserves between 11% and 16%, Europa had raised her visor.

'A few minutes later she gave us an account of how she'd laboured to take several breaths before slamming her visor shut. The atmosphere was unpleasant smelling and tasted bitter, but there was no stinging to her eyes or airways, unlike Crete's earlier experience.

'Matrix paced up and down behind me in the lifeboat, theorising that warmer, expanding gases, including the oxygen in the rising steam, must be trapped in underground chambers, resulting in pressure being contained – as evidenced by the increasingly forceful escape of compressed gases via small vents deeper down. In other words, a natural process replicating what we've accomplished in the arks, lifeboats, suits and sustainers.

'With ankles soothed and oxygen almost spent, there was no more time to waste. Zephyr told us there were other streams flowing from the lake into three sizeable portals within twenty paces of where they'd entered the cavern. Mirage carved a large arrow into the lichen (as Zephyr was now calling it, whether it was living or not) next to the middle portal, which promised a steeper, albeit possibly more hazardous descent.

'Shortly after resuming, Shard complained that his odour-neutralising filter wasn't working. Rubella, our suit technician, quipped that it was hardly surprising, as the suit was constructed over a thousand years ago. There was certainly nothing she could do or advise from the lifeboat.

'Shard found his own solution, though. Whether out of desperation or necessity, he became the third in the party to raise his visor. We heard him gasping and spluttering for a full minute before he sealed it again; but it didn't take him long to recover from the ordeal, which was more unpleasant than debilitating. Meanwhile, M4, with its sustainer vents still open, was not only alive, but by all accounts behaving quite normally – a further indication that the atmosphere was becoming more breathable.

'From that point on, and with the external oxygen readings nudging 20%, each of the team took it in turns to switch their oxygen supplies off and raise their visors for one minute, and then a little longer, until they felt the benefit of acclimatisation and were confident enough to manage without oxygen from their tanks for several minutes at a time – while also learning to live with the pungent smell and bitter taste.

'Fogging on the inside of the resealed visors was a problem initially. However, the suits' dehumidifiers soon took care of that – except for Shard's, which was malfunctioning along with his deodorising unit. Only able to wipe the outside, he stumbled along blindly at the rear, tugging on the rope attached to Europa for as long as could stand it before daring to take a chance on keeping his visor up. In doing so, he was at least able to conserve his remaining oxygen in case of an emergency.'

'Galleon, Swift and Kodiak were absent from the lifeboat during this time. They'd gone to find out more about the other craft and bring back more artefacts for study. Galleon's detailed reports are here in the audio files "Galleon014" to "Galleon025". The bottom line is that the ship's exact origin, approximate date of departure from Earth and arrival here, and the fate of its crew remain subjects for conjecture. Galleon and Swift, with their combined expertise in electrical and mechanical engineering, couldn't even gain sufficient access to determine its method of propulsion.

'On their return, the trio carried out a thorough examination of the exterior of the lifeboat, but were unable to identify anything other than minor collision damage and superficial scarring caused by heat. There was no evidence of anything externally that would have disabled our surface-to-orbit communications.

'That sortie was Kodiak's first. By the end of it he was unable to conceal the physical discomfort caused by three hours of downward pressure on his neck. He was actually too tall for the suit, despite the less than optimal fit having been approved by Rubella. As each other's chosen partners, they were reluctant to be separated, so Rubella's position as one of the ark's suit technicians greenlit Kodiak's status as a colonist.

'I don't know how it'll work on the other arks, but on ours the selection of colonists is determined first and foremost by their ability to fit into a suit. Of those who can, the fifty-six youngest of each gender are selected, unless ineligible due to disability or ill health – the priorities being survival and procreation.

'It seems that the suits' designers had anticipated everything except the extent of human evolution during fifty generations in space. The expandable midsection allows for additional height, but that wasn't enough for the eight strong and healthy young men and women who will be separated from their desired breeding partners and remain in orbit with the nonbreeding couples, small children, the elderly and those who are differently enabled or otherwise proportioned. Druid and Matrix, the only established breeding pair on the surface, are fortunate that their twelve-year-old daughter is just tall enough to be allocated a seat alongside her older sister. Not so fortunate for their two young sons, though.

'Inevitably some of the younger ones left on the ark will procreate, condemning subsequent generations to life in orbit, or elsewhere, with no hope of ever reaching the planet's surface, like every generation prior to ours – a fate that Kodiak escaped at the expense of the next oldest male who would otherwise have been eligible.

'Meanwhile, any colonist whose chosen partner is ineligible for transportation due to physical attributes outside the suits' design parameters is reassigned, as Kerid, Crete, Trebuchet and I were.

'Opus, if you can hear this, I miss you.'

'It took the advance party another five hours after resuming to reach a second, and much bigger cavern. They'd been able to conserve oxygen by breathing the atmosphere for increasing lengths of time the deeper they went. Shard hardly relied on his at all, only closing his visor briefly for the occasional boost.

'On arrival they were all exhausted. Zephyr said they'd reached their limit and needed to rest. She didn't have the strength to give us any more information at that point. They had to sleep – and they had to sleep while breathing Proxima b's subterranean gases for however many hours they slept, with no certainty that they'd even wake up.

'Having no idea how long it would take before the resumption of communications, the rest of us in the lifeboat caught up on some sleep ourselves, dimming the lights and lowering the volume on all six channels so that we could just about hear everyone's breathing, snoring and semi-conscious comments.'

'By the time I was nudged on the resumption of

day mode, half the crew were awake and staring at the speakers, straining to pick up any of the barely audible utterances from underground. Zephyr's voice was the most prominent as she asked each of the others how they were feeling.

'Regardless of anyone still dozing, I turned the volume up so that we could listen to whatever comments were exchanged until Zephyr was ready to address us in the lifeboat. Here's her account of their experience of waking up in the second cavern.'

'We're not suffering any adverse effects from sleeping for six to seven hours without reliance on our oxygen reserves. The oxygen content here is more than adequate, and atmospheric pressure is no longer a problem ... I'll leave you to figure that one out, Matrix.

'The smell and the taste of this ... air ... is the most unpleasant aspect – but at least we're alive. No-one's complaining of being unwell. We're all just very tired – and hopefully not because of what we've been breathing.

'Our next priority will be determining if the liquid down here is drinkable ... and then finding food.'

'I'll skip to Zephyr's next file, recorded a few minutes later.'

'Let me tell you about this place ...

'First of all, we can see without our lights. The walls are covered in a similar luminescent lichen-like substance to what we saw in the cavern above, but it's chunkier here, and more luminous. The whole cavern is brighter. The fog is denser, too, which might explain why we can breathe more easily. The downside is that we can't see so far, but everything close by is clear enough ... And because the fog's thicker, every-

thing's wetter ... The soil underfoot is slushy ... And we're soaking wet inside our suits after having our visors open for so long ... but probably also because we've been sweating more, as it's warmer. The ambient temperature is 22° Celsius ... and we have an oxygen reading of 23% on both sensors.

'There's a lake here, too, just like in the upper cavern, but we won't have any idea how far the shoreline extends until we venture beyond the immediate vicinity.

'As in the first cavern, there's steam whistling through vents all around ... It's particularly noisy overhead ... And there's vapour drifting in through several other passageways leading even deeper down. At the same time, liquid is overflowing from pools formed by constant showers from the ceiling and run-off from the walls.

'I think we'll take some time to explore. The consensus among the group is that we need to acclimatise and conserve our energy after such an arduous descent. At least we can breathe comfortably down here.

'Our most pressing needs now are to test this liquid and look for a food source.'

'The team set up a base camp close to the shore of the lake – essentially unloading all of their equipment and supplies in one spot, including their detached ropes.

'With no time to waste, Zephyr took a sample of liquid from the lake to study under the microscope. Her full analysis is in audio file "Zephyr009". To cut a long story short, the sample contained living microorganisms, but nothing resembling anything that she or Kerid had encountered on the ark or could recall from the biological database. The water – as they were now calling it – was alkaline, which Zephyr thought was curious, because the moisture they were inhaling tasted acidic.

'Zephyr and Mirage discussed the possibility of using their flints to create a spark with a view to boiling the water, but they reasoned that it would be either futile or unwise. Even if they could kindle a spark in the dampness, their only potential fuel would be the lichen or the soil, which were too wet anyway. In the unlikely event of success, the chemical reaction in the unknown gases would be impossible to predict. In an enclosed environment where adapting to unfamiliar substances was vital, they didn't want to jeopardise their chances of survival by poisoning or igniting the atmosphere. So, with no way of sterilising the water, a volunteer was needed to test for a reaction – first to external application and then to consumption.

'Uncharacteristically for the group, no-one was eager to step forward. Perhaps it was because of the quantity of moisture in the mist that no-one was desperately thirsty. In the event, the first mouthful of extraterrestrial life was offered to M4 in the palm of Kerid's glove.

'The mouse drank enthusiastically, and we listened keenly for news of the slightest change in its behaviour. We picked up a few comments about nothing happening, and then there was silence for a while, until the focus of everyone's attention shifted.

'Waning interest in one experiment was surpassed by interest in the next, as Kerid and Mirage ventured briefly into the lake – fully protected within their suits, of course. They waded knee-deep, half a dozen paces from the shore, lingering only long enough to take a temperature reading. It was 36° Celsius where they stood, although it was probably warmer farther out, where more steam was likely evidence of more heat.

'An hour or so later, with M4 still seemingly unaffected, Crete marched impatiently into the lake, cupped his gloved hands, scooped up some water and splashed it into his open mouth. Here's his response to Zephyr's reprimand.'

'Hell, we either drink this or we don't drink it. If we don't, sooner or later we'll die of thirst anyway ... Might as well find out now ... M4 seems OK.'

'As a biologist, Zephyr hadn't been expecting an instant reaction to M4's consumption of Proxima b's microorganisms; but now, sooner than anticipated, she and Kerid had a human test subject to monitor, as well as a rodent.

'Crete described the liquid as bitter tasting and slightly oily. He wondered if the water dripping from the walls and ceiling would be any purer than what he'd just swallowed. Perhaps it had deposited some of its less palatable properties in the process of nourishing the lichen. Kerid postulated that it was just as likely that toxins were leaching from the lichen into the pools. Typically for Crete, though, in for a gram, in for a kilogram, he collected a sample from a pool near the edge of the cavern for comparison. It was slightly less bitter, he judged – less oily, and definitely preferable. Despite his assessment, his words were followed by some forceful spitting.

'The advance party spent the remainder of that day resting and acclimatising, while also exploring the immediate vicinity of the camp.

'When I say the remainder of the day, I mean our day – the ark's day. It was noticeable how the group seemed to lose track of our simulated day-night cycle soon after their arrival in the second cavern, sleeping for short periods at all hours, but awake most of the time.

'I should also mention that neither Crete nor M4 displayed any outward signs of intolerance to the liquid that they'd consumed that day. It was only after ascertaining the next day that there was less microorganic activity in the puddles than in the lake that Zephyr declared the purified pool water to be safer for consumption.'

'By the time we in the lifeboat awoke from our next night, half of the advance party's oxygen tanks were empty. For Zephyr, Kerid and Mirage there was no longer the option of alternating between their own supply and the steam, or having a back-up in the event of an emergency. By the end of the day, Shard and Europa were the only ones with any reserves left.

'The most significant news on a day of acclimatisation and little further exploration was that everyone had begun drinking the pool water.

'There was also plenty of time for reflection on their first full day in the lower cavern. I'd like to share Europa's thoughts with you, as I feel it's important for future colonists to recognise that there's more to colonisation than managing the practicalities.

'So this was on day six.'

'This is Europa of the UK Ark, Lifeboat 1, for anyone out there interested in hearing the thoughts of one of the first fourteen colonists on Proxima b, and one of the six-member advance party ... currently sit-

ting uncomfortably against a rock wall in a thick fog, somewhere inside the planet's crust, tired and aching.

'If you're listening to this, you've probably heard some of our previous recordings describing our adventures, discoveries and observations ... and you'll have heard our complaints of discomfort and fatigue ... but no-one's really talked yet about how they're coping emotionally.

'I'd like to tell the entire fleet, and anyone else in this star system, exactly how I'm feeling right now.

'Aside from the aching ... and chafing ... and swelling ... I'm mentally drained ... but above everything, I'm thankful to be alive ... thankful that we're all in good health and still have a chance of survival.

'I'm also scared ... It frightens me that there's no way back from here ... There never has been any way back ... no way back to the ark as soon as the lifeboat was launched ... no way of climbing back up to the surface once our oxygen tanks were more than half empty ... and no alternative now but to remain at this depth or deeper for the rest of our lives ... which could be days ... or it could be decades.

'With little to do today but reflect, the realisation has sunk in that this is my new life ... in my new, permanent home ... bathed in moisture, breathing acrid steam in a glowing fog, drinking a bitter liquid, and facing the prospect of foraging for a food source that will be equally distasteful ... And for recreation ... gambling ... gambling with our lives every time we touch something, or consume something, or venture further into the unknown.

'If the water doesn't poison us, and if we find food to sustain us, and if those following in our footsteps can bring some lambs and chicks with them, and if the lambs and chicks can also survive down here, and breed, and supplement our food source, then Mirage and I will proceed with our plan to procreate, and we'll work to establish a migrant colony underground, where future generations will never see the stars.

'But of course, unlike us, they never will have seen the stars, so they won't miss that ... "What are stars?" they'll ask us.

'We'll tell our children the stories of the stars that our parents told us ... And we'll teach them about the Reactor, whose power has sustained us since the beginning of the time that matters and has guided us safely to our destination. Although our descendants will never see the ark, they'll know that the Reactor is still with us, all around us, and looking after our distant cousins as they watch over us from above ... and we'll teach our children to be thankful every day for our very existence, so that they and their children and their children's children never forget how our civilisation came into being.

'It won't be easy for the first generation. The subterranean environment is harsh. I already miss the comfort of the ark ... my dormpod ... my extensive rack of smocks ... all those smooth, sanitised surfaces ... the freedom to choose zero gravity ... the sweetness of the air ... the unappreciated purity of the water ... not being wet all the time ... and being able to see as far away as the stars.

'Shard and I are the only ones with any oxygen left. I'm on 7%. I've been breathing the atmosphere as much as possible to conserve what remains of this precious commodity, and now I'm going to relish it more than ever ... Not all at once, though ... a little to *send me to sleep later with a smile on my face ... and a small indulgence on waking – just enough to satisfy my craving for a fleeting sensation of the life that we've left behind.'*

'For us in the lifeboat, Europa's words were food for thought, which we digested with a greater appreciation of the need to steel ourselves mentally, as well as physically, ahead of our own descent.

'During the middle of that day communication became patchy for the first time, but it was still better than we'd hoped for at the outset. The interruption to the signal certainly wasn't due to the relocation of either party, so we attributed the interference to atmospheric conditions.'

'Seventy-two hours after setting out, Shard and Zephyr's waste management receptacles were full. As Shard's odour absorption unit had also long since ceased functioning, they decided to detach and discard their catheters, urine sacks and faecal pouches. Of course, removing their attachments also involved removing their suits for the first time outside the lifeboat.

'Crete provided us with a commentary on their departure, beginning with some crude remarks about chafing flesh and watering eyes, before coming up with a more eloquent description of their disappearance into the embrace of a swirling shroud, which escorted them away to bathe in private and soothe their sores in a stream draining from a pool at the edge of the cavern.

'He honed the cutting edge of his humour once more on the pair's rematerialisation minus their suits ...'

'... *their emerging outlines glistening green in the reflected glow of the lichen as they model their rinsed and wrung-out thermal unitards, discreetly, yet stylishly buttoned underneath.*'

'The volume of Zephyr's voice increased as she approached Crete's communicator to comment via his channel on how remarkably effective the fabric was at displacing fluid.'

'With diminishing food rations in mind, and while still protected within their suits, Kerid and Mirage returned to the lake to try their luck at fishing, as Kerid put it.'

'... *water's thicker than our ark water. Mirage says it's due to the gravity ... and it probably feels heavier because we're in waist-high now and dragging our fully laden legs around in it ... but you can also see it's thicker by the way it runs off our gloves in oily globules.*'

'And then she and Europa started philosophising. This is also from Kerid's channel.'

'*I know what you mean, Ropes. We may be a long way from the ark, but I feel that we're still drawing spiritual strength from the Reactor ...*

'*Exactly ... It's incredible to think that its power has kept fifty generations alive and guided us all to our destiny. It's given us ambition and purpose – for me the inspiration to study medicine, and for our colony the desire to rise to the challenge of survival and multiplication ...*

'*Oh, I don't doubt it ... and I'm convinced that I owe my personal survival here to the quickness of mind that enabled me to hook my axe into that crack in the crevice when I slipped, and to Crete and Mi-*

rage's combined physical strength in pulling me back up ...

'I believe that our collective being is fortified with the power of the Reactor ... and although we'll never physically feel its warmth again, our civilisation will be guided by its inextinguishable light ...

'You're right, Ropes, we should honour it down here ... maybe carve symbols into the stone, like the one you saw on the abandoned spaceship – you know, the one you thought might have represented the Reactor.'

'Kerid paused to report that there was no sign of life in the water, and then we listened to more of Europa's reflections before lowering the volume and adjusting the dimmer.'

'Following that period of subdued light, Zephyr donned her helmet to tell us that she'd planted most of the seeds and seedlings that she'd been carrying – various fruits, vegetables and grasses that had been cultivated in hydroponic gardens in low light on the ark, and which we now hoped would flourish in the dim glow of the lichen, our only natural light source underground.

'We also learned that Zephyr and Shard, so far the only ones without their suits on, had ventured into the lake in their unitards. Here's an extract from Zephyr's description of what they discovered.'

'It felt furry in the water ... as if my toes were being pampered ... It was like running them through the thick pile rug next to my dormpod.

'But now it's out of the water, it's gone flat, and it's not at all soft with the liquid squeezed out – certainly not how I imagined it when walking on it ... It's black

... and it looks dead ... I'm guessing it was alive, and maybe we killed it when we stepped on it or tore handfuls away to bring ashore ... or maybe it just can't survive out of the water.

'Even though it was firmly anchored to the lake bed, I can't be sure yet whether it's flora or fauna.'

'Zephyr went on to say that it resembled aquatic moss – something that used to grow on Earth. None of us had any knowledge of that, as there was no such thing on the ark. Druid remarked that we were fortunate to have someone with us who'd studied ancient botany and knew what to call it – otherwise we'd have to name it after its discoverers. Swift proposed "zephyrshard".

'Apart from the luminescent lichen, which by all accounts looked about as appetising as ovine lubricant, this ... moss – as we're now calling it – is so far our only potential native food source.

'M4, as always, had first refusal ... and did refuse. It showed no inclination to eat anything unfamiliar, since it still had a supply of its own food in the sustainer. So Zephyr confiscated the mouse mix with the intention of waiting a few hours until M4 was hungry enough to eat anything.

'Shard, impatient as ever for results, threw caution to the stellar wind and sank his teeth into the underside of a clump, which he considered less unappealing than the side that they'd been trampling on. Here's how he described the experience.'

'The texture's similar to mycoprotein patties, but chewier ... and there's a lot of bitter, oily moisture oozing out – hopefully just the lake water.

'Mmm ... sure is chewy ...

'But once the bitterness is squeezed out, there's an

unusual flavour ... like nothing I've experienced before ... It's not unpleasant ... savoury, rather than sweet.'

'Everyone else avoided the zephyrshard, and there were no more discoveries to report, although the group did split into pairs to undertake some further exploration of nearby streams and passageways. It also gave the other four an opportunity to remove their suits, bathe, and rinse their unitards, while taking care to flush away their waste in streams flowing out of the lake, so as not to pollute the drinking water.

'On her return to the camp with Shard, ahead of the others, Zephyr reflected on their first hundred hours underground and the colony's food prospects.'

'I can only imagine how thick the porous crust of this planet is. We're surely still only at its outer edge, yet we may have already reached the point where we're as warm and wet and fog-bound as we can tolerate. If these seedlings don't grow and we need to go beyond this place in search of a food supply, so be it. Something in the lakes is producing oxygen. It might just be the moss, or there might be something else. We need to find it, whether it's at this level or deeper, as we're unlikely to survive for long on a monotrophic diet – assuming that we can even digest the moss. Shard has impressed upon us the need for variety. We can't simply wait until the lambs and chicks get here – and then grow. In any case, we'll have to find something nutritious for them to eat in time for their arrival, or they won't survive.'

'Zephyr's thoughts started me wondering what plant and animal species might have survived on the other arks, and whether their crews would have selected and bred them to adapt to the anticipated conditions on Proxima b. We know that the successful transplantation of vegetation will be vital for the animals that we've considered essential for our long-term requirements, but the composition of the soil, or silt – whatever we're going to call it – is so far unknown. Somehow we'll need to cultivate corn for the chicks, which, if they thrive in sufficient numbers, will supplement our diet with eggs and flesh; and we'll endeavour to grow grass for the lambs so that they can provide us with the wool that we'll need in the future to replace our worn-out smocks and blankets. If we can establish sustainable poultry and sheep populations, they'll be our primary food sources for generations to come.

'As we have ample reserves of corn on our ark and can transport more than enough for the crews to carry, the first chicks can be brought down without further delay. However, the grass will have to be widely propagated and highly resilient before the lambs can be loaded as planned onto the last two lifeboats, otherwise they'll have to adapt to a moss diet ... or perish.

'In addition, though, now that we're able to report the presence of large bodies of subterranean water, subsequent lifeboat crews can also bring down fish, which hopefully will be able to find enough aquatic nourishment to enable them to populate the lakes.

'Due to the limitations on portability, the adult sheep and all of the cattle will remain on the ark to sustain the orbiting remnants of our interstellar civilisation.'

'While the focus underground was on exploitation of the lake bed, Matrix, Rubella and Druid explored the terrain on the far side of the mystery craft, looking for clues as to where its crew might have gone. They found no footprints, scuff marks, vehicle tracks or evidence of an attack, and there were no alien objects more than fifty paces from the ship – the farthest being an erect tripod with nothing attached. There was no sign of a trail, nor was there any obvious destination to head for. The escarpment dropped off sharply on the far side of the plateau, two hundred paces beyond the landing site, so any journey in that direction would appear to be more arduous and hazardous than the descent into the canyon. That said, the ship's crew might have undertaken it for reasons of their own.

'Following that, twelve of the sixteen suits were now confirmed as functioning in surface conditions. Only Trebuchet and I hadn't yet been outside the lifeboat, so only two male and two female suits remained unused, including the spares.

'By the end of that day – day in the lifeboat, that is, as there was no longer any distinction between day and night below ground – the last of the advance party's food rations were exhausted.'

'Our next update included the news that Shard, Crete and M4 were still experiencing no ill effects from the substances and organisms that they'd consumed.

'M4 appeared to be in good health and had been released from its sustainer. After a thorough exploration of its new habitat, it was tempted back for a nibble of mouse mix, which was lasting much longer than expected.

'Zephyr and Shard returned to the lake to harvest more of the ... well, they were calling it moss, but I agreed with Swift that we should name it zephyrshard as a tribute to their pioneering spirit. It seems that it's more prevalent farther from shore, where the bed slopes gently into deeper, warmer water. Interestingly, Shard remarked that he found breathing easier in the denser fog.

'Zephyr and Kerid later discussed the possibility of the microorganisms in the water being nutritious, as there had been little sensation of hunger so far in any of the team, and no pressing need to eat anything after the rations had run out. Observing that Shard was still in good health after eating the moss, Zephyr and Europa decided to indulge in a sample themselves.

'Meanwhile, Mirage attempted to feed some flakes of lichen to M4. Like the rest of us, M4 didn't seem hungry – or perhaps it was perturbed by the odour, or the luminosity. In fact, M4 appeared not only healthy, but especially lively, drinking willingly despite continuing to refuse the lichen and moss, no matter how they were served up. It was also barely touching its own food, which added weight to the theory that the microorganisms in the water contained nutrients, some of which we might even be inhaling.

'Not to be denied some kind of test on the lichen, Mirage tasted a flake himself, which he promptly spat out, declaring that he'd never eaten anything that glowed before. He described it as brittle, intensely bitter, and producing a mild stinging sensation on the tip of his tongue.

'Later that day, assured that the lake was non-toxic and not inhabited by anything likely to prey on humans, all six enjoyed a swim, and most agreed with Shard that breathing was easier farther from the shore.

'By the time we switched to night mode on the surface, Kerid, Crete and Mirage had consumed a modest quantity of lichen, ground into a damp powder and mixed with pool water to create a paste that was more palatable than the raw flakes that Mirage had spat out.

'Meanwhile, Zephyr, Shard and Europa continued to eat moss – the idea being to test the effects of each potential food source on separate halves of the team.

'It wasn't long, however, before Kerid, Crete and Mirage reported swelling in their mouths and throats, which restricted their breathing and swallowing for up to an hour. Some degree of inflammation in their upper respiratory tracts persisted for the rest of the day, but it was later surpassed by increasing discomfort in their digestive systems. Their pain was eased by expelling waste after drinking copious quantities of pool water, but the relief was only temporary. Consequently, the lichen was declared unsafe for consumption pending further investigation. There had been no indication from Mirage that the lichen was toxic when he sampled it earlier – but then he'd only tried a small amount before spitting it out.'

'The following forty-eight hours were designated as a period of further acclimatisation and experimentation for those underground, and preparation above ground for the next group's descent.

'While we in the lifeboat slept prior to the departure of the second party, Zephyr and Shard revealed to the others a skin irritation that they'd initially dismissed as chafing beneath their unitards. However, during the previous twelve hours it had begun manifesting itself as a crimson rash and was spreading from their torsos to their thighs and upper arms. On being shown the rash, all four of the others confessed that they'd begun itching, too.

'Meanwhile, even though Crete, Kerid and Mirage continued to complain of recurring stomach aches and feeling nauseous, despite having eaten nothing but lichen since their rations ran out, the rate of decline in their health was so gradual that there was no suggestion from anyone in the advance party that they wouldn't recover.

'Worst of all, though, day eleven was the day when we lost Druid.

'After a period of smooth sailing, the proverbial excrement tornado had unleashed its full fury.

'I'll get back to the rash later, and also how Crete, Kerid and Mirage's sickness progressed, as there's so much more to tell ... but first I need to relate what happened to Druid.'

'After we'd received the advance party's update, the second party – Druid, Matrix, Kodiak, Swift and Rubella, led by Galleon – loaded themselves up with the remaining tools, seeds and seedlings and set out to follow the trail of arrows.

'Less than an hour in, Druid noticed that his oxygen consumption was excessive. It was already down 15%, compared with the others' 8 to 10%.

'Half an hour later, a quarter of his supply was gone, while the others had only consumed 12 to 15%.

'A further twenty minutes swallowed up another 10%. His gauge showed 65% remaining, while those of the other five ranged from 82 to 85%.

'With no doubt that there was a defect somewhere – either in the suit or in the regulation of the oxygen supply – Druid and Matrix, his established breeding partner, agreed that he should return to the lifeboat for the spare male suit and replacement tank, while the other five continued their descent. Considering that the advance party's first mouse had perished at the entrance to the canyon, only an hour and a half from where the second group was at that point, it seemed unwise for him to continue the journey and risk prematurely breathing steam that was unlikely to support life. With an estimated two and a half hours to return to the lifeboat, climbing instead of descending, alone and without a rope, it was hoped that 60% in the tank would be sufficient – but Druid had to leave immediately. What hadn't been adequately factored in was that he'd been losing oxygen at an exponential rate.

'From the lifeboat, Trebuchet and I listened to Druid's infrequent commentaries on the exhausting climb as he hauled the weight of his suit, on-board supplies and axe up instead of down. He gave no details of his diminishing oxygen until he saw stars through an opening overhead, by which time he was down to 4%. I was already suited up and in the airlock, but between the lifeboat and the canyon I heard only his laboured breathing ... and words of encouragement from Matrix.

'Ten minutes later I looked down from the edge of the canyon, spare oxygen tank in hand. Druid was lying face up on the ledge, motionless, eyes and mouth wide open, just two paces away from M2 ... his arm stretched out towards the mouse.'

'I'm so sorry, Rhea and Xanthe, to have to tell you of the tragic loss of your father. He was a courageous man and a skilful pilot who set us all safely down on the surface.

'It's fitting now more than ever that you and your future partners have been confirmed as colonists to be transported on the last four lifeboats. It's a shame, though, that neither of your brothers will have an opportunity to follow in your father's footsteps. Nevertheless, I'm sure they'll grow up to be fine young men, whatever lives they make for themselves on the ark. Your mother is displaying remarkable strength and is looking forward to being reunited with you both in the near future, as soon as it's safe for you to join her. Be assured that your father's passing will not be in vain.'

'I'd initially thought of Druid's death as the first loss of human life on Proxima b, until I remembered the other vessel, which was almost certainly abandoned decades ago, if not centuries.'

'Nine and a half hours after setting out, the five surviving members of the second party reached the first cavern, where they heeded the advance party's warning about the lichen. It was considered safe for them to raise their visors periodically to alternate between oxygen and steam to conserve oxygen; however, Europa advised them to keep their suits on, stay out of the lake and avoid the pool water unless anyone's supply was critically low.'

'We heard later that Zephyr and Shard's rashes had spread to their necks, forearms and lower legs, and had become extremely itchy.'

'After we next awoke, Trebuchet and I listened to

Europa describing a grey fungus growing on Shard and Zephyr's rashes – predominantly around Shard's waist and under Zephyr's arms and around her midriff. The rashes themselves were now covering about half their bodies.

'More worrying still was the news that rashes were spreading on the other four. We deduced that direct exposure to the water in the lake and / or moisture in the atmosphere was the cause, since all six were affected. Consumption of the moss and lichen could be discounted, since half hadn't eaten any moss and the others hadn't eaten any lichen.

'For Mirage, Crete and Kerid, who were experiencing increasingly acute abdominal pains that no amount of drinking or expulsion of waste would alleviate, the rash was of little concern.

'All the advance party could do was monitor the progression of the skin condition, eat what little moss had already been brought ashore, and keep hydrated by drinking only pool water.

'By the end of the day, Mirage, Crete and Kerid, who still hadn't touched the moss, were in extreme discomfort and vomiting. Trebuchet and I found their cries so distressing when they were near their helmets that we had to mute their channels.

'Meanwhile, knowing that the atmosphere in the first cavern was breathable, however unpleasant, and also that the second cavern was only five hours away, the second party spent our twelfth day resting and acclimatising instead of pushing on.

'Oh, and Zephyr also mentioned that the seeds that she'd planted five days earlier had not yet germinated. There was no mention of the seedlings.

'Incidentally, I'm not playing any recordings from

these difficult days for obvious reasons.'

'I next awoke to see Trebuchet staring statuesque through the window at a portentous Proxima Centauri, set ominously on the horizon like an ancient doomstone. The scene's stone-cold silence announced another death.

'It was Mirage.

'And before the second party reached the lower cavern later that day, Crete and Kerid had also succumbed to the lichen's poison.

'Galleon subsequently revealed that, of the three survivors from the advance party, Zephyr and Shard had no uninfected area of skin visible, and at least half of their rash had metamorphosed into fungus. He also noticed that there was as much hair on the ground as on their heads. The couple themselves described the itching as torment beyond purgatory, and told Galleon how they'd tried scraping some of the fungus off – but that only caused bleeding and compounded the irritation with an intense soreness.

'Europa, whose initial exposure to the lake water was a day and a half after Zephyr and Shard had first waded in, was now the only fully coherent member of the trio. She explained that the fungus was absorbing its hosts' blood and exudate, which congealed to form a bed of moist fungal scab clusters, on which a new layer of fungus began growing almost immediately.

'In despair, and believing the lake to be the most likely cause of their affliction, Zephyr and Shard sought refuge in a large pool that was constantly refreshed by run-off and showers. They hoped that the steam rising from the lake had left behind whatever substances had caused their skin condition, and that the lichen was absorbing any residue, leaving the pooled water uncontaminated. There was also a chance that the fungus wouldn't be able to grow while submerged.

'The first signs were encouraging. Bathing softened and soothed the scabs, but for Shard the itching resumed soon after he stepped out; so he returned to the pool, where he and Zephyr kept themselves immersed for several hours in the hope that the fresh flowing water would provide lasting relief while inhibiting further growth.

'On detecting the first trace of fungus on her own rapidly spreading rash, Europa joined the others in the pool.

'She had this message for the fleet.'

'Monarch, make sure the fleet knows about this. Tell them that we have nothing in our medical kits that's effective in treating the rash or preventing the fungal growth. Zephyr and Shard used their balms early on, but that didn't help. Once established, the fungus can't be scraped off or cut out without causing more harm. In fact, what appears to be happening now is the fungus is consuming Zephyr and Shard's flesh, so it has to be left intact to prevent bleeding. The pool water is soothing, but it's not likely to be a cure. I can only hope that immersing myself at a less advanced stage than the others will slow the spread until Kodiak comes up with a remedy. If you can make contact with any of the arks, tell them it's imperative that they send down the widest possible range of herbs and balms in their lifeboats.'

'On seeing the state of the survivors, the new arrivals had no inclination to remove their suits, and only partially raised their visors for breathing. Kodiak was the exception, completely detaching his helmet from his poorly-fitting suit for some much needed relief from the downward pressure and constant jolting that had caused him severe neck pain during the descent.

'Galleon said that they'd try to manage for as long as possible without consuming anything other than their remaining food and water supplies, and would only resort to drinking from the pools at the point of extreme dehydration. They had to be sure that the steam, while sustaining human life in the short term by providing oxygen, didn't also contain toxic elements that would ultimately extinguish life.

'While Galleon was reflecting on their hopes and fears, our communications were disrupted again, this time fading out completely for almost two hours before a faint, intermittent signal was restored. We picked up enough to establish that there'd been no significant improvement or decline in anyone's condition.

'I asked Galleon what they were going to do with the bodies of Mirage, Crete and Kerid. This was what came back.'

'... beneath the soil is too hard to dig up, even ... the axes, so we dragged the bodies to a recess ... cavern wall, about thirty paces back from the shore ... laid them side by side ... them in soil ... collected using their helmets ... placed their helmets together ... head of their resting place.'

'Communications worsened again during our last couple of hours in day mode, to the extent that Trebuchet and I resigned ourselves to receiving no more news until the next day.'

'By the time the cabin was illuminated again, atmospheric conditions had improved considerably.

'All three survivors from the advance party were exhausted from lack of sleep, having spent most of the interim period immersed in pooled run-off. Zephyr and Shard had shown admirable restraint in gently massaging their softened fungal scabs rather than scratching them, but in their semi-conscious state they surrendered to the occasional wild urge, inadvertently breaking off chunks to leave oozing sores which required further bathing. What they actually needed was the formation of crusts to seal the wounds and promote healing, but the ambient moisture and frequent soaking prevented the fungus-infused blood from hardening.

'As if Zephyr and Shard's plight wasn't dire enough, the next report, which came from Kodiak – now our only surviving medic – was alarming to say the least. He observed what he suspected might be the next stage in the development of the fungal infestation.'

'... fungus in multiple fallen scab fragments has continued to grow on the sodden soil.

'After only a few hours on the ground, particles of the mixture of blood and fungus appear to have germinated, as if grown from seeds, and are taking root, almost plant-like.

'They're growing vertically and remarkably quickly, although the tallest is no more than five centimetres at the moment.

'It's as if we're witnessing the genesis of some hybrid life form.'

'Seemingly oblivious to what their by-products were doing, Zephyr and Shard had no alternative but to continue drinking from the fresh run-off pools and eating squeezed and rinsed moss, if only for distraction from the rest of their miserable existence, which consisted of cleansing their wounds in streams and immersing themselves in pools – all the while taking care to support their heads above the water's surface to avoid falling asleep and drowning. When on the shore they lay on rocks, rather than the soil, to minimise the absorption of moisture through their blankets and smocks. Galleon described the pair as being in constant distress, unable to sleep on the uneven rocks while pawing at every accessible square centimetre of their bodies.

'Zephyr later made a determined effort to stop interfering with her scabs, as the soreness caused by the repeated massaging and scratching had exceeded the discomfort from the itching itself. At the same time she resisted the urge to bathe, in the hope of giving her suppurating sores a chance to dry. Despairing of finding any relief, she even resorted to crushing a handful of lichen and rubbing the crumbled flakes into the wounds of one arm in an attempt to discover whether the luminescent organism, while poisonous to ingest, had any beneficial properties that could be applied externally.

'Significantly, there were no signs so far of skin irritation on the faces or necks of the second party, who had been exposed to the steam intermittently for more than sixty hours, but had not yet been in contact with any other liquid.

'Most of the communications that Trebuchet and I were receiving by this time were from members of the second party, who were all still wearing their suits. Europa was coping better than expected and kept her helmet close by so that she could keep talking to us. Meanwhile, all we could hear of the other two was their unabated cries of agony in the background.

'Amid the turmoil, we'd given hardly any thought to Matrix, who had been suffering in silence since the loss of Druid.

'As a footnote to the events of the day, M4 went missing and hasn't been mentioned since. That was day fourteen – exactly a week ago.'

'The next day, Kodiak began testing the moss for medicinal properties, ably assisted by his makeshift medical team consisting of our mechanical engineer, electrical engineer, suit technician and astrophysicist. Still in their suits, despite their waste receptacles being full to overflowing, the four of them harvested copious quantities of the substance, squeezed the liquid out and cleansed it thoroughly by sponging up water from a pool designated only for rinsing. Kodiak then mashed the moss and applied the resulting black paste to the fungating sores on the legs and feet of Zephyr, Shard and Europa.

'They also tried making use of the soggy soil – or silt, as Mirage had called it – which they applied to the arms and hands of all three.

'Finally, the faces, necks and the rest of the afflicted bodies were coated with a blend of soil, moss and water. There was nothing else to try – just those three combinations of the only ingredients not yet known to be noxious.

'We received this from Galleon.'

'A strange thing's happening. We're noticing more of the plant-like objects sprouting up along a trail between where Zephyr, Shard and Europa have been bathing and the rocks that they've been lying on.

There are more than a dozen of them now. The tallest ones are up to knee height already and have grown a distinctly bulbous top. Below this, two stubby shoots have appeared on opposite sides of the stem. Curiously, the objects are covered in a grey fungus remarkably similar to that growing on Zephyr, Shard and Europa.'

'As the day progressed, Swift described how a division was appearing in the bottom half of the stems of some of them; and then, by the end of the day, how the two sides of the lower stem had separated completely. As the organisms increased in height, their bulbous tops expanded, while the two offshoots continued extending outwards. Swift wondered if the bulbs were likely to flower, and, if so, what they'd produce.

'Galleon gave us a final update before another routine day in the lifeboat drew to a close.'

'Zephyr is resisting scratching in an attempt to leave her scabs intact. Shard has been clawing frantically at his, breaking them off and causing considerable bleeding. He's aware of the risk of infection, but he's finding the itching insufferable. Europa's condition is less advanced, as you know, but the irritation is still driving her crazy. All three are staying out of the pools now, so as to properly test the potential remedies.

'If anything, Shard and Europa have been scratching their legs less, but it's too soon to tell whether that's an indication that the moss and pool water mixture is having some effect. We'll continue with the treatment in the same way with all three concoctions and give you an update tomorrow ... I take it you two are going to sleep now.

'We have no sense of day or night down here, or any other measure of time. It's only by counting your daily greetings that we know it's been five Earth days and four Earth nights since we set out. As soon as you leave the lifeboat, Earth time will be finally consigned to the past – without the intended transition to Proxima time. Even if we had an antique mechanical chronometer, we wouldn't be able to simulate a day-night cycle in an underground environment where light and sound are constant. With no awareness of planetary motion, the concept of time is meaningless.

'Enjoy your silent slumbers while you can in your padded reclining seats, wrapped in dry blankets and breathing sweet, purified air. It's hard to get any kind of rest down here, forever rolling over to find the least uncomfortable device or container to lie on, inhaling the pungent atmosphere and the stench of overflowing waste running up our legs from our raised boots, while stuffing our ears with corners cut off our blankets to muffle the incessant sound of steam hissing and screeching through the vents all around us.

'And then there's the thirst. The fog has kept us hydrated to a certain extent, but we're desperate enough to start drinking the pool water now.'

'The next time the plant-like growths were mentioned, the tallest ones were above waist height. Their bulbous protrusions at the top were now twisting and rocking from side to side, but nothing about them gave the impression that they were going to flower. The two branches near the top of the trunk were no longer rigidly perpendicular, but had begun flexing up and down, and the branches on some of the more developed ones had become jointed halfway along. A bend had also appeared at the top of the dual, lower half of the trunk, while a further joint was evident halfway down both sides of the divide. Kodiak speculated that this might be a highly significant stage in the emergence of this new life form – if indeed it was a new life form. He counted two dozen or more of what he was now calling fungoids.

'Here's Kodiak's medical update, twenty-one hours after the commencement of the three experimental treatments.'

'There's been little or no observable progression in the fungal condition on the legs and feet of Zephyr, Shard or Europa. However, the fungus is proliferating unchecked elsewhere, and is rife across the bodies of Zephyr and Shard. I can't say yet if there's any improvement on anyone's legs and feet – only that there's no apparent deterioration.

'It wasn't long after you two last spoke to Galleon that Europa declared that she'd seen enough. She washed off all three experimental preparations and asked me to apply the moss and pool water paste all over her body, which I duly did. For her, the early signs are encouraging.

'For Shard and Zephyr, though, the prognosis is grim. The fungus was visible in their mouths when we arrived, but it wasn't impeding their breathing at that stage. Now it's firmly embedded, not only in their mouths, but in and around their other facial orifices, to the extent that respiration is becoming increasingly laboured. Neither of them can see now. Zephyr's eyelids are closed, as if knitted together by the fungus; and Shard's eyes are such a mess from scratching that I can't tell if his eyelids are open or closed – or

even if he still has eyelids.

'Galleon has declared their status to be terminal.'

'Although uncertain yet of the effect that the moss and pool water mixture was having on Europa's rash, it was decided that the experiment should be extended to some of the members of the second party. All five agreed that it was time to get out of their suits anyway, as the overflow from their receptacles was turning their suits from the waist down into mobile cesspits which produced an undesirable backflow when reclining with legs elevated.

'However, before removing their suits they needed to stock up on moss, which for Kodiak meant entering the lake for the first time. And, yes, the irony hadn't escaped any of us that the best chance of a cure for a deadly disease caused by the lake was in the lake.

'It was considered inevitable that everyone would be afflicted with the rash sooner or later, whether they came into direct contact with the lake liquid or not, so the moss and pool water mixture was seen as a potential preventive measure, if not a cure. In the interests of experimentation, only Kodiak and Rubella were coated with the fresh batch. By delaying the treatment of Galleon, Swift and Matrix, it would be possible to draw conclusions about the compound's effectiveness on Kodiak and Rubella if a rash were to break out on the other three – and possibly prove its efficacy in mitigating or preventing an outbreak if Kodiak and Rubella were unaffected, or less affected.

'Whatever the outcome, at the first sign of itching, the others would begin the treatment anyway.

'By the way, "moss and pool water mixture" was too much of a mouthful, so we didn't call it that for much longer. It was Kodiak's concoction, so he was given the credit and it was renamed Kodiak cream. When I get down there I'll insist that the main ingredient is named zephyrshard after its discoverers.

'We didn't hear much after that, as communication became increasingly difficult towards the end of the day. Before giving up trying to make sense of the few wayward words that we could pick out, we were in no doubt that something dreadful had happened.'

'It wasn't until four hours after we awoke on day seventeen that the atmospheric conditions improved sufficiently for us to piece together a message confirming that Zephyr had suffocated about twelve hours earlier. Shard was also barely breathing by then and didn't outlive his lifelong companion by more than an hour. Both had been laid to rest in the growing graveyard alongside Crete, Kerid and Mirage.

'The mood thereafter was sombre, both in the cavern and the lifeboat. Later, with the signal having improved, Trebuchet and I listened as Swift lamented their plight ... our plight ... the plight of the entire fleet. You might like to hear what she said. It sums up how we all felt that day, and puts our precarious existence into perspective.'

'2,464.
'How many now?
'Eight lifeboats per ark ...
'Fourteen seats on a lifeboat ...
'112 colonists per ark ...
'Five arks ... 560 colonists.
'Six lost already down here ...
'That leaves 554.
'A colony of 554 is the most that we can hope for now ... That's all that remains from a fleet of twenty-

two identical arks, designed so that their original crews of seventy-five breeding pairs and their descendants would procreate in transit but maintain their populations within the dormpod capacity of 200 until Proxima b was reached more than a millennium later.

'It's ironic that our commanders' strategy of overpopulating the UK Ark in the decades prior to arrival, knowing that most of our inhabitants would be unable to disembark, was preferable to the risk of underpopulation and a struggle to establish a depleted colony.

'So here we are, 1,268 Earth years later, and 554 is our best case scenario – a long way short of the original target of 2,464, which would only have been attained if every ark had reached Proxima b with at least 112 crew members able to fit into defect-free millennium-year-old suits, and with all lifeboats fully functional and piloted to a successful landing.

'We can send another ninety-eight down in our seven remaining lifeboats, but what about the other four arks? We don't know if they can even get a lifeboat to the surface.

'How long's it been since there was any verbal interaction with the US Ark, Galleon?

'Before your parents were born?

'Yeah, and mine.

'Hard to believe that we once spoke the same language. Our grandparents and theirs simply gave up trying to understand each other and resorted to transcribing and translating recorded messages – until the messages became so infrequent as the decades passed that the art of transcription and translation was lost ... so we don't know anything about the current status of their crew or their equipment.

'Then there's the Indian Ark. The latest information we have is from a 320-year-old census relayed to us before the last Anglo-Punjabi speaker died. According to the data received back then, the ark was perilously underpopulated, with males outnumbering females by five to one. If that trend has continued, there must be very few females of child-bearing age now.

'What's that, Europa?

'Yeah, maybe none. We've only ever heard male voices through that channel.

'Not good for establishing a colony.

'And the Russians ... We've been side by side all the way and our channels have been open the whole time. We hear their voices, but no-one has any idea what they're saying.

'As for the Korean Ark, all we know is that it's years behind, but still on course for a rendezvous.

'Can you imagine how our five cultures will cohabit in a subterranean environment? How have the other four civilisations evolved? Will we be able to live together with so little in common and no basis for communication, or will there be tribal conflict?

'Matrix thinks they'll all choose different landing sites half a world away, so territorial claims and resources won't be an issue.'

'There have been no more deaths in the four days since the loss of Zephyr and Shard – at least there hadn't when I last heard from Galleon twenty hours ago ... and there's still no sign of Trebuchet.

'The other news has been mixed. The latest I have on Europa is that her condition had stabilised. Galleon, Swift and Matrix started itching within twenty-four hours of removing their suits, so Swift and Matrix promptly applied the Kodiak cream; but Galleon delayed his treatment for about half a day to compare the progress of his condition with theirs. Up to yesterday, Kodiak and Rubella, having continually reapplied the cream for three days, still hadn't developed any symptoms.

'Trebuchet and I couldn't figure out why communications cut out abruptly yesterday. Previously, whenever we'd experienced problems, the signal had become intermittent, and gradually faded until there was nothing intelligible; but there was always something ... some kind of crackling ... never nothing. It's either a very different kind of atmospheric disturbance, or something has happened below to block the signals from the six channels that are still active – or were still active.

'There was growing concern about the fungoids – "Proximans", they started calling them – dozens of them, the largest at least shoulder height. This is what we listened to at the end of the day that had begun with the terrible news of Zephyr and Shard ... on Swift's channel.'

'Look at this one!

'Galleon! ... Everyone! ... Come and look at this!

'It's uprooting itself!

'Can you hear this, Monarch?

'Trebuchet?

'The biggest fungoid is pulling itself up out of the soil ... as if it has legs.

'It's lifting one of them up, clear of the ground.

'Incredible!

'It lost balance for a moment and put its ... whatever it is down ... but stayed upright.

'What is that?

'It doesn't have roots ... It's not a plant ... It's all fungus, just like what grew on Zephyr and Shard ... but it's shaped like us!

'The bulbous top isn't a bulb at all ... It isn't going to flower like a plant ... It's more like a head ... and the branches aren't branches ... and the dual lower trunk ...'

'Galleon cut in to check that we were recording. Fortunately, we hadn't yet gone into night mode, so we caught everything that Swift described.'

'It's raising and lowering its ... What can we call them? ... They're just like legs – totally detached from the ground ... and it's waving its branches ...

'It's lost its balance and has fallen forward ... supporting itself unsteadily on all fours like a newborn ...

'Keep back, Matrix. We don't know what it's capable of.

'Monarch, Trebuchet, are you still getting this?

'It's pulling itself along on its branches, dragging the divided trunk behind it ...

'Now it's trying to push itself upright ...

'It's unsteady, but it's done it ...

'Now it's fallen forward again.'

'The commentary continued for some time until, incredibly, the fungoid established a sufficient degree of stability to walk, they said, like a toddler, frequently falling forward, but pushing itself upright, and getting better every time with practice.

'It was aimless, though. It had no eyes, and no apparent sense of direction, so it bumped into and tripped over rocks and several of the two dozen other fungoids that were as yet immobile; but every time it toppled forward, it righted itself and resumed its progress.

'Neither Trebuchet nor I slept well that night. We dimmed the lights and muted the speakers, leaving the six below to monitor the walking fungoid, while no doubt keeping a watchful eye on the others that were still rooted ... actually not rooted in the ground.'

'On resumption of communications, we learned that five more fungoids were mobile and stumbling around, bumping into each other and the cave walls like blind children taking their first steps, struggling for balance, tripping and tumbling. Some of them waded into the lake, fell over and floated on the surface. One of them was last seen drifting into the mist.

'Kodiak, the only remaining member of our crew with any substantial biological knowledge, speculated as to what might have occurred.'

'Good question, Monarch ... and I don't pretend to have an answer, but this is what I have by way of a theory so far.

'If the fungi on Proxima b are anything like the fungi on the ark, it's conceivable that they reproduce by means of spores. We know that the first cases of skin irritation and rash occurred following immersion in the lake. Assuming that spores are present in the lake, every member of the advance party would have been covered in thousands, possibly millions of them when they came ashore. That would certainly account for the itching and subsequent rash.

'By scratching and tearing their skin, Zephyr and Shard allowed the spores to merge with their body fluids, effectively mixing the fungal DNA with our alien human DNA. The mutating scabs were then scratched off and discarded in the soil along a trail between where Zephyr, Shard and Europa were bath-

ing and the rocks where they tried to sleep and stay dry. This is where most of the fungoids have emerged, but with a greater concentration nearer the rocks. I can only assume that something in the soil stimulated growth in the fungal scab fragments, transforming them into these humanoid-fungal creatures, a fusion of two life forms – one native to Proxima b, and the other ... us.'

'It was just a theory, he said, but it sounded as though he was right about witnessing the genesis of a new life form.

'As the hours passed, more and more of the fungoids liberated themselves from the soil, while the remainder continued to grow. Curiously, there appeared to be no new ones cropping up, probably because there were no fresh scabs being sown.

'Europa's condition is now stable. She'd initially experienced some fungal growth, but she hadn't caused herself any significant harm by scratching. When we last heard, the itching had eased, thanks to the all-pervading power of the Reactor, she said – or perhaps it was the Kodiak cream.

'Rubella and Kodiak were still rash-free, and the outbreak on the others was kept under control with repeated applications of Kodiak's black salve. We can only wonder if the formula will keep the condition at bay long enough to enable the human body to produce antibodies to fight the fungus by itself.

'Kodiak's musings extended to the matter of the species' life cycle, if it had one. Its birth had been witnessed, and now its infancy was being observed. Presumably its fungal properties were enabling it to absorb nutrients and grow without the need to ingest anything that its human characteristics might require

– otherwise it would have a mouth.

'Having monitored the fungoids' rapid development over the previous four to five days, Kodiak confronted us with a plethora of unanswerable questions which he must have been pondering for some time, as he had them all cued up for us. This for starters.'

'When will the creatures stop growing? They've adopted our basic human shape, but they've far exceeded our growth rate. The biggest ones are already as tall as I am.'

'Nobody commented on that. So then there was this one.'

'What are they feeding on? Something in the atmosphere? Or in the soil? Or both?'

'Everyone reflected silently, including Kodiak himself, so I'll skip to the next file.'

'If the species is to survive, sooner or later these individuals will need to reproduce. There are no obvious openings or appendages as yet, so unless some human-like organs develop prior to sexual maturity – whenever that might be – they'll have to propagate as a fungus. If that happens, will the release of genetically modified spores pose a greater threat to our colony than the native ones that we've been exposed to already?'

'Again no response, other than a perceptible sense of dread.

'And this.'

'At the moment, the Proximans appear to be acting on instinct, just as infant mammals would; but how much of our physiology is there beneath the fungal exterior, and to what extent will their human qualities develop?

'Does the fungoid physiology have a nervous sys-

tem? Can the hybrids feel pain?

'Is there any semblance of a brain in their equivalent of a head? If so, will the evolving Proximans develop cognitive abilities? And if they do, how quickly will they learn?

'Are they likely to become aggressive with maturity, or dangerously defensive? Should we eliminate them now as a precaution, or should we plan to live alongside them in the hope that it'll be safe for us and future generations to do so?'

'Well, if our medic didn't have the answers, who else would?

'Rubella, her grounded sense of practicality keeping a rein on her partner's theoretical meanderings, wondered if the fungoids might be edible. Could we control their reproduction and farm them to establish a food supply? Or would that constitute cannibalism?

'Her input sparked a lively discussion which included a proposal to cut open one of the smaller ones to test for a reaction and find out what's actually inside, how close it is to human ... and if it's edible.

'The consensus was that we'll only have to tackle these kinds of moral and ethical dilemmas if we find ourselves under threat; for example, if we're faced with a species capable of rapid reproduction to the extent that they vastly outnumber us in the competition for resources and put us at risk of starvation. If the Proximans don't consider us in any way essential to their survival, or a threat to their survival, or they remain totally unaware of us, we might live independently of each other in our shared new world without conflict.'

'Before our day was done, Kodiak and Rubella decided to explore one of the portals that led deeper into the planet's crust. A stream flowing from a run-off pool would guarantee a water supply for as long as they and the stream continued along the same path. Trebuchet and I switched to night mode just after they set out, so we caught up with their news when we were rested and refreshed.'

'The next day was the last time that we heard from anyone below. It was a period that began with the fungus and the fungoids seemingly under control, and ended with all of us in a state of indecision and disunity.

'The first thing we learned was that the rest of the Proximans were mobile. Swift counted twenty-three in all, including two that were later seen drifting away on the lake. The older ones hadn't grown any taller, but they were steadier on their ... whatever they have for feet. They were silent, docile, still tripping over blindly, and seemingly oblivious to the presence of the crew, each other and everything else in the cavern. They didn't appear to be posing an immediate threat; nevertheless, everyone took care to avoid physical contact, including sleeping in their flushed-out suits with their visors only slightly open, for fear of contracting a rash and initiating the whole contamination process again.

'With no new shoots visible, the fungoid population seemed to have been capped at around two dozen – until Galleon's discovery.

'Uproar erupted around midday. At first, no-one was close enough to a helmet for us to make any sense of the garbled cries; but eventually Galleon picked one up and came through on Matrix's channel.'

'Trebuchet, Monarch, get this!

'There's a forest of them! ... They're all over the burial mound!'

'After that thump, all we heard was a babble of agitated voices until Galleon came back on.'

'No-one's been in there for two days ... Why would they? ... I was kicking the soil around on the shore, making sure that there were no new growths, when I had a chilling thought ... so I ran to the recess to check on the bodies.

'One side of the burial mound is covered in new shoots ... hundreds of them!

'This didn't happen after we buried Kerid, Crete and Mirage. There was nothing growing there when we took the bodies of Zephyr and Shard in ... four days, you said, after we buried the first three.

'If you could see this ... Two hundred at least ... clumped together on the side of the mound covering Zephyr and Shard – but still nothing on the other three.

'So why has all of this sprouted within two days of burying Zephyr and Shard? And why did it take me, or any of us, two days to even consider that this might happen? We should have known that their fungal scabs would still be active.

'Kodiak at least should have anticipated this. He says now that nothing grew on Mirage, Crete and Kerid because they died of lichen poisoning before their rashes had developed into a fungus.

'So this confirms his theory that the biological reaction is triggered when the blood-soaked fungus makes contact with the soil ... and we shovelled soil all over their scab-encrusted bodies!'

'I'll pause at that point, because there's some information from earlier that I've skipped and need to include, as it has a bearing on the rest of the day's events.

'After Swift had initially allayed our concerns regarding the fungoid population, Rubella and Kodiak gave us an account of their expedition, which for us had occurred during night mode.

'They'd followed what became a fast-flowing stream down a steeply descending passage for about three kilopaces before the downward pressure and constant jarring on Kodiak's neck forced them to turn back.

'As there was no lichen to light the way, and the two torches in the lifeboat had been deemed surplus to requirements and left behind by both parties, the pair had to endure the increasing heat and humidity in their suits.

'With hindsight, fully integrated suit lighting has proved to be an impediment rather than a convenience, compounded by the need to wear helmets for communication.

'They didn't discover a new cavern, but they said that the passageway widened considerably at the point where they felt compelled to return. Visibility was down to five paces there, and they described some of the high-pressure jets as ear-piercing, suggesting that there might be another chamber directly below.

'Based on Rubella and Kodiak's report, and before anyone had any idea of what was later found in the recess, Galleon informed us that he, Swift and Europa had decided to resume their descent into the planet's crust. He emphasised the need to find food sources other than the moss – an inadequate diet that could only be supplemented in the medium term by farming the Proximans – and stressed the importance of establishing whether the organisms in the lakes were the only producers of oxygen.'

'Swift, Europa and I feel that we're ready to continue the journey and have decided to set out before the end of your day in the lifeboat. Europa insists that she's sufficiently recovered, and Kodiak thinks she may have some degree of immunity now.

'We'll wear our suits for lighting and protection, and we'll take our smocks, blankets, axes, twelve paces of rope, and plentiful supplies of moss, pool water and Kodiak cream. Swift and I will wear our helmets for communication as well as lighting, but Europa will leave hers behind, as the batteries are almost dead.

'Having set out from the lifeboat seven days after Europa and the others, the rest of us can't be sure if we even have seven days of power left in our helmet and wrist lights – so we either press on now or we'll be confined to this cavern forever.

'Kodiak, Rubella and Matrix will wait here for you to join them. I think this is as far as Matrix will go in any case. She said she'll remain for as long as it takes her daughters to get here. I also get the impression that Kodiak and Rubella have seen enough to know that they've reached the end of their quest for somewhere to begin a new life – and I can't see Kodiak going any further with that helmet torturing his spine.

'If we find a more hospitable environment with an alternative food source, we'll report back to say that we're establishing a new settlement there. If not, depending on our assessment of conditions deeper down, we'll either keep going or, power permitting,

turn back.'

'Hours later, following the burial mound discovery, Galleon, Swift and Europa revised their plan, agreeing with the others that the imminent liberation of two hundred fungoids needed to be addressed before the group split up.

'We discussed at length the question of what to do with the Proximans, considering all the moral issues raised by every potential scenario.

'Were we prepared to pre-emptively hack down the new growths to safeguard our own survival – in effect committing speciocide?

'If not, and if the fungoids should turn out to be predatory, Kodiak, Matrix and Rubella would be overwhelmed by hundreds of them, and Trebuchet and I would have to limit our descent to the upper cavern, or explore elsewhere. The wrong course of action now, or any undue hesitation, could prove fatal – not only for our landing party, but for our entire species.

'Kodiak argued that we'd be unwise to contemplate any such drastic action based on insufficient knowledge.'

'We don't know anything yet about the physiology of the Proximans or the interaction between the human and fungal components. For example, is the relationship symbiotic or parasitic? If the fungus is parasitic, will it ultimately consume everything of the human host? If symbiotic, might we be witnessing the interplanetary evolution of the human race in its only viable form? We can't possibly predict the long-term effects of an alien monotrophic diet on the human body, nor the effects of our consumption of the microorganisms in the water, so this might be the only way

forward for our species.'

'The astrophysicist in Matrix agreed that our survival prospects looked slim, lamenting that without a Geiger counter we can only guess at the effectiveness of the planet's porous crust as a radiation shield. However, Matrix the mother voiced her concerns regarding her daughters living among fungoids and risking the same fate as Zephyr and Shard. She remarked with revulsion that human-fungal hybrids possessing her family's DNA were not the grandchildren she'd envisaged.

'Kodiak took the astrophysicist's first point as reinforcement.'

'What if it turns out that this is the only way humans can adapt to the conditions on this planet and survive as a species – through symbiosis?

'Think of what we're witnessing here, people ... a rapid mutation of native organisms and human body fluids into a hybrid entity with a newly evolved DNA – human characteristics infused with native properties that are UV-resistant and better adapted to absorb nutrients and survive in Proxima b's subterranean environment than we are in our current form.'

'Trebuchet and I wondered to what extent our six crewmates were already affected by radiation sickness, poor nutrition and lack of sleep.

'Kodiak expanded on his argument by suggesting that these might be intelligent creatures, and that some kind of communication might even be possible, given time. Further, he questioned our right to unnecessarily extinguish the life of any sentient being – "unnecessarily" being the key word, since his medical training had accustomed him to experimentation on non-human subjects whose lives were extinguished for the benefit of humankind.

'Rubella, as true to Kodiak as she was when approving the fit of his suit, proposed restraining, observing and experimenting on a limited number of fungoids, and then, depending on the results, either making use of or eradicating the remainder. She thought eight lengths of rope ought to be sufficient to keep a select few captive while assessing their value as livestock.

'It was clear that Kodiak and Rubella saw opportunities for exploitation of the Proximans; and while they had no qualms about terminating as many as necessary in the name of science, they were not in favour of wiping them out entirely ... whereas it became increasing evident that Matrix was.

'Galleon, on the other hand, was uncharacteristically hesitant. He recognised the fungoids' potential worth to our survival, but was wary of allowing such a large number of them to roam free.'

'While the infant forms appear to be harmless right now, we can't predict how the juveniles and adults will behave. If we let them live and they become a threat, how easy will it be to overpower them once they're mature and fully mobile?

'Sure, we have a range of tools with points and blades, but using those would likely entail bloodshed – or the release of spores, depending on their composition – but then what will be the consequences of their fluids reacting with the soil ... or their spores entering our lungs?'

'Galleon's indecisiveness, according to Kodiak, was a perfect demonstration of the need for vital questions to be answered before an informed decision could be made – and who but Kodiak himself, with his medical training and Zephyr's microscope, was better equipped to provide the answers?

'Trebuchet, while unable to deny the logic behind Kodiak's reasoning, openly declared his opposition to sparing the lives of any of the hybrids. He concluded that the most prudent option would be to eliminate all of them now and carry out research on the remains. We know how to produce them, he reminded us, and could do so again under controlled conditions if they prove to be of nutritional value.

'Swift instantly quashed that notion, arguing that the current crop was produced at the expense of the lives of two of our crew, and that further production would necessitate the prolonged and agonising death of another colonist – either by misfortune, as with Zephyr and Shard, or through a deliberate act of self-sacrifice ... or sacrifice.

'Matrix, hypothesising with more than a hint of wishfulness that this new life form might not even be capable of surviving in the long term, insisted that it would be a waste not to exploit the fungoids immediately as a food resource.

'Rubella seemed to change direction with the suggestion of experimenting on some of the lambs and chicks when they're eventually transported down.

'By which time we might not be here, was the unified response to that idea – precisely what Rubella and Kodiak wanted to hear.

'The thought of fungal sheep hybrids and fungal chicken hybrids prompted Europa to raise a question that no-one had considered up to that point. If these rapidly multiplying and fast growing fungoids are the result of direct human exposure to the lake, what's become of M4?

'The question hung in the air as discussion gave way to contemplation and a much needed opportunity for us to reflect on our nature as human beings.

'Do we have the moral right to slaughter these creatures out of ignorance or fear, or because they don't serve our interests? If they prove to be edible, can we justify their preservation solely as a food source? If so, will we expect those who follow in our footsteps to embrace our quasi-cannibalism? As semi-endemic hybrids, are the Proximans not better adapted and therefore more entitled to exist on this planet than we aliens are? Do we suddenly abandon the code of ethics that has guided our civilisation on the ark for centuries? Are we humans actually no better than any other organism driven by primal instincts to survive and ensure the survival of its species at all costs?

'The argument for self-preservation – a euphemism for speciocide, according to Kodiak and Rubella – was gaining momentum by the time Trebuchet and I retired. Swift's infrequent input revealed her to be a third member of the pro-Proximan camp; while at the other end of the spectrum Matrix remained vehemently opposed to the blending of species or any recognition of the fungoids' status. Galleon and Europa were still non-committal when Trebuchet and I cast our votes in favour of self-preservation.

'Anticipating no further need for communication, we switched to night mode, leaving those below to reach a democratic outcome and avert the colony's first civil war.'

'We spent most of yesterday trying to re-establish contact with our crewmates, while also preparing for the final disembarkation.

'Trebuchet searched for faults outside, while I ran checks inside. All systems appeared to be functioning as they were the day before. There was no evidence of any extraordinary stellar activity while we were in night mode, and it was highly unlikely that the batteries in most of the second party's helmets would have failed simultaneously, so we could only conclude that there'd been an incident underground.'

'We delayed today's departure in order to record and relay this final transmission, but also in the hope of hearing something other than the unsettling shuffling on Swift's channel – the only one still active.

'It didn't take two, so Trebuchet took the opportunity to explore the abandoned craft and scavenge for anything easily portable that might be useful below. A forty-minute walk each way would allow him up to seventy minutes to examine some more artefacts and search for clues as to the fate of the crew.

'When he set out, there was no indication that Proxima Centauri's corona was any more volatile than it had been in the previous three weeks, or that a flare of such intensity was imminent.

'If anyone in the fleet is receiving this, I assume you're tracking any coronal mass ejection that might have accompanied that flare. I have no such data, and I don't have Matrix to advise me.

'I currently have no contact with anyone.'

'I've reconsidered my plan.

'As Trebuchet's survival seems unlikely ...

'I don't know how long I have, and I can't predict the impact of a CME, so I'll head straight for the canyon and take refuge from whatever matter and energy is hurtling this way.

'Hopefully the surface temperature will have dropped a little more by the time I get out there.

'I'll finish this transmission by including some brief recordings of Trebuchet's observations at the landing site, some of his findings inside the ship, and his last comments which were interrupted by the flare. It's not much, and it's rather fragmented ... but anyway ...'

'... no tracks or footprints outside, other than ours ...

'I wonder if they all left together ... or split up and made their way to different destinations, including the canyon ...

'Could've been hundreds of years ago ...

'Maybe we'll find some sign of them or their descendants deeper in the planet's crust ...

'Maybe there's a whole civilisation down there.'

'Then this, once he was inside.'

'... guess everything of any use was taken by the crew ... There are some ripped-out circuits in here ... an empty canister ... a carabiner ... Maybe I'll bring that ...

'The suits are no use ... No power ... Too heavy anyway ...

'I can't see how to open this doorway to the midsection ... If we could get into the crew's main quarters, we'd know how many were on board ...

'Maybe there's access to the propulsion system internally from there ...

'Galleon and Swift couldn't find a way in, so I'll leave it.'

'Then he found something that aroused his curiosity.'

'A box ... with a handle ... clasped shut ...
'Doesn't seem to be locked ...
'Might be a medical kit ...
'No symbols on it, though ...
'Can't get a grip on it with these gloves on ...
'I'll bring it back ... There's something in it, but I can't get it open.'

'After a few more minutes of rummaging, he remarked that it was getting warm in there. I lowered the shield to see the corona flaring up, and warned him to stay inside and avert his eyes from any external light. He acknowledged, and we waited.

'When he came back on, he said that it was too hot to stay inside. I checked the external temperature ... It was 42° Celsius.

'For the next few minutes I heard only clambering sounds, followed by a thud ... and then this.'

'Look at the star ...
'Monarch ... look at the star!'

'I'd been watching it indirectly, but even through maximum tinting it had become so bright that I had to raise the shield.

'I sensed that Trebuchet was outside the ship, but before I could urge him to get back into the cargo bay and take cover, his channel fizzed and fell silent.

'The outside temperature peaked at 115°. The suits weren't designed to withstand that.

'It's fifty-eight out there now ... Should be a few degrees lower by the time I get out ... hopefully not so hot in the canyon ... and the deeper the better before the CME strikes.

'M5's ready to go, waiting patiently in its sustainer next to the hatch, alongside our two ex-packs, axes, torches and a six-pace length of rope.

'I'll leave the rope.'

'I can't help but feel frustration and bitterness at what our ancestors did to our home planet to put us all through this – not only those of us in what remains of the fleet, but thousands of others in the seventeen arks that didn't make it this far – from the crew of the Japanese ark wiped out by a virus within two years of their departure, to the South Africans who made it through more than twelve centuries, only to suffer a hull rupture five years before I was born.

'Our exodus has pushed our species to the brink of extinction.

'If I were optimistic, I'd say that we're on the eve of a radical evolution. The fungoids have four limbs and something resembling a head. They have a sense of balance and are able to walk upright, which indicates that they've adopted some human characteristics, if not instincts – but do they have a consciousness? Will the hybrids retain or develop any of their human traits, or, as Kodiak postulated, will all traces of humanity be suppressed or extinguished in a process of symbiosis or parasitism?

'It seems that if Proxima b is ever to be colonised by humans, it won't be in the way any of us intended.

'Anyway ...

'Hopefully the art of transcription and translation has been kept alive on some of the other arks and someone can make sense of our language and dialect, whether via this speculative surface-to-orbit transmission, or on retrieving these recordings physically from this isolated plateau.

'Monarch of the UK Ark, Lifeboat 1, signing off.'

THE MATRYOSHKA LOOP

Iseropus

Pinned facing the cave wall, his eyes streaming in the stinging wind whistling across the glistening granite, Dayne groaned under the pressure being exerted on his diaphragm from behind as a pair of mandibles assaulted him with relentless volleys to the back of the head, intermittently pinching his shoulders and hammering at his kidneys with all the zeal of a sadistic masseur. Yet it wasn't what the iseropus was doing behind his head and shoulders that worried him so much as what it was repositioning itself to do lower down his back.

He had little chance now of escaping what was becoming the inevitable. His only hope would be a moment of inattention, or some kind of distraction – but who or what could deny an iseropus the ultimate climax that would elevate it from its primal function to the zenith of its existence? The other three would have fled, exactly as Dayne had intended on diverting the beast away from them. He didn't expect that any of them would have turned back to follow him into the cave with the iseropus scuffing at his heels – and clearly they hadn't.

The team knew from the outset that most of them, if not all, might live to regret their choice – or worse, that they might not. Four adventurers setting out to discover and hopefully return with evidence of creatures that had been rumoured for centuries to exist inside a gigantic caldera in a vast expanse of uncharted wilderness, from which no explorer had ever returned, and of which no reliable account, description or proof could be found anywhere. This was their Bigfoot ... their Loch Ness monster.

Battered, bleeding, and bruised under the increasing pressure of the probing around his sacrum, Dayne's mind began conducting a futile analysis of events leading to the pivotal decision that had condemned him to this ordeal while sparing the others – futile, since what had been done could not be undone. Nevertheless, his recollections served to direct his thoughts away from what was happening behind him.

Assembled seven days earlier beside the Hummer, having unloaded their packs after reaching the point beyond which no vehicle, including The Beast with all of its modifications, would take them, each one eyed the other three up and down. Their determined demeanour confirmed their collective assurance that whatever qualities or skills any individual lacked were more than adequately compensated for in the other three.

Rusty, red-headed, as the name suggests, a twenty-nine-year-old rock climber with a black belt, third dan in karate – twice ladies' state champion. Over six feet tall and fit as any marine, she could outpace, outclimb and outlast the best of them. Equipped with her rope, carabiners and axe, if there was any climbing or abseiling to be done, she'd be the one to lead the way.

Doc, they called him – not a doctor, but a forty-year-old research scientist with two decades of experience in entomology. He'd be the team's knowledge bank and the guardian of the tranquiliser gun, ammunition, storage jars, net and first-aid kit. Slightly built, but a finisher of countless marathons and half-marathons, he'd be better suited for endurance than most.

Ebbeny, a strikingly bronzed thirty-eight-year-old former infantry major with training and experience in jungle warfare. As an ex-army officer, she'd be their strategist. Adept offensively and defensively in the finer points of sharpened steel, and with the physique to adroitly offset the weight of a combat knife in one fist with a machete in the other, she'd spearhead the group through the untamed terrain.

And Dayne, the youngest, also known as Tank, or Mountain – six foot nine, and two hundred and fifty pounds of mostly high-tensile muscle amassed from the age of twelve because Paw wanted his boy to be a third-generation champion woodchopper, and so pumped him full of steroids throughout his teenage years. Contributing his strength to the venture, Dayne would carry the bulk of the food supplies, the electronic equipment and their heaviest and most expensive piece of defensive hardware known affectionately as the zapper.

Amid the publicity leading up to the team's departure, the story of how this elite foursome came together, and the bond that united them, became worldwide news – namely, their common obsession with the legend of the mutant ichneumonids, giant parasitoid wasps that have featured in folklore for centuries, living on through tales that have become so distorted as to be widely dismissed now with a sceptical guffaw or grunt.

Few of those who consider themselves enlightened would dare to speak of the fabled monstrosities – better to remain a silent witness than to have your credibility shredded in public. Yet a small group of those captivated by the legend banded together in an online forum entitled *Ichneumonidae Gigantae*.

In the course of his research, Doc was the first of the team to discover the forum, and he was soon installed as one of its leading authorities. Ebbeny, Rusty and Dayne stumbled across it while following a trail of inconspicuous links, and all four subsequently became avid contributors.

Unanswerable questions abounded online for months until Doc, no longer satisfied with the confines of hearsay and speculation, suggested mounting an expedition. While the forum's founders were willing to act as online advisers, they would have no part in Doc's proposed escapade, warning that no-one who had previously embarked on such a mission had been heard from again. Whenever quizzed as to the source of their knowledge, or the foundation for their beliefs, the hosts would only insist that the existence of huge winged insects was, for them, simply beyond doubt – a question of faith.

Lured by talk of an expedition, Rusty, Ebbeny and Dayne were hooked, and Doc reeled them in. All four had long since settled on what they wanted to believe, as had the forum's faceless founders and legions of passing and peripheral contributors. Having pieced together scraps of stories fed to them at various stages of their lives, they chose to accept something for which there could be no rationale, but upon which they were prepared to stake their lives.

Gasping at the bitter breeze biting his face, and trying to gulp some oxygen into lungs hampered by the frenetic pummelling from behind, Dayne recalled the day that the four of them and The Beast were airdropped into a flat, rocky clearing 11,500 feet above sea level, almost twenty miles from the volcano. That was the closest that they could safely land in favourable weather conditions to what appeared in images captured by reconnaissance drones to be a honeycomb of caves opening onto a cliff face jutting out from the centre of the crater. Depending on the terrain concealed beneath the unbroken canopy that stretched from the drop zone to the very foot of the escarpment, and depending on how much of that could be covered in the Hummer, a two-week return trip was envisaged, with four weeks' supply of provisions to sustain them if needed.

As it turned out, the Hummer had to be abandoned before the end of day one, with barely two miles covered. Even using both chainsaws it made no sense to attempt to carve a corridor any wider than was necessary for Dayne, fully laden, to pass through.

Having made the decision to leave the unwieldy chainsaws and fuel canisters with The Beast and just take two machetes, it was a further six days of hacking through the dense vegetation and surmounting and sliding down muddy, rocky, root-bound slopes before the caves were sighted just after midday from a clearing on a ridge overlooking an undulating patchwork of foliage. Ebbeny estimated the rock wall to be little more than a mile, and less than two hours' steep, downward trek away.

A broad sweep with the binoculars revealed no signs of life. In the week that had passed, the team had heard numerous birds, although they had seen very few, and they had encountered a handful of snakes and lizards, with which they had supplemented their diet. They had, however, seen no trace of any mammals. By contrast, they had been plagued day and night by insects – although nothing approaching the size of those that they were seeking. At last, tantalising glimpses of what they hoped were entrances to labyrinthine tunnels promised so much more.

Their promise was fulfilled. Now, incarcerated in one of those caverns, Dayne's thoughts flashed back to the moment of their final scramble up the rocks beneath the lowest and most easily accessible of the caves.

Enthused by the proximity of their goal, and despite his heavier load, Dayne overtook Rusty, quickly opening up a ten-foot gap and leaving the others a further ten feet below her. He was about to hoist himself up onto the ledge along the front of the cave when they heard the scuttling of displaced stones from above. Fragments cascaded over them, ricocheting off their helmets as a high-pitched buzz drilled through the air.

Ebbeny chanced an upward glance and stifled a shriek. Dayne watched from above as she slid down past Doc, face to the wall, her limbs splayed and rigid. She'd seen something.

Doc looked up, shielding his face against the spray of dust and debris.

Rusty was motionless, her right arm supporting her against the rock wall, while her left hand was pressed over a bloody ear.

Ebbeny gasped and turned in panic, releasing her tenuous hold and skidding down further on her side.

Doc's eyes widened in horror as he stared beyond the two above him.

At that moment the buzzing broke off just long

enough for Dayne to catch the four-syllable word exhaled from below.

'Iseropus.'

Dayne dared to look up. No more than fifteen feet away, in the mouth of the cave to the right of the one that he was about to haul himself into, he saw a pair of antennae, four feet long at least, flailing haphazardly around two glistening globules of compound eyes. The creature's head twitched as if in alarm at the myriad of visions of the four intruders laying siege to its lair from below.

As the buzzing resumed, Dayne could see the semi-transparent blur of a wing and feel its downdraught. The force was insufficient to generate lift. Nevertheless, the thorax edged into view, and then the abdomen appeared as the whirring monstrosity propelled itself forward with all the grace of a hovercraft on a pebbled beach. The colossal insect was slowly being drawn out – either by curiosity or by an instinctive compulsion to defend its territory.

Suddenly the wings stopped. Silence ensued for an instant of treacherous tranquillity before a foreleg swept out, scattering more rocks and dust over the edge. Dayne closed his eyes for a second, then opened them to see a spiky tarsus resting on the ledge directly in front of him, endowed with claws ideally adapted for shredding soft animal tissue.

He looked down. Ebbeny had gone. Rusty, the left side of her face smeared red, was staring up, as was Doc below her. A decision had to be made. With little time for reflection, Dayne pulled himself up – equipment and supplies, including the zapper, strapped to his back. He gave the tarsal claws the widest possible berth as he crawled into the opening next to the one from which the iseropus had emerged.

'Go!' he shouted down to the others. 'Find cover! I'll distract it and lead it away!'

And that was it. That was the pivotal moment.

Once out of the shadows, the iseropus was drawn towards Dayne's movements – or the sound or smell of him. With its wings beating sporadically, it used its front and middle legs to cling to the partition between the caves, and then swung awkwardly round the edge of the precipice into the opening where Dayne, still fully laden, was now on his feet and backing into the darkness.

'The zapper!' Dayne reminded himself out loud.

Breaking off his retreat, he unhooked the entire pack from his left shoulder. It swung round heavily behind him and clattered on the ground to his right. The iseropus paused momentarily, its wings beating so fast now as to be invisible. The draught forced Dayne to stagger backwards. He caught his heel on a loose strap, tripped, instinctively rolled over and made for the cover of the nearest large rock. That was a mistake. The zapper was out of reach and the parasitoid wasp was closing in. He'd left himself defenceless.

Sweeping ever closer in random arcs and loops, one of the antennae made contact with its quarry, brushing against Dayne's thigh before whipping round and lashing the side of his head. With nowhere to go, Dayne retracted his limbs and closed his eyes until he felt the insect's vibrating head nuzzling his upper arm, and heard its mandibles grinding and its proboscis slurping, as if it were tasting the fabric of his jacket. He opened his eyes to see the beast take an exploratory hold on his right shoulder with its multiple mouth parts, gripping and twisting as both predator and prey rubbed their coarse cheeks together.

Dayne had to fight back. With his vision impaired by clouds of dust, he aimed a left hook at the middle of one of the creature's surprisingly soft compound eyes, causing it to let go momentarily. It quickly readjusted and clamped a claw onto Dayne's ankle, making him wince at the intensity of the pincer-like grip. There was no escape now. The iseropus proceeded to drag its prisoner deeper into the cave by the leg, scuffing him with ease along the ground, despite his size, and buffeting his upper body and head against every rocky obstacle. Dayne felt his ankle snap just before his skull cracked against the cave wall.

That was all he could remember of the course of action that had led him into his current predicament. Now, ten, maybe fifteen minutes after regaining consciousness, he could feel the searing pain of his broken ankle surpassing that of the bruising around his head and upper body. Of more concern to him, though, was the pressure low down behind him, and the increasingly concentrated soreness. The ovipositor was no longer probing all around the back of Dayne's jeans. It had settled on the optimal location and was drilling through the fabric several inches below his waistline.

Dayne recalled Doc giving the team a lecture on the reproductive propensities of parasites, but nothing had prepared him for the moment when the ovipositor broke through both denim and flesh, or the subsequent sickly bloated feeling in the few seconds before he passed out again.

Driftwood

'Daddy!'

Dayne opened his eyes to a blinding brightness and instinctively raised his left arm to diffuse the sunlight.

'Daddy's awake!'

He kept his eyes shielded behind the shadow of his forearm to allow them time to adjust to the unexpected light, while he dispatched his other senses on a mission to reconnoitre an environment that he wasn't expecting to wake up in.

His right hand raked over the surface beside him and reported that he was lying on sand. The grains were warm, as was the breeze, in stark contrast to the biting wind in the cave. But it wasn't the warm sand that surprised him so much as the fact that he was lying on his back.

'He's had a good sleep.'

Dayne could hear several voices – children, and a woman. There were others, too, in the background.

'He's pretending to still be asleep.'

It didn't take Dayne long to realise that the pain was still there at the base of his spine. It was more of a dull ache now, though – less intense.

'Shall I give him a shake?'

'No, sweetie. He'll get up when he's ready.'

The woman's voice didn't sound like Ebbeny's or Rusty's, so Dayne's curiosity compelled him to lower his arm. Squinting as his eyes emerged from the shade, he jerked his head to one side and winced at the shock that was relayed via his backbone to the sensitive nerves around his sacrum. As his eyes became accustomed to the light, he could see two small children, one kneeling on each side of him – a girl to his right, with straight, black, shoulder-length hair, and a tawny, tousled tyke to his left. Neither could have been of school age. Dayne guessed that the boy was slightly younger.

'What am I lying on?' he asked, with no idea who he was talking to.

'Sweetheart, it's just the shrapnel.'

Dayne looked beyond the boy to focus on the slender silhouette of a woman kneeling with her back to them, busily folding something like a towel, which she shook out high against the sunlight. Her hair, flowing freely halfway down her back and blowing in the breeze, was similar to the girl's, but there was something odd about the outline of her head. The shape was more heraldic than round – flatter on top and at the sides, and wider and higher than a human head should be. It was as if she were wearing a mask. Dayne's eyes were taking too long to adjust for his liking. Sweetheart? Shrapnel? Where was the iseropus?

'Come on, let's go and get tea,' she suggested, still facing away from them.

Dayne jacked himself up awkwardly with his right arm, turning laboriously onto his left side, from where he managed to lever himself uncomfortably into a precarious seating position. Head bowed, he caught sight of a naked midriff that he didn't recognise.

'What's wrong, Daddy?' the girl enquired.

Daddy? Was she actually talking to Dayne? She was looking straight at him and waiting for a response.

But he didn't have any children.

'I'm OK,' he replied to avoid appearing rude.

Returning the girl's concerned smile with one of his own, Dayne sensed the woman turning towards them. 'Here's your shirt, darling.'

Darling? Who was this woman? He glanced over to her and froze.

She was indeed wearing a mask! Dayne scrutinised its entire surface in two seconds, while trying to avoid staring or betraying any emotion. It reminded him of voodoo masks that he'd seen in movies set in African jungles or the Caribbean. Carved out of a single piece of wood, it was wider and flatter on top than a human head, while narrowing almost to a point two or three inches below the chin. It seemed to have been hollowed out for the purpose of assimilating the wearer's face. Each eye hole was smaller than a dime and so deep that it was impossible to see the woman's eyes – at least in this light with the sun at her back. Her mouth was similarly obscured behind the rectangular, horizontal orifice. A vertical black smear represented a nose, and random scratches were stained red to suggest scars. There was nothing about the shapes of the eye or mouth holes to suggest any kind of emotion or intention. The expression was entirely neutral.

Dayne took the shirt and put it on, noticing as he did that his chest was considerably less expansive, and his arms were thinner. He was almost hairless, too. What had become of the bulk of the man that they called Tank? Had he been unconscious for so long that he'd lost all that weight? What had happened in the meantime? Did Rusty, Ebbeny and Doc rescue him after all? He hauled himself unsteadily to his feet, observing as he did so that he was on a beach with dozens of others on a warm, sunny, late afternoon or early evening, facing west.

'This way,' the woman pointed, rising to her feet, swinging her beach bag over her shoulder and striding ahead.

Dayne, barely beginning to process the host of questions that were queuing up to be asked, duly followed. The children skipped and jumped merrily alongside him and the woman, who presumably was their mother – or perhaps not.

A walk of less than five minutes led them to a small, whitewashed timber building standing alone at the roadside, with a board outside reading, 'Sunshine Shack Snacks'.

'Get one of those tables outside, kids,' their mother instructed. 'Daddy and I'll go and order.'

Daddy? Dayne was no nearer to fathoming any of this out, but some way closer to the first of his many questions.

'Can we talk?' he asked the woman as she led him into the café.

She paused just inside the doorway and turned to face him. 'It's all gone again, hasn't it?'

'I'm not sure what you mean,' Dayne frowned, still unable to see her eyes or mouth, despite his proximity and the change of light.

'It's OK. I'll explain it to you ... again. Let's eat first, and then the children can go and play while we talk.'

Dayne paused for a moment's thought, and then whispered, 'Who are you?'

'I'll tell you everything just as soon as we've eaten,' she smiled. 'Just be patient, Lee.'

'Lee!'

'Sorry ... Look, let's just have tea, and then we can talk afterwards.'

Dayne hung back, thrusting his fists hard into his pockets, elbows locked straight, shoulders hunched and brow furrowed as he watched the children's mother collect and pay for a tray full of cold snacks and drinks. On rejoining the children at the table, Dayne could hear her whisper to them, 'Daddy's ...' something or other.

The food and drinks were consumed in almost complete silence and with minimal eye contact. Dayne watched curiously out of the corner of his eye as the woman inserted various pieces of dried fruit and freshly cut vegetables into the two-inch-wide slot and drank her milkshake through a straw. He had nothing to say until he could find out what he wanted to know, and the other three, for reasons of their own, opened their mouths only to eat.

The scrunching of the last napkin was the cue for the children to clamber down from their chairs. Acknowledging their mother's instructions to take care and stay in sight, they ran off gleefully to the play area. She watched them until they reached the swings.

Meanwhile, Dayne, observing the woman from the side, was still unable to see anything of her face behind the mask, which was a perfect fit, reaching back almost as far as her ears. It was then that he noticed that her hair was lighter than the girl's – more like the boy's brown waves, only straight. She turned towards the bewildered man seated next to her.

'What do you remember?' she asked.

Dayne chose his words carefully. 'I was in a cave,' he began.

'About us!' the woman interrupted impatiently. Then, more calmly, 'What do you remember about us?'

Thrown by the woman's tone, Dayne paused to reflect before replying, 'I'm sorry, I don't know who you are.'

The woman inhaled sharply and pressed a hand over the mouth opening. Dayne sensed the stifling of emotion behind the mask. It was half a minute before she could speak again.

'We'll have to go back to Doctor Reinhardt,' she said.

Mindful of the effect that his last words had had on her, Dayne remained silent, but attempted to appear as concerned for her sake as he was for his.

'My name,' she swallowed, 'is Mina ... Does that mean anything to you?'

Dayne's eyes offered nothing.

'I'll have to tell you everything again, just like I did last time – like Doctor Reinhardt said I'd have to do again sooner or later. I just didn't think it would be this soon. Six months? Seven? I hoped that you'd hang on a little longer, or that maybe this time everything would be all right – that you'd recovered.'

Mina knew that she'd have to begin the whole painful process of recreating her husband's world for him, just as she and the children had with the help of Doctor Reinhardt a few months earlier, the first time that Lee had relapsed after a year of rehabilitation following his tour of the Middle East.

Despite having gone through this before, she felt unprepared for their return home and her husband's inevitable outburst of rage on seeing himself in the bathroom mirror – unless he catches sight of his face in one of the car mirrors, or a window, in which case she'd have no idea how to deal with his reaction in public.

She should phone Doctor Reinhardt before returning to the car. Perhaps she, or someone, could be at home waiting for them. Or maybe it would be better not to leave it that long, in case Lee needs to go to the gents here. He keeps looking at his arms – just like last time.

'Call me any time, day or night,' Mina recalled the doctor urging her. This was an emergency. She'd have to call her now. She could go to the ladies, make the call, come back and keep Lee talking until Doctor Reinhardt gets here. It could be a long wait, though, and Mina sensed that her husband was likely to snap and black out before the doctor's arrival.

'He's coming round, Doctor,' a woman with a Spanish accent announced.

Dayne opened his eyes, blinking in the light of the lamp that arched over him.

'How are you feeling, Lee?' This was a different voice to the first one, although he couldn't place the accent. He could see the woman standing to the right of the bed – around fifty, chestnut brown hair, obviously not natural, or perhaps it was the light. She was staring into his eyes with an expression of concern and curiosity.

Feeling drowsy and a little nauseous, and having no idea where he was or what was going on, he answered, 'OK.'

He looked down to see that he was in a green, short-sleeved gown, with no visible opening at the front. A tube was feeding something into his left arm.

As his eyes became accustomed to the light, the woman with the Spanish accent fluttered around his peripheral vision, while the one that she'd addressed as 'Doctor' leaned in closer and resumed speaking.

'We had to sedate you, Lee. Do you remember what happened?'

Dayne struggled to recall the events of his most recent past.

'Tell me what you remember,' she pressed.

Dayne scrabbled around in his head for any pieces that he could find. His speech was as fragmented as his memory.

'The cave ... the iseropus ... the beach ... the mask ... and the children.' He contorted his face on adding, 'The mirror!'

'That was when we had to sedate you, Lee. You broke the car mirror. It upset the children. You needed to rest. We brought you here last night. You've had a good, long sleep.'

She went on, 'Now we have to continue with your rehabilitation. We need to help you to remember Mina and the children.'

Dayne listened, but said nothing.

'We're going to give you a relaxant to take away all the anxiety that's been hindering your thought processes. And then I'm going to help you to remember who you are.'

She nodded at the other woman. Dayne was vaguely aware of one bag of fluid being replaced by another, and this being attached to the tube that led into his arm. In an instant it felt disconcertingly cold, but soon all of the sharp edges around him appeared smoother as he listened to the doctor's fuzzy utterances.

She held up a spinning light, which they watched together in silence for a minute, and then she resumed.

'Lee, you were born thirty-four years ago in Broken Arrow, Oklahoma. You grew up with your father, mother and sister, Zia. Here's a picture of you all together.

'You lived in a lovely little house, surrounded by fields that were green all year round. You were very happy there. You remember that house, Lee. Here's a photo of the house and the garden that you and Zia used to play in.

'You had your own room, too. Picture your bedroom, Lee, with your toy trucks and tanks deployed strategically around the room, and model aeroplanes from different eras suspended in battle formation from the ceiling. You were very good at model making. You had such a passion for military vehicles.

'Your mother and father knew that you'd join the military some day. They were so proud of you when you graduated from the Tulsa Technology Center and decided to join the US Army.'

Doctor Reinhardt proceeded to outline and colour in the missing details of Lee's life, from childhood, through adolescence and into manhood, all the while evoking emotions linked to past achievements and failures. In the pulsating light, Lee's face flickered with emotions ranging from joy to sadness as the doctor reminisced with him over the three decades that he seemed to have forgotten. It was as if his life was under construction. Block by block, people, pets, places and events were being manufactured and assembled in his mind, while each muffled word and hazy image was injected into his tingling cardiovascular system to be deposited and stored in his brain – and all at the bidding of a voice emanating from a spinning light.

It was clear now. He was Lee Chan. A thirty-four-year-old war veteran, honourably discharged on medical grounds following an incident during operations in Iraq. Married for five years to Mina. Two adorable children, Leah and Kane. He'd been unable to work since his discharge, due to PTSD and the shrapnel embedded at the base of his spine.

'A very lucky man,' Doctor Reinhardt continued. 'Your family loves you very much. Mina, Leah and Kane are at home. They can't wait to see you.'

Lee began reflecting on his good fortune – aside from his ordeal in the Middle East – at having led such a fulfilling and happy life. Now, floating in a pool of numb relaxation, immersed in sumptuous sounds and comforted by the fading flickering light, he closed his eyes. He was overwhelmed by the relief of having recovered his missing life. The emptiness had gone. The void had been filled. His life had been restored. Where confusion once reigned, clarity now prevailed.

His thoughts drifted contentedly towards his two young children.

'Can you hear me?'

The Santa María

'Can yo' hear me?'

Lee was revelling in his game of Saint George and the two dragons with Leah and Kane and resented the intrusion by the ethereal voice addressing him in surround-sound.

'Hey! Can yo' hear me?'

He envisaged the invading words as pendulums suspended in the air all around him, swinging irregularly to and fro, their tempo disconcertingly out of time with the undulating background droning. He hadn't previously noticed the droning above the hissing and snarling of the dragons, but now it was gaining in intensity, and Lee sensed it encroaching with the intention of enveloping him. He'd been aware of an omnipresent disembodied voice in the recent past, but now its tone had changed. It had become deeper, masculine, more urgent. The accent was different, too.

'Hey, Marshall! C'mown! Wake up!'

The hand that shook Lee's shoulder frightened the dragons away and made him acutely aware of a soreness in his backside. Had one of the beasts bitten him there without his knowing? He opened his eyes for half a second before closing them again tightly, keeping them forced shut as he tried to figure out why the brief exposure to light hadn't given him a snapshot of his bedroom with Mina lying beside him and Leah and Kane slinking around the bed, pretending to breathe fire.

'Ah saw y'open yo' eyes, man! C'mown, wake up!'

Lee parted his eyelids slowly. The light was unnatural – a dull fluorescence from various sources around the peculiarly-shaped, metallic-looking room. He could actually feel the droning now, or humming, or buzzing, or whatever it was, and he guessed that the shadowy, unshaven, perpendicular figure was the source of those dangling, disjointed words.

'Y'OK, man?'

Lee was confused. In the blink of an eye, the queen-sized bed in his Oklahoma home had metamorphosed into a padded slab in an opened capsule fixed to the centre of what resembled the inside of a giant discarded beer can. Seeing the rough-hewn, weather-worn physiognomy of a man aged around forty eyeballing him from no more than a foot away made him clench his buttocks, which sent a sharp pain shooting in all directions from his tailbone.

'What's up, man? Y'OK?' the stranger asked again, his look of consternation drifting eerily upwards, along with the rest of him.

'Where am I?' Lee asked, half expecting to reopen his already open eyes and see Mina leaning over him, stroking his forehead and nuzzling his cheek to ease him gently into another Sunday morning.

'Yo' two days out from Mars, that's where yo' are.'

The constant humming and the pain in Lee's lower back as he lay on the slab in the middle of the artificially lit aluminium can were not conducive to any kind of coherent response to the news, 'Yo' two days out from Mars.'

The stranger continued, 'Yo' need to pull yo' leads out, get yo' coccyx clamp off an' get yo' muscles workin' again.'

Coccyx clamp?

Troubled by the lack of response to his words of motivation, the stranger proceeded to remove the leads and tubes that were taped onto and inserted into Lee's forearms, chest and neck. A red droplet oozed out of the pin-sized hole in his arm, turned spherical and hovered above the vein.

'Yo' gonna have to take the clamp off yo'self an' get that catheter out. Let's get these straps undone.'

The stranger unclipped a buckle, splitting in two a strap that Lee hadn't been aware of running across his chest and disappearing under his armpits. A peculiar sensation prompted Lee to grab at the surface beneath him, but his palm slapped the slab and caused his upper body to rise, while the strap that was still securing his thighs held his lower half in place. He gasped as if falling.

'Ah'll just loosen this one a bit so yo' can turn,' the stranger said, and proceeded to do so.

Lee, coming to terms with his unexpected weightlessness, found a handrail to cling to, which enabled him to turn onto his side. The green gown draped around him was open at the back, so he was able to feel around for the clamp. A prominent button released it easily and provided Lee with some relief from the pressure, but as he probed around the back and front he found that there were other insertions to be removed. He guessed that these must be drainage tubes for waste disposal. He eased the rear one out gently with a squelch before turning his attention to the urinary catheter, which required considerable tugging before it worked its way free as globules floated out of his tear ducts.

'That's it. Yo' can sit up now,' the stranger told him while unbuckling the leg strap.

Lee had no intention of sitting. He may have been unencumbered now, but his posterior region was still very sore. Then, realising that he wasn't going to be putting any weight on the sensitive area, he swung his legs round with far more momentum than necessary in a zero-gravity environment.

'No, no, no, man! Yo' been in cryo for seven months. Yo' can't control yo' legs yet. Ah came out yesterday an' ah only been swingin' them around safely since this mownin'.'

'Cryo? What? Seven months?'

'Yo' know where yo' are, don't yo'?'

'You said two days out from Mars. What does that

mean?'

'It means that the day after tomorrow we kiss this bucket goodbye – with yo' help and the help o' the others, 's long as none o' them's havin' trouble gettin' their brains in gear like yo' are.'

'What others?' Lee asked, pushing down on the bench with his knuckles, and then pawing awkwardly at the lid of his capsule to pull himself back down again.

'The rest o' the crew, man! Amira an' Teak. Amira's in the recovery tube – 's where yo' 'n' Teak are gonna be takin' turns spendin' the rest o' the day, buildin' up yo' muscles.'

'Teak?'

'Teak's over there. He ain't come out yet.'

'And what's your name?' Lee asked, trying with minimal success to get his floating feet to respond to various commands from his brain.

'Yo' forgotten that, too?' the stranger asked, eyebrows raised. 'Cade. Leroy Cade. That mean anythin' to yo'?'

'I've never seen you before in my life – and I don't know the name Cade.'

'That's a worry, man. An' ah suppose yo' ain't never heard o' the Santa María, an' don't know how to assemble her cargo own that red rock up there?' Cade gestured towards what Lee thought must be the front of the vessel, although there was no window that he could see any 'rock' through.

'I don't know about any of this,' Lee mumbled, craning his neck upwards to track Cade, who had rotated sideways above him. 'It's a dream, right? Doctor Reinhardt's got me under, hasn't she?'

'Ah dunno what yo' sayin', Marshall. Maybe yo'

just need mo' time to come round. We need to get yo' into the recovery tube. C'mown, get own this chair. Gimme yo' hand.'

With that, Lee allowed Cade, now upside-down, to ease him into the seat of a plastic cubic frame, about four feet across, which seemed to be somehow attached to the floor. Affixed to each of the cube's eight vertices was a rubber ball, the size of a tennis ball, presumably to cushion the occupant against impact from any angle, whichever way up.

Bundled into positon, Lee winced as Cade buckled and tightened the waist strap, pressing Lee's bruised backside mercilessly onto the ribbed surface of the seat.

Lee pondered for a moment. 'Marshall.'

'What?'

'You called me Marshall.'

'So what?'

'I'm not Marshall.'

'We all been callin' yo' Marshall for the last two years.'

'Not me. My name's Chan. Lee Chan.'

'Yo' don't look like no Chan to me.'

Lee shook his head before explaining, 'You've got the wrong person.'

'Where's yo' suit?' Cade asked, allowing a hint of impatience to creep into his voice. 'There. I'll get it.'

He tugged at some wall fittings and launched himself three or four feet towards the head of Lee's pod. Lee watched curiously as Cade pulled out a neatly folded bluish garment, which he shook out in slow motion to reveal a one-piece suit similar to the one that Cade himself was wearing. With a kick to the side, he drifted back, deliberately colliding with the cubic frame, which he used to help himself turn. Once stabilised, he pressed both thumbs into the back of the suit directly behind the identification tag, which he aimed at Lee's face. He read the name aloud: 'Zachary Marshall.'

'And presumably,' Lee cut in with an air of invincibility, 'That's a photo of Zachary Marshall.'

'Correct.'

'Well, then, where is he?' Lee asked.

'It's yo', man!' Cade fired back.

'That's not me.'

'Yo' need a mirror? We got a mirror!' And with that Cade tugged on the plastic frame, detaching it from the floor to which it had seemingly been magnetised, and towed it and its reluctant passenger towards a small, bare section of reflective wall panel, which both Cade and the cube clattered into. The rubber balls on the corners were indeed a good idea. Cade reoriented himself and lined up the frame so that its occupant could see his reflection in the aluminium. To Lee's dismay, he saw eyes that matched those in the photo. Marshall's eyes. The rest of the face was unrecognisable behind the coir-like beard and overgrown hair – hair which should have been short, black and straight, but which was long, brown and haphazard.

He ran his hand over his face, watching as the reflection did the same. Unconvinced, he pulled the hair floating around his right ear forward, so that he could see directly in front of his eye that it was indeed brown.

'Ah'll leave yo' two to get acquainted some,' Cade sighed, on seeing his crewmate's stunned reaction; and with that he propelled himself out of view.

For the man in front of the mirror, the evidence was stacking up. He didn't appear to be who he thought he was, and the ID tag confirmed that he wasn't. He was Zachary Marshall. It would seem to any independent observer that he'd dreamt that he was Lee Chan at home in Oklahoma, Earth, playing with his two children, while all the time he had been aboard a ship called the Santa María, approaching Mars.

He, Lee, Zach, was still unsure. Was he in reality on a psychiatrist's couch being hypnotised, dreaming first of home and then of this? He remembered, or remembered a dream about a Doctor Reinhardt, who was trying to help him recover the missing fragments of a life which, according to her, had been broken up and strewn around his mind as a result of trauma. So was all of this around him, including Cade, a product of that hypnosis? Or had he, as Cade had claimed, been in cryogenic suspension for seven months, during which he'd dreamt up an elaborate, if incomplete, alternative existence, while all the memories of his actual life as an interplanetary traveller were being erased in the process? Was everything that he was now experiencing in his mind a side-effect of long-term induced sleep – in space?

The answers were not to be found anywhere in Zachary Marshall's reflection. It would take a while to unravel these strands of confusion. For the moment, the facts attested to the existence of four people on board a vessel approaching Mars and due to touch down on the red planet the day after tomorrow. The undeniable discomfort that he'd experienced on having his leads and tubes removed, the sickly feeling of weightlessness in his internal organs, and an overwhelming hunger all supported this. The wiry image frowning back at him from the aluminium, combined with the name under that same face on the ID tag, and Cade's so far credible account of their mission were sufficient to persuade him for the time being that he might indeed be Zachary Marshall – astronaut.

Zach spent the next two days adapting to zero gravity, grappling with the muscle-building apparatus in the recovery tube, developing a taste for unfamiliar food and getting to know Leroy, Amira and Teak. The support that they offered when not engaged in landing preparations enabled him to take the first steps towards accepting his newly found, or rediscovered, reality.

A series of revelations ensued – the most disconcerting being that this was the first crewed mission to Mars, and there was to be no return trip. Teak told him that tons of hardware and organic matter had been transported in advance, but this was to be the first landing of humankind on another planet. Other settlers would soon follow, but so much depended on a successful first touchdown to get the base's systems up and running and continue the work started by the robots and rovers that had already been deployed.

Leroy and Amira, it turned out, were a couple. That made sense, since this was a one-way voyage and the purpose was to establish a new colony. What didn't make sense to Zach was Amira's remark that only couples were being selected as colonists – not only for reproduction, but for emotional support. That being the case, he wondered why he and Teak had been chosen among a crew of three men and one woman. In view of the curious way that Teak had been looking at him since their reunion, and his often measured and hesitant manner when speaking to him, Zach thought it wise to postpone any further questions on the subject for the time being.

Of his other discoveries, the most worrying was that that he himself was a doctor – a medical practitioner with no medical skills or knowledge whatsoever. He also learned, or relearned, that Teak was a botanist, Amira was a geologist and Leroy was an engineer. All four of them were trained in piloting the lander manually, should the need arise, although Teak and Amira would be at the controls during the descent.

Strapped into the landing module on the final countdown before launching into the Martian atmosphere, Zach's thoughts were predominantly of the family and life that he still sensed he'd lost. If he closed his eyes, he could picture Mina, Leah and Kane as clearly as he could Leroy, Amira and Teak. The images were fresh and vivid – not at all like the dissipating wisps of a dream.

The incompleteness, though, of his 'memories' of a previous life persuaded him that these were the effects of cryosleep, rather than this alternative existence, with its multitude of sensations right here and now, being the product of hypnotherapy occurring concurrently on another plane of consciousness.

The other three, despite their expressions of support, clearly regarded him as a dead weight as far as the mission was concerned. In the forty hours or so since their reunion at the end of their seven-month voyage, it had become apparent that the mental capacity of a quarter of their crew had been jettisoned.

Zach had no recollection of signing up for this, nor of the rigorous assessment and training process which would have resulted in his selection as a crew member on the first mission to Mars, of which he also had no knowledge until the day before yesterday. The crew knew that his survival, and theirs, too, would depend on his ability to adapt to circumstances and an environment for which he was no longer prepared.

'5 – 4 – 3 – 2 – 1 – module disengaged,' Teak reported as the landing module jolted on separation.

The first stage of the approach to Mars seemed timeless, although Teak provided periodic updates and data for the benefit of those who were able to understand them. For Zach, though, seated directly behind Teak and to the left of Leroy, and having no role to play in the guidance of their vessel towards the surface, this was a time for reflection.

The sight of Mars's transformation from a not-so-distant orb into an encroaching land mass fast filling every portal was spectacular beyond imagination. As the features of its terrain became more prominent, the temperature climbed and the ride became bumpier. Zach gasped to keep his breathing in line with his accelerating heart rate, and fought to fend off the rapidly increasing internal and external images besieging his brain. His eyes witnessed the growth of rust-coloured, mountainous ridges and valleys, while his mind overlaid these with the faces of Mina, Leah and Kane. Panic and doubt compelled him once again to question the reality of his situation, but only left him floundering in a flood of perspiration. Had there really been some kind of malfunction or medical crisis during his cryogenic sleep that had caused him to remember nothing but what he'd dreamt from that point on? Or were the remnants of that 'dream' the fragments of a real life that another fragment, namely Doctor Reinhardt, was trying to reassemble?

Teak's now rapid-fire commentary struggled to keep pace with the constantly changing data. His words were swallowed up by the turbulence, their significance lost in the gravity of their plight as the small craft spun in an alarmingly steep trajectory towards a range of mountains.

With control of the lander in the hands of fate, a sudden backwards jolt confirmed the deployment of the first parachute. Hopes of a successful landing were boosted as the craft stopped spinning and instead began spiralling. The angle of descent had changed, too. They were no longer hurtling towards mountains. A rugged, but flatter terrain lay directly below. Zach could feel the gravity now. Mars was sucking them in, although still too fast and too steeply, with the single parachute straining to hold them aloft. Something was shouted about other parachutes having not yet deployed. Time was running out as Zach closed his eyes and resolved to keep them closed.

Another upwards jolt ... more buffeting ... swinging ... a side impact ... spinning ... another side impact ... tumbling ... Zach was almost pleading to hear the words, 'When I snap my fingers, you will wake up.'

Protandry

Zach opened his eyes to a darkness dotted with red, green and white lights, some of them flashing, some flickering, others constant – but they weren't the stars that he was expecting to see.

Wherever he was, and whatever had happened during landing, he was thankful that the life support systems were still working. The temperature was comfortable and he had no difficulty in breathing.

Without warning, the speckles expanded into a spectral blur and faded completely from view, giving way to a softly illuminated panoramic slide show depicting amorphous life forms drifting diagonally downwards from left to right. Zach found himself immersed in a pool of tranquillity until his ethereal idyll was contaminated by an infusion of shimmering shadows and vague vocalisations that seemed to exist on not quite the same plane as the floating amoebic matter.

Disoriented in the dark, Zach concentrated on whatever shapes and sounds he could fix his attention on. He theorised that the panoramic display might be internal rather than external – perhaps on the inside of his eyelids. If this was the case and his eyes were closed, he wasn't prepared to open them and risk revealing his conscious state to the sources of the incoherent vocal resonations until he had more information about them. Soon, he hoped, he'd be able to understand their words and learn more – assuming that their language was his language – but for now their codes were indecipherable.

Attempting to orient himself psychologically, as well as physically, Zach recalled his previous prolonged period of consciousness, shuddering as he relived the intense anxiety and extreme discomfort of shooting through the Martian atmosphere in an interplanetary ballistic pressure cooker. Although distressing, the clarity of the recollection signalled to him that his mind was functioning better than he'd initially thought.

Still unwilling to open his eyes, he turned his attention to his physical condition and whatever he could perceive of his immediate environment. From the evenly applied pressure behind his head and down his back, he deduced that there was gravity, and that he was supine with his head raised slightly. His skin felt comfortable – not hot, not cold, not bruised, not itching. He could tell that he was lightly covered from the neck down, with his arms under cover at his sides. He rubbed the thumb and fingers of his left hand together, hoping that the movement would not be obvious from the outside. Repeating the exercise on the other side confirmed that there was a slight numbness in the digits of both hands. Taking a chance, he licked his lips. They were dry. He tried to moisten them while listening for any disruption to the voice patterns which would indicate that their sources had become aware of his movements, but he was unable to produce enough saliva, so he ground his teeth together gently, generating a reassuring vibration inside his head.

The external discussion continued. The sounds were mobile – at least two, maybe three feminine voices. One of them must have been Amira – the only female member of the crew. She could only be talking to Leroy or Teak. Yet the more intently that Zach listened, the more he was sure that both, if not all three voices, were female.

He tried to wiggle his toes and rub them together, as he had done with his fingers and thumbs, but there was no sensation. The pressure behind his head and down his back was perceptible only as far as his waist. He tried to flex his buttock muscles, but his brain received no acknowledgement of any such instruction. Perspiration prickled his brow. To find out more, he knew that he had to open his eyes.

Allowing light to filter through his eyelashes, Zach looked down to see a dual mound that was consistent in shape and location with the presence of two feet. At the same time, he was aware of two figures in the room, one on each side of him. His relief at seeing the twin humps quickly gave way to silent alarm as, no longer intent on feigning unconsciousness, he tried unsuccessfully to move his feet. Not only was there no feeling, there was no movement.

Keeping his head still, he rolled his eyes to the left to observe a young woman standing side-on to him beside a desk, studying the screen of a hand-held electronic device. He was captivated by her elegantly sculpted charcoal hair, which accentuated her smoothly carved mahogany profile, and was struck by the contrasting clinical functionality of the light blue uniform.

Rotating his eyeballs to the right, he strained his lateral rectus muscles to focus on the worried, pale complexion of a grey-haired woman seated close to the bed, apparently occupied with something lower down, beyond his field of vision.

Neither of them was Amira.

A shaft of sunlight streaking through the half-open Venetian blinds had already begun encroaching upon Zach's cheek and was now beginning to illuminate his nose. From this he ascertained that evening was approaching. As his eyelids flickered, the woman to his right sprang to her feet with a gasp.

'Mama!'

The younger woman, presumably Mama, dashed towards him.

The grey-haired woman exclaimed, 'She's awake!'

She? Zach realised now that their words were no longer incomprehensible, even if his interpretation of them was somewhat askew. The younger woman busied herself on the left side of the bed, juggling with leads, devices and receptacles, while the other arched over him from the right.

'How are you feeling?' the younger one enquired with a look of concern.

Zach inhaled with the intention of replying, but he didn't have an answer, so he just let his breath go. How was he feeling? Confused, and terribly thirsty. He didn't know these women. He couldn't identify the room. He had no idea how he came to be there, or why he couldn't feel his legs.

'You've been asleep for a very long time, dear,' the older woman said in a calmer tone as she began stroking the hair on top of Zach's head while gazing earnestly into his eyes. 'You were very lucky to survive all those years ago. We're so thankful that you're still here ... and awake now.'

Zach couldn't imagine where 'here' was. The only way to find out would be to ask. He took a long, slow breath.

'Where ...?' He cut the question short with a splutter on hearing a voice that seemed not to be his own. Had he sustained damage to his throat during landing? Or had his hearing been impaired?

'Where?' the older woman picked up the question. 'You're in the hospital, dear.'

Zach said nothing, but stared into the space between the two women.

'Do you remember anything about the accident, Mama?'

Mama? Wasn't that what she called the other woman? Why was she looking at him if she was talking to her? Why should she ask her if she remembered anything about the accident? And why did Mama appear not to acknowledge that she was being spoken to?

With no reply to her question, the older woman resumed, 'Is she all right, nurse?'

Puzzled, Zach became increasingly agitated and began shaking his head from side to side. He wanted to get up and walk out, but his arms didn't have the strength to raise his upper body from the bed, and he felt as though he didn't have any legs at all. Frustrated, he let out an anguished cry.

'She'll have to be sedated, I'm afraid,' were the last words that Zach was able to make out before he felt the inside of his left arm go cold. He watched as the shapes and colours of the room rippled disconcertingly and swirled around him, mixing with an echoing vortex that sucked him from one realm of consciousness into the next.

It appeared to be night time. The blinds were closed and the lights were on. The older woman was still sitting in the chair at his bedside, only now she was wearing a pink top. She'd already noticed that he was awake.

'Hello, again,' she said, rising to perch on the edge of the bed. After pausing for a moment, she leaned towards him, 'I thought we'd lost you again, but it seems you just needed a few more days' sleep,' she smiled. 'So how are you feeling today?'

'I don't know,' Zach replied before he'd even contemplated answering. The horror that distorted his face made the woman pull back. The voice was still wrong.

'It's OK, Mama. You just need time to get used to things as they are now. We'll all help you, but you mustn't get excited like last time, or I'll have to call the nurse and she'll have to sedate you again.

Mama. Wasn't that the name of the nurse? Zach didn't want to be sedated again. He was confused enough. He wanted to understand what had happened to him and find out about his voice and his legs ... and the rest of the crew. He had to stay calm, no matter what.

'Do you remember anything, dear?'

Zach braced himself to hear the alien sounds coming out of his mouth again.

'I remember ...'

'What do you remember? Do you remember the accident?'

'Yes ... I remember.' Zach hesitated. The quavering tone was more feminine than masculine. He was reluctant to hear more, but he had to maintain his self-control if he was to find out what he needed to know.

'Go on, dear.'

'I remember leaving the Santa María.'

'Was that a bar?'

'What?'

'A restaurant?'

'No, a space ship.'

The woman gazed down at him, nibbling the inside of her lower lip, carefully considering her next question.

'And what did you do when you left the Santa María?' she resumed.

'We took off in the landing module and headed for Mars.'

The woman's lips parted and twitched.

'So it wasn't a car? You don't remember getting into a car?'

Zach scowled. 'No, not a car!'

'And the others?' the woman pressed.

'What about the others?' Zach frowned, as much at the sound of his voice as at the line of questioning.

'Do you remember them? ... Do you remember who was with you?'

'Of course: Leroy, Amira and Teak.'

The woman pressed her lips together, and then sighed. 'Don't you mean Mostyn, Tamara and Blair?'

Zach didn't know how to respond. Why would she come up with three completely different names?

'Mostyn was driving, wasn't he?' she went on. 'Tell me what you remember, Mama? Tell me what happened.'

It was clear to Zach that this woman, whoever she was, had been misinformed on all fronts, including as to his identity. Feeling obliged to provide her with an accurate account, he proceeded to describe the events leading up to what he could now only assume was a crash landing.

'Amira and Teak were at the controls, but the lander was on autopilot. We went down fast. It was extremely bumpy.' He paused, still troubled by his voice. 'Then we started spinning, and it became unbearably hot. I don't think all of the parachutes worked properly. We must have crashed into the mountains, but I don't remember that.'

'Oh, my dear, you've been dreaming! After all this time, that's how you remember it! Yes, you did crash, but that's not exactly how it happened, is it? It's been so long that you've got it all muddled up with a dream.'

Zach's eyes narrowed. 'I don't understand.' He pulled his left hand out from under the covers to massage his temples with his thumb and middle finger. Then he stretched his arm out in front of him and looked at the back of his hand. It was withered and speckled – an old woman's hand. Was he hallucinating?

'Let me tell you what we know,' the woman continued. 'We know that Mostyn was driving, and Tamara was sitting beside him, and you and Blair were in the back. We just don't know why Mostyn lost control and how you came to be thrown clear just in time.' She broke off, choking back her next words, before resuming. 'If the top had been up and your belt had been done up … Something must have happened in the car, because we know from Mostyn's blood tests that he wasn't under the influence of anything, and the investigators found no mechanical faults. It's been a mystery all these years. We hoped that one day you'd be able to tell us more.'

'Where are the others?'

The woman paused, pursing her lips. 'Of course, you don't know yet, do you, dear? I'm so sorry, Mama. You were the only survivor.'

'My legs …'

'You were found beside a tree.' She paused for a moment's reflection. 'Perhaps I should get a nurse, Mama.'

Mama? Why did she keep calling him that? She

was not at all familiar to him, yet she was talking as though she knew him.

'Who are you?' he asked.

The woman was taken aback by his question.

'Don't you recognise me, Mama? It's me, your little girl, Celine – all grown up.'

Zach stared incredulously as she continued.

'I have three grown-up children of my own now – and one of them has a little boy.' Then with a hint of pride she announced, 'You're a great-grandmother, Mama.'

Zach examined his hand again and snapped, 'I need a mirror!'

Tears welled up in Celine's eyes. Without acknowledging the request, she replied, 'I'll be right back.' Then, pressing her fingers over her mouth, she headed for the door.

Zach was left to contemplate the possibility that the Mars mission was nothing more than a dream that was the product of a coma that was the result of a critical injury in a car accident that must have happened decades ago – in which case, the Santa María's landing module was a transfiguration of the convertible, while Leroy, Amira and Teak were ghosts of the car's other three occupants.

The door opened. A woman in a white coat led the way – not the nurse he'd previously known as Mama, but a more robust, authoritative figure – followed by Celine. Holding what appeared to be a hand mirror with the glass towards her, the woman in white approached the left side of the bed, while Celine took up her customary position on the right.

'How are you feeling today, Emily?' she asked, without introducing herself.

Emily? So that was his ... her name. Zach ... Emily ... didn't respond.

'Emily, you've been asleep for a very long time. Your daughter has just told me that you didn't recognise her. Of course you didn't. She was very much younger when you saw her last.' The sleeves of the white coat crossed, as if in expectation of some kind of reaction, which wasn't forthcoming. 'You're older, too, Emily. I want you to understand that ... before I give you the mirror. When you see yourself, you'll look very different. You need to be prepared for that. I'll only hand you the mirror when I'm sure you're ready.

Zach ... Emily ... needed the final confirmation that only the reflection would provide, ready or not.

'Please let me see.'

The woman in white complied, hesitantly passing the mirror face down to the expectant recipient.

As the object turned very slowly, the first visible reflection was of the legs of the desk across the room, followed by the bottom of the window and some charts or posters. Rising and rotating unsteadily, the mirror centred momentarily on a transparent bag of clear fluid with a tube hanging out of the bottom. A slight twist brought the edge of a pillow into view, with a shoulder resting on it. Straggly strands of grey did little to conceal a wrinkled ear, while a rivulet ran down a shrivelled cheek and vanished into the pillow. A bloodshot eye enfolded in furrowed flesh revealed itself to be the source of the rivulet as the mirror continued panning to expose the horrified face of an elderly woman.

It was undeniable. Zach, the young space pioneer, was a character in a dream that had seemed to span only two days. She was Emily, an old woman who had been disabled decades ago in a car accident and had inexplicably, and regrettably, emerged from a coma.

The rivers flowed freely as Emily began sobbing. Her cries turned into convulsions as she threw the mirror to the floor, screaming and flailing her skeletal arms.

'It was too soon, Celine. I'm sorry. She wasn't ready. I'll have to sedate her.'

As the woman in white busied herself, Celine looked on helplessly.

Emily felt the inside of her left arm turn cold. She watched the pink and white figures ripple disconcertingly, swirl around her and mix with an echoing vortex that licked its lips audibly before sucking the consciousness out of her.

Zaglyptus

Emily spat out a mouthful of dirt, thinking that she must be somewhere between sleep and another spell of tedium in her hospital cell. Resisting the force that was dragging her like a dead weight from her slumber, she resolved to keep her eyes closed, not yet prepared to be confronted by whoever was at her bedside on this particular occasion, whatever time of day it was.

She pressed her tongue against her palate. It felt gritty. The probing muscle explored around her gums from top to bottom and along both sides. Tiny particles crunched between her teeth. She turned her head to one side before spitting again, to ensure that the saliva-sodden shower didn't rain back down on her face – not that the previous spray had. But as she did, instead of feeling the right side of her face cosseted by a cotton-covered pillow, her nose and left cheek scraped against a sharp, stony surface that stung her with the realisation that she was lying face down.

She must have fallen out of bed – but onto what?

Half awake, but determined to cling to the dissipating remnants of a sleep in which all of this was surely a dream, she tried turning her head again to find a more comfortable position. This time, instead of nestling into a cushion of foam, her forehead grated across the same jagged surface. She stopped halfway, nose pressed to the ground. Her face was sore, the back of her head felt bruised, and she was cold. The harshness and stark reality of the environment made it impossible for her to claw her way back to the realm of subconscious comfort that she had been so cruelly expelled from. Yet, shouldn't this be the other way round – an unpleasant dream giving way to the relief of waking? She cleared her throat, swilled what little saliva she could muster around her front teeth, and spat again.

Emily's attempts to shut reality out by keeping her eyes closed were futile. Her other senses had already ushered it in. Raising her head and blinking in the half-light to focus on whatever was immediately below her face, she strained to make out the features of a partially exposed patch of rock sprinkled with dust, splattered with fresh spittle and dotted with damp red clots. Turning her head to the left, while taking care this time not to graze her right cheek, she surveyed the darkened recesses of her stony enclosure, and listened.

Her ears picked up sounds other than those of her own respiration – background sounds that she hadn't been aware of until now. They certainly weren't the voices that she would otherwise have expected to hear on waking, but scuffling, slurping and squelching, coming from behind her to the right. Perhaps whatever was making the noises had just arrived – and was advancing. She'd have to look back the other way to see who or what it was. But did she want to? Was it safe to look? Was there any alternative if she wanted to find a way out of this?

Emily forced her palms down and pushed upwards, turning her head cautiously from left to right as her arms straightened. A speck of dust blew into her right eye, inducing a gasp. Both her eyes began watering in the cold air as she rolled her eyeballs in an effort to dislodge the foreign body. Fortunately, her tears had the desired effect. She squinted to squeeze the excess fluid out along with the dust, and then blinked rapidly to bring her blurred surroundings into focus.

What she saw ten or fifteen yards away, clearly defined against the contrasting background light, simply could not be. She inhaled and exhaled sharply, cutting short a throaty growl. This must be a dream, she thought – a dreadful nightmare.

At first, Emily spotted only one of the enormous insects, the only one that was moving. It was at least as big as she was – probably much bigger. It was hard to judge the creature's relative size from her perspective. The giant insect – if that was what it was – seemed preoccupied with something that it was scuffing around and nuzzling, while randomly waving its antennae.

Uncomfortable maintaining the push-up position while straining to look back over her shoulder, it occurred to Emily that such exertion should have been impossible for an old woman with frail arms and muscles wasted from decades of disuse. She glanced down to see two disproportionally large hands with stubby fingers and thumbs supporting her at the ends of what appeared to be a pair of amply filled sleeves. Slowly bending her left elbow to the ground while twisting her torso, she stifled a groan on feeling immense outward pressure inside her abdomen. She tried to sit up, but her swollen middle prevented her from bending sufficiently at the waist. It felt like a severe case of constipation, but looked more like the latter stages of pregnancy – at her age!

As she settled into a semi-reclined position, propped up on one elbow, she noticed that her backside was in a puddle, and that the jeans that she'd never have imagined herself wearing were saturated from the waist to the knees. Out of curiosity, she ran her inflated fingers through the fluid. It was sticky, like honey.

Looking up, she tried again to make sense of the shadowy lump lying motionless in front of the mutant insect, which thankfully didn't seem interested in her at all. Her eyes widened as she realised that it was another six-legged freak of nature. As the first one continued nudging the second, which failed to respond in any way, she assumed that the one on the ground was dead. But what were they?

She could do nothing but watch as the Brobdingnagian bug danced triumphantly around its prey – or perhaps its mate – and she noticed the flickering of a pair of wings that hadn't been obvious up to now. A wasp, she thought. On closer inspection she discovered that the other one also had wings, although these were skewed at an awkward angle, confirming her suspicion that it was dead.

If this was a dream, Emily thought, now would be a good time to wake up. Was it a dream, though? Everything that she could see and feel was so real: her grazed face, the bruise at the back of her head, the dirt in her mouth, the cold wind in her eyes, the abnormal bloating, and those two monstrosities. On the other hand, if she wasn't dreaming, how did she get there?

It was time to make a move. As long as the wasp was distracted, she might be able to turn and drag her paraplegic body out of the cave and find help, or at least refuge, before any others of the species turn up. Of course, if this was a dream, she might be able to get up and run out – but that wisp of hope vanished instantly as Emily established that there was no more feeling in her lower body than there had been in the hospital bed. There was just a sickening sensation as far down her back as she could feel. She'd just have to do the best she could using her arms and the muscles of her upper torso, which surprisingly seemed as though they might be up to the task.

Emily decided that now was as good a time as any. As she braced herself to roll over and press her palms down on the ground again, she heard a different kind of scuffling coming from outside. Was it already too late? Could it be another wasp? Or a swarm of them? Or a spider!

Petrified, she stared at the cave entrance, scanning the periphery of the opening for whatever was approaching. A clattering of rocks signalled its arrival as an unidentifiable part of its anatomy appeared low down on the right. It was small – not unlike a human hand. After a slight pause, a white object popped up, resembling a helmeted head. Then an arm swung a climbing axe over as a semi-silhouetted figure hauled itself up and scrambled sideways onto the ledge, where it lay prone for a while, presumably surveying the interior of the cave.

Surprised, but relieved to see another human being, Emily revealed her presence with a gentle 'Psst!'

'Keep down!' was the muted reply. It was a woman's voice. 'I'll come to you.'

Satisfied that her appearance hadn't attracted any unwanted attention, the new arrival set out to cross the twenty yards or so between her and Emily on her elbows and knees.

Meanwhile, the wasp continued nudging and nuzzling the carcass, as if unaware that it had company.

As her would-be saviour reached halfway and emerged from her silhouette, Emily was able to make out a smooth, pale complexion and red hair, which was tied back beneath the helmet into a short ponytail that dangled beside her neck as she edged closer on all fours. Her left ear was bloodied.

'It's a zaglyptus!' the young woman whispered.

That meant nothing to Emily.

'It must have killed the iseropus.'

Unable to make any use of the information, Emily looked on blankly, gave a little shrug and turned her thoughts to how the two of them were going to escape undetected. Plan A had been to roll over and crawl to the mouth of the cave on her bloated belly, but that was as far as her thinking had taken her. Now, miraculously, an ally had appeared, but it wouldn't be easy for them to get out of there together. Emily's legs were useless and her body felt incredibly heavy. She couldn't be carried, so she'd have to be dragged somehow. She reasoned that the most effective strategy would be to use her arms to assist her rescuer in some way. To do that, she'd have to be face down, and the woman would have to carry or drag Emily's legs, either pulling her from the front, or pushing her from behind.

Emily's image of herself as a human wheelbarrow was shattered by a clattering of metal on rock. The woman, now only five or six yards away, had picked up something that must have been lying near a discarded backpack that Emily had been only vaguely aware of until now. The metallic object, resembling a ray gun from a science fiction movie, had slipped from the woman's grasp, and her vain attempt to catch it had only compounded the calamity.

Emily wasn't the only one that had been startled. The two of them looked across to see that the wasp was no longer attending to its victim. It had turned and was facing them, seemingly observing them with a compound glint its eye. The young woman crouched, forehead to the ground, motionless. Emily held her breath, hoping that they were inconspicuous enough and the flailing antennae weren't picking up any signals. After a minute that seemed like an eternity, the beast's wings whirred and it twirled back towards its prey.

With no time to lose, Emily rolled over face down, exposing the tread of her boots to the woman who had wasted no time in resuming her approach. Emily listened as the crunching of stones under elbows and knees drew closer, until she heard the voice of the woman immediately behind her.

'C'mon, Dayne, let's get you outta here!'

EAT THY NEIGHBOUR

'Jazlyn, you seem troubled. Would you like to talk about it?'

'I dunno, Head Chef.'

'Are you having second thoughts about being a kitchenmate?'

'I dunno.'

'Something's bothering you, Jazlyn, I can tell ... Is it Damien?'

'Sort of.'

'Would you like to share your concerns?'

'I guess I'm findin' it a bit hard ... harder than I thought it'd be.'

'Harder than it was in weeks one and two?'

'Week one was a buzz. It was fun comin' into the kitchen with the studio audience cheerin', an' knowin' that millions were watchin' live ... an' it was great meetin' all the other kitchenmates. The first week was all about us gettin' to know each other, an' as a group we got on really well.'

'And how did you feel in week two?'

'Week two was OK. I didn't really know Sinnita as well as the others, an' anyway we were all so excited about the first one an' all the plannin' an' everythin' that we didn't really give her much thought – at least I didn't. She was there for a week an' then she was gone.'

'So what's changed?'

'I didn't know how much harder it'd get each week as you get to know everyone in person. It's not like watchin' it on TV. I swear I'm gonna scream on Saturday night when I hear the announcer say, "Which kitchenmate will we marinate?" I used to think it was funny hearin' it every week when I watched the show at home, but now I'm a kitchenmate myself an' have helped in the actual processin', the thought of hearin' that again makes me wanna puke ... an' now I'm dreadin' the week when it might be me.'

'So what made you apply to be a kitchenmate, Jazlyn?'

'Same as everyone else, I s'pose. We all like food, an' I like to try different things.'

'How did you feel about the first season?'

'I loved watchin' it last year! We all did. A lot o' people thought it was a bit sick, but it was just a different kind o' reality TV.'

'You obviously didn't agree with the public outcry, or you wouldn't be here.'

'No way. All the kitchenmates went on the show knowin' what they were doin'. No-one was forced to do it. It's not like there was any crime being committed, an' it's only on 18+ pay TV an' streamin', so no harm's bein' done.'

'And the chance of winning free meals for two in any participating restaurant in the world for life.'

'Yeah, that'd be cool!'

'A one in ten chance, but a risk worth taking?'

'Sure. All that fame an' fortune ... an' free food for ever. When you look at where we've all come from, it's not like there's much to lose anyway.'

'But now you seem to have reservations. Tell me what's changed so much between the end of week one and the middle of week three?'

'Gettin' to know the people who were nominated

for the award ... an' bein' part o' the processin'.'

'Getting to know Damien, you mean.

'I guess.'

'But you enjoyed the food preparation in week two: the creative methods of cooking and presentation; planning the week's menu; the exotic flavours and newly discovered textures; and the camaraderie, Jazlyn ... the thrill of nominating for the weekly award.'

'I didn't know Sinnita that well. I hardly talked to her.'

'But we all saw how you got to know Damien.'

'Sure, everyone's gettin' to know everyone now.'

'You said it yourself, Jazlyn, no crime's being committed. Everyone's here of their own free will, and you all know what the odds are, and so did Damien and Sinnita.'

'All the same ... seein' 'em hangin' upside-down like that ... then havin' to stun 'em ... an' the screamin'.'

'It's all over very quickly, though, as you saw live on TV last year and have seen twice up close this year.'

'Damien seemed to take ages.'

'The processing meets the minimum standards for the USA and Europe.'

'All the same, I ain't never heard screamin' like it ... not even poppin' dogs.'

'You pop dogs?'

'Only the little ones ... There's too many of 'em anyhow.'

'But Damien's processing wouldn't have been a problem for you if you hadn't seen it, or if you'd detached yourself emotionally. He would have gone the way he did, regardless of whether you were there or knew how he ended up. It only seems to be bothering you now because you've seen in person how it's done, and because you'd formed an attachment with the following week's main ingredient.'

'So it's my fault I'm feelin' like this?'

'Well, the only difference between week one and week three is your perspective. We can all choose to switch our feelings on or off for any person, situation or issue we like. All your life up to now your feelings have probably been switched off regarding this kind of processing, but now you've switched them on for your fellow kitchenmates. You probably have feelings for your dog, too. You do have a dog, don't you?'

'Yeah.'

'But you pop dogs.'

'I only pop dogs that I don't know.'

'That's my point exactly, Jazlyn. You select your attitude towards the brutal treatment of any creature depending on how you'd like to feel. It's all about you. You'd feel bad about popping a dog that you know, or about witnessing the processing of a kitchenmate that you like, or any other mammal, bird or fish, but because you don't like to feel uncomfortable you decide that you'd rather not think about it than share in any collective responsibility for their wellbeing. You simply flick the switch in your mind that shields you from reality and prevents you from feeling bad. Meanwhile, the processing in the real world continues, regardless of whether you choose to care about it or not.'

'Yeah, but when you buy meat already packaged at the supermarket, or from the butcher's trays, you don't think about how it got there or what the animals went through … 'cause you didn't see 'em or get to know 'em. You wouldn't eat your dog, 'cause you know it.'

'So is it only bad if you know the animal … or the person?'

'It makes it worse.'

'It makes it worse for whom?'

'It's just worse.'

'It makes no difference to the kitchenmate chosen to be on the following week's menu. He or she – or you – will be processed in exactly the same way in week nine as in week two, according to strictly applied industry standards designed to ensure that the stunning is effective and the first cut is as incisive as possible, with two or three cuts at the most.'

'If it goes right.'

'Let me show you a couple of video clips from the first two weeks' awards announcements to illustrate my point. Here's the first one ... take a look.'

'Must we?'

'Bear with me, Jazlyn ... Now, this is all of you gathered together on the Saturday before last for the announcement of the first week's award. I'm sure you wouldn't have given any thought at the time to what the cameras were focusing on, but this is what everyone at home saw. As you said, no-one really had time to get to know Sinnita or form an attachment – except maybe Amy. Look at how the cameras pick up each of your individual reactions. First there's an all-round cheer as everyone but Sinnita discovers that they've made it for at least one more week ... then there's a close-up of Sinnita, who's smiling ... but look at the desolation in her eyes. Then watch as the camera pans. All the other kitchenmates are either smiling, cheering or clapping, except Amy. She's frowning and wiping tears away ... and now Sinnita's started crying ... and now they're hugging each other ... and look at you ... fists pumping, jumping up and down, whooping at the top of your voice.'

'So?'

'So now I'll show you a clip of you the next evening, enjoying Sinnita's calf ...'

'You don't need to show me that.'

'I'd like you to see it anyway ... Here it is ... There you are in the middle, next to Damien.'

'I didn't know I'd get to watch any of this.'

'See how you're enjoying that?'

'Everybody enjoyed it – even Amy.'

'Listen to what you said.'

'This is the best roast ever! It's a shame that Sinnita's missin' out on this ... Imagine goin' first an' not even gettin' a finger!'

'And here's a bit more, just after Damien makes a comment about whoever gets the award next being able to go happy having "pigged out on Sinnita" all week ... Here it is ... Listen.'

'Yeah, but I won't be satisfied unless I'm the one that spends the next nine weeks feastin' on all o' you, and then gets free meals for life!'

'What are you getting' at, Head Chef?'

'That'll become clear after we've watched the next clip, recorded six days later.'

'What, you're gonna show me Damien gettin' the award?'

'You guessed it.'

'I don't need to watch that.'

'I think you do, Jazlyn, because you'll see something you probably weren't aware of at the time ... Here we go ... Look, everyone's standing in a circle this time, holding hands. You're squeezing Damien's hand, as you'll no doubt remember ... and there's the announcement ... Look at Damien's reaction ... Well, you saw his face, of course ... Utter disbelief ... and now he looks very angry. I'll go back a bit and pause it ... there, close-up.'

'He wanted to go all the way. It was too soon for him.'

'You obviously weren't expecting it either, judging by your expression – but he did say that whoever went second could go happy. Presumably that included him, and maybe deep down he actually did go happy, even though he didn't make the processing easy for the rest of you.'

'I was sure either Taj or Stephanie would get the vote. They weren't involved in hardly anythin' in week two, keepin' themselves mostly to themselves. No-one likes Stephanie ... The things she was sayin' about Sinnita last week! ... "No good alive or dead," she said ... She sure tucked in, though ... Bitch!'

'Let's just go back a little so we can have a look at Amy.'

'Why?'

'There ... No, not there ... Back just a little more ... Now look ... What's she doing?'

'She's clappin' and cheerin'.'

'Why do you think that is, Jazlyn, when she was so upset the week before?'

'Prob'ly 'cause she liked Sinnita and didn't care about Damien.'

'Or she just hadn't got to know Damien.'

'So you think she'd have been upset if she knew Damien better?'

'What do you think, Jazlyn?'

'I think you think I need to flick the switch off?'
'Here's one more clip – dinner time the next day.'
'No more! ... Come on! Why are you doin' this?'
'Just watch, Jazlyn ... Watch everyone in general, then look at the close-up of you eating vegetables.'
'Yes, I know I haven't had any of Damien. I just couldn't.'
'And you didn't contribute anything to the processing. Even Amy helped out with Sinnita's processing, although she found it difficult.'
'I wasn't plannin' to have any of Damien, so I didn't want anythin' to do with any of his processin'. It was bad enough just bein' there watchin' – an' that was only 'cause Damien said he wanted me there.'
'So how do you feel about taking part in next week's processing – assuming that you're not the third award winner yourself? After all, by not helping out with Damien's processing and not participating in any of this week's games, you've put yourself in the position that you rightly said Taj and Stephanie were in last week. Most of the kitchenmates expected them and Amy to be nominated last week, but no-one expected Damien to be nominated, let alone get the vote. It's no surprise to anyone that you're on the list this week, along with Taj and Stephanie, and I don't think anyone will be surprised if you're this week's recipient.'
'Amy got over it. I'll get over it.'
'I'm sure you will, Jazlyn. You're just feeling a little down because you've experienced first-hand some of the more confronting aspects of being a kitchenmate, and your emotions have come as a shock. Most kitchenmates go through that at some stage.'
'So what can I do about it, Head Chef? I know I

need to get involved in tomorrow's challenge, but I don't know what I can do about the way I'm feelin' right now.'

'Why don't we focus on some of the positives? As you've said yourself, Jazlyn, fame and fortune, all those flavours, and so much fun! ... Tell me, what was the highlight of season one for you?'

'I'm not sure.'

'Which of the weekly challenges did you think was the most fun?'

'Um ... the taxidermy challenge, I guess.'

'See, that got you smiling, just thinking about it. Why did you enjoy that one in particular?'

'Because o' how the four of 'em just couldn't agree on what Ruskin's face was s'posed to look like.'

'They had to do it from memory, of course.'

'Yeah, an' their memories weren't that good. The nose was puffy an' the lips were out o' shape, the glass eyes didn't look in the same direction, an' one kept fallin' out, an' the skin was all wrinkly an' stained.'

'In their defence, the instructions in the do-it-yourself taxidermy kit weren't particularly easy for novices to follow – even though the kitchenmates didn't have to start from scratch with a new mould, since they had the skull. They only had to preserve the skin, stretch it over the skull, touch up the face, stick the hair back on and mount the head on a plaque.'

'An' they made a right pig's ear o' the whole thing!'

'The main problem was with the chemicals discolouring Ruskin's face, and the wrinkling, of course, and the sagging – but the head looked quite realistic as far as the hair and beard were concerned.'

'Yeah, at least it looked like a head.'

'And once it was mounted on a plaque it was a nice memento for the organisers to present to Ruskin's fiancée after the show's finale. At least it was some consolation for missing out on her share of free meals for life.'

'I wonder if she keeps it on her bedroom wall.'

'I can't think why she wouldn't.'

'Will we have a taxidermy challenge this year?'

'Would you like that, Jazlyn?'

'I'd love to have a go at stuffin' Stephanie's head!'

'You see, you're feeling more positive already. I'm afraid I can't reveal what other kitchen games and challenges are lined up this year, but I can assure you that there's plenty to look forward to.'

'I also liked the sacrifice thing last year.'

'Ah, the sacrificial rites in week six. There was a lot of positive feedback from the viewers after that. It gave the processing a novel angle.'

'The kitchenmates really got into it.'

'It was one of their favourite challenges. It took considerable imagination and creativity for each of them to make an item of ceremonial jewellery and a musical instrument out of the by-products left over from weeks two to five.'

'The jewellery was cool.'

'Yes, necklaces made of teeth and strung together with finely sliced intestines ...'

'Not only teeth – finger an' toe bones, too.'

'Rings carved from cross sections of hollowed-out leg bones.'

'Bangles made from plaited hair.'

'Painted patella brooches.'

'An' those earrings that Cassidy made out o' bits o'

backbone. I dunno what she strung 'em together with.'

'And Ryan's pelvic headdress decorated with finger and toenails that had already been painted.'

'That was the coolest!'

'And some of the musical instruments were ingenious: the humerus flutes, the pelvis and rib cage drumkit played with tibia sticks, the spinophone with the fibula mallets ...'

'The scapula castanets.'

'And the phalanx-filled skull maracas.'

'An' they actually sounded pretty good. The kitchenmates really got into the sacrificial ceremony thing. It was like some genuine pagan ritual, like they really believed they were offerin' up a sacrifice to the gods.'

'So you don't have a problem with making new products out of the remains of bodies that have been used for meat?'

'Nah, there's no sense in lettin' stuff go to waste.'

'So what if, one week, we didn't use the flesh and just made something out of the skeleton?'

'Like Bryony last year, you mean?'

'Exactly. Everyone worked exceptionally well together as a team to make that lovely coat stand out of Bryony's skeleton – something nice for Bryony's family to remember her by.'

'But that was after the Bryony barbecue.'

'So how would you have felt if they'd had enough leftovers from the previous weeks for the barbecue and didn't use Bryony for that?'

'What, just threw it away?'

'If it wasn't needed.'

'So just use Bryony for parts for makin' stuff out of?'

'Like the coat stand, or anything else.'

'That sure was a beautiful coat stand.'

'If a kitchenmate has already agreed ... it's just another kind of consumption, which we do anyway. After all, we humans make all sorts of things out of animals that we haven't necessarily eaten first, don't we?'

'I s'pose.'

'So, apart from making costume jewellery and musical instruments out of discarded body parts, imagine what else the kitchenmates could come up with.'

'I remember last year Marina used the leftover chemicals from the taxidermy challenge to make a drawstring purse from the skin of Malik's buttocks.'

'So she did ... and there's a whole world of other useful items that could be made.'

'Like what?'

'Well, we know that ancient civilisations used to make tools out of bones.'

'Yeah, gardenin' tools ... like shoulder blades for diggin', maybe.'

'You've got it ... and kitchen utensils, too.

'An' what about making a bowl out o' the top of a skull?'

'Sure! Why not? Or something ornamental ... a work of art.'

'You could stretch a face out flat, then paint it an' put it in a frame.'

'I suppose you could. Not many would have thought of that.'

'Sinnita had lovely hair. You could weave it into a doyly.'

'You see, Jazlyn, you're absolutely bursting with creativity!'

'I dunno if it's right, though, Head Chef, wastin' a

body just on makin' stuff if you don't need it for food.'

'It's what we humans do, though. Poachers rob elephants of their tusks because traders are able to convince potential buyers that ivory ornaments are highly desirable and worth exorbitant asking prices. We do the same with rhinos because of the widespread belief that the horns have healing or aphrodisiac qualities. And then there's the prestige and admiration that are all but guaranteed when sporting a crocodile-skin handbag or a pearl necklace.'

'An' fur.'

'Yes, and there are many individuals who thrive on the glory of posing for photos with dead animals, or preserving and mounting the bodies or heads of their kills as trophies to ensure that their friends know how skilful and courageous they are – and also to make themselves more attractive to the right kind of sexual partner.'

'You mean someone who likes a tumble on a leopard-skin rug.'

'Exactly, Jazlyn. Whatever the use, as long as there's plenty of demand, the money will keep rolling in.'

'An' we couldn't go without leather clothes.'

'Of course not. So you can see that there's plenty of justification for using any number of any creatures we like to make anything out of, for whatever reason suits us, even if there's no use for the flesh.'

'Yeah, prob'ly ... but that wasn't what we signed up for. We agreed that when our time's up we'll be the main ingredient on the menus for the next week, an' we're OK with the leftover bits bein' used, rather than just throwin' 'em away, but I don't know about us just bein' used for ornaments an' tools an' musical instruments. That's not the point of bein' a kitchenmate, is it? I mean, it's not about the kitchen then, is it?'

'It's still entertainment, though, Jazlyn, and if it attracts large audiences, sponsors will pay big money to advertise, and they'll offer generous prizes. Who do you think pays for the winner's meals for life? You see, the value of an individual life isn't really that important in commercial terms when it comes to satisfying the majority's desire for luxury items and entertainment.'

'I know what you're sayin', Head Chef, but to be honest, I don't think humans should be used just to make things out of, like animals are. If we start doin' that, where will it all lead to? We'll go back to treatin' people like they did thousands of years ago, like gladiators an' slaves.'

'Many would argue that that wouldn't be a step backwards, but a natural progression, and that the human race has finally evolved to the point where it's ready to treat all species equally, so that there's no distinction between throwing humans into an arena and making them fight to the death, and putting spurs on cockerels, or spiked collars on dogs, and encouraging the public to gamble on which one's going to rip the other to shreds first.'

'But that's barbaric. We don't do that any more.'

'We certainly do, Jazlyn, and much more besides. Countless animals are captured or bred to be enslaved and are only kept alive for human pleasure and amusement for as long as they continue to be useful.'

'Useful for what?'

'Well, take mammals for example. Consider the lives of circus elephants, dancing bears, fighting bulls, racehorses and orangutan sex slaves, to name just a few. While many would argue that the treatment of humans in the same way as other species would be a regression to the barbaric practices of the past, the consensus in the corridors of power is that inclusivity is progress. More and more advanced societies are beginning to acknowledge that a life is a life, of equal value whatever the species – and it's that belief that justifies the exploitation of humans in exactly the same way as the exploitation of any other creature.'

'I don't know nothin' about dancin' orangutans or any o' that other stuff ... 'cep' circus elephants ... an' bull fightin' I s'pose ... but people fight bulls an' work in circuses already, so they already have the same rights as the animals.'

'But they're not treated equally, Jazlyn. Circus performers are provided with cages and whips, and matadors have swords and spears. Humans will never achieve true equality until they're granted the right to compete or perform on an equal footing with the rest of the animal kingdom.'

'The humans would get torn to pieces.'

'The price of equality, Jazlyn. Progressive entrepreneurs would argue that if sufficient demand can be generated for the kinds of entertainment we provide here, and if the public is willing to buy tickets or subscribe, or gamble high stakes on the outcomes, and if sponsors offer huge prize money, and bookmakers give generous odds, and all with government support in return for a lucrative source of tax revenue, then surely the practice is justified – just as what we do in the kitchen is justified. You must agree with that, Jazlyn, or you wouldn't be here.'

'Yeah, but I'm sayin' that it's OK for entertainment

as long as it's for food as well – but not if it's just for arts and crafts or sport.'

'But, Jazlyn, it's justified all the more in sport and the arts, because this is a novel development of an old trend, and one that nobody this century has experienced before. People have a voracious appetite for anything new, and are always willing to pay. Of course, there'll always be stuck-in-the-mud minorities who'll say that this or that is unethical and immoral, but in the end it all comes down to how much profit can be made. Lives are less important than profit to magnates and oligarchs. That's the way it's always been, and that's the way it always will be.'

'It's all wrong, though.'

'What's wrong exactly?'

'Well, I think that whatever happens to animals an' people is OK as long as people agree to it – 'cause they at least know what's goin' on – an' only if it's for feedin' people an' pets or zoo animals first, an' then it's OK usin' the leftovers for whatever, like what we've been doin' ... but not changin' the rules now we've all signed up.'

'Jazlyn, listen to me. Humans have always generated wealth and power by exploiting other creatures, including weaker humans – and not just for food. Admittedly, in the last few hundred years the trend has been away from expending human life for sport and entertainment, but what we're doing in this centre of culinary excellence is a clear reflection of the recent reversal in that trend and a shift towards species equality.'

'But how can you say that all creatures should be treated equally, includin' humans? ... So a human should be treated the same as a crab?'

'Not necessarily tied up and thrown into a pot of boiling water – although that's not so very different to what we do here on Sunday mornings when you think about it.'

'All right, so are you sayin' then that we should have people sittin' on the backs of other people, racin' 'em round in circles an' whippin' em' till they have a heart attack or break an arm or a leg?'

'My question for you, Jazlyn, is how can anyone justify placing different values on different lives?'

'What do you mean?'

'Well, you mentioned people sitting on the backs of other people and racing them around and whipping them, so let's compare the treatment of humans and horses as an example. Thousands of years ago ... even two or three hundred years ago, it was widely considered acceptable to whip both human and equine slaves. Most populations today would be outraged at the thought of enslaving or whipping a human, but horses continue to be whipped, whether for sport, entertainment or labour. There's a growing school of thought which argues that if there are any mammals with no legal protection from physical abuse, then no mammals should be exempt from mistreatment.'

'What's sauce for the horse, is sauce for the brander.'

'That's a very good culinary analogy, Jazlyn!'

'Pff.'

'But the discussion isn't just limited to mammals, is it?'

'It ain't?'

'Certainly not. Would you agree that most people would marvel at the beauty of a butterfly, but wouldn't hesitate to stamp contemptuously on a cockroach?'

'Yeah, I s'pose.'
'Why would that be?'
'One's pretty and one's ugly.'
'Says who?'
'Prob'ly everyone.'
'Everyone? ... Humans, you mean.'
'Yeah ... wouldn't they?'

'So because a cockroach is ugly to a human it deserves to die. But would a cockroach think another cockroach was ugly?'

'Nah, a cockroach would think another cockroach was sexy.'

'So do you think a cockroach would think another cockroach deserves to die because of the way it looks?'

'Prob'ly not.'

'What about a sweet little mouse and a dirty fat rat? Stroke the adorable mouse and keep it as a pet, and poison the filthy rat?'

'I would.'

'Why? Because one's small and looks cute and the other isn't and doesn't?'

'Yeah.'

'In your opinion, Jazlyn.'

'Yeah, in my opinion an' most other people's.'

'But would a rat think that a mouse was sweet? And would a mouse think that a rat was dirty?'

'They prob'ly wouldn't give each other much thought.'

'No, they'd most likely be going about their business, like every other creature on the planet, including us, striving to survive and reproduce, and feed and protect their young. Like all of us, their own lives and the survival of their species would be their number one priority.'

'Anyway, I don't s'pose they have opinions like we do.'

'So is it our opinions that give us the right to judge the value of other creatures?'

'How do you mean?'

'Most humans tend to adore cats and dogs, and pet owners love and care for them as companions. You have a dog yourself, yet you pop little dogs. Isn't that you making your own decision about what different dogs are worth?'

'I s'pose so.'

'Based on their size and how well you know them?'

'I guess.'

'Would you pop a human baby?'

'That's disgustin'!'

'You're right, Jazlyn, it is disgusting – to a human. What I'm getting at is that humans generally value human lives more highly than they value the lives of other species. Would you agree?'

'Sure.'

'Not only that, humans tend to rank other species according to human values, such as intelligence – but intelligence that's based on human criteria for assessing intelligence, including how that kind of intelligence might meet human needs.'

'Like guide dogs an' guard dogs, you mean.'

'Yes, good examples! And the less intelligent a creature is, according to human criteria for measuring intelligence, the less it's assumed that it will suffer from pain, emotional trauma or deprivation of liberty. Do you follow?'

'I s'pose so.'

'That self-imposed belief conveniently clears the

conscience of all those whose primary consideration is the commercial value of whatever species they're exploiting – like we talked about earlier.'

'Like you talked about earlier.'

'The point is, Jazlyn, the relative importance of other species is judged by how closely they're related to us biologically, or how similar or different their nervous systems are, and whether or not they're more or less susceptible to physical suffering – but based solely on comparisons with human anatomy and the human concept of suffering. We're brought up to believe that the intelligence of cattle, sheep, pigs and chickens, for example, is so inferior to human intelligence, and their needs are so dissimilar to ours, that they're incapable of grieving for the loss of their young in the way that we do; and because they know nothing of freedom, they're less affected by what we'd call deprivation of liberty; and because their nervous systems are different to ours, they're less susceptible to the crushing, slashing and shocking sensations of grinders, blades and wires.'

'Well, lots of animals don't feel pain like we do.'

'Exactly, Jazlyn! You just hit the nail on the head: "like we do" – judgement based on human criteria.'

'It's prob'ly 'cause we actually are superior. That's what we've always been taught, ain't it?'

'But what we're not taught, Jazlyn, is what gives us the right to establish a hierarchy for the entire animal kingdom and assign values in the first place – and not only for non-humans. Subjugation and exploitation of people and populations for the purposes of accumulating wealth and exerting power have been prevalent throughout history to justify invasion, colonisation, marginalisation, segregation, slavery, and genocide, with the imposition of a hierarchy of entitlement to rights based on ethnic, religious, social or biological factors. Examples abound: the Nazis' mass destruction of Jews; Pol Pot's extermination of educated Cambodians; Qin's persecution of Chinese scholars; ancient Rome's maltreatment of Christians; apartheid in South Africa; European colonial slavery and the destruction of indigenous populations; disregard for the welfare of particular ethnic groups by certain law enforcement officers in the US; and contempt worldwide for those whose sexuality doesn't conform to traditional norms or scriptures. The modern world has striven with mixed success to eliminate human inequality and heal the festering wounds of prejudice. Now, at last, we have a progressive movement that is advocating for equality between species – and our kitchen is a part of that revolution, Jazlyn.'

'I don't know about all o' that, Head Chef. I'm really only in it for the free meals.'

'You must see, though, that while we've been led to believe that humans are superior, we're only superior in ways that matter to humans. The truth is that we're just different – and at long last the world's more evolved societies are beginning to recognise the injustice of maintaining this obsolete hierarchy of rights based on the valuation of species according to human criteria.'

'And ...'

'And another of those criteria is how many of them there are – increasing or decreasing the value of a creature's life depending on whether its species is abundant or endangered. Can you imagine a starling thinking that its life is worth less than a white rhino's because of how many other starlings there are and how few white rhinos there are?'

'As if a starling would even think about that!'

'Not in the same way as humans, naturally, but its life and the lives of its offspring would be more important to it than the life of any other creature on Earth, regardless of any human valuation of starlings based on how they look, how many of them there are, how useful they can be to us, or how much money can be earned from them. There's no denying that every species values its own kind above any other. As Darwin demonstrated, the priority of every living being is the survival of the species. In order to achieve that, it must first ensure its own survival, so that it can reproduce and then nourish and protect its progeny. Few humans would consider the life of one creature to be equal in value to the life of a different creature – least of all that one human life to a human is equal to one rat life to a rat, and one cockroach life to a cockroach ... the value of each of those lives being what, Jazlyn?'

'One?'

'Exactly. It's a matter of perspective, you see, and every creature has its own perspective, but the number of lives it has is the same as any other – and the value is always one.'

'It sort o' makes sense when you put it like that.'

'Of course it does! So why aren't there millions of female humans designated as breeding stock and locked in cages from infancy until they're mature enough to be impregnated by the few males spared from the cleaver? Why shouldn't those women then spend the rest of their fertile lives in a cycle of childbirth, milk provision and hair production? And why shouldn't a selection of their male offspring be removed prematurely for the consumption of their succulent flesh, while the remaining boys are farmed in close confinement with hundreds or thousands of others for the later production of less tender but higher protein morsels, while a tiny proportion are earmarked for breeding and kept alive for as long as they're fit for the purpose?'

'Meanin' what exactly?'

'Meaning other creatures shouldn't be entitled exclusively to treatment that has been denied to humans for so long.'

'So that's why we have all these rights in the kitchen.'

'Precisely ... By the way, Jazlyn, do you know where pearls come from?'

'From oysters ... What's that got to do with anythin'?'

'Yes, from oysters, but do you know how the pearls are produced?'

'Don't they just catch the oysters in fishin' nets an' take the pearls out?'

'Not exactly.'

'How, then?'

'When young oysters are old enough, a fragment of shell is surgically implanted into their reproductive organs. They're then strung up in a submerged net with thousands of other oysters for two to five years. Their internal organs react to the irritant by secreting a substance called nacre, which builds up layer upon layer around the foreign body. When the farmers determine the time is right, the pearls that meet the highest standards are cut out of the surviving oysters, and the oysters that don't make the grade are simply discarded – wasted after spending their lives hung up in a net.'

'That sounds cruel!'

'Not at all, or so the oyster farmers would have you believe. Oysters don't have human intelligence, and they don't have a nervous system like ours, so they can't possibly experience pain or suffering or deprivation of liberty like we do. It's not as if the survivors of the scalpel are left screaming in agony, feeling trapped with no respite from intensifying pain as a lump grows inside them for two to five years.'

'You can't know they don't feel anythin' just 'cause they're not like us.'

'The point is, Jazlyn, our show's producer doesn't believe that humans should be denied the same rights and privileges enjoyed by the rest of the animal kingdom, such as the opportunity to grow a precious spherical object inside your reproductive organs. She's come up with the idea of trying to create a thing of beauty inside a human by inserting a fragment of tooth into an ovary or a testicle. The results wouldn't be evident during the course of a twelve-week season, so whoever volunteers would almost certainly be guaranteed an appearance in the following season. It's an exciting prospect, with free food for the entire forty weeks between seasons, but the participant would have to agree to be strapped to a wall and streamed live for the duration. Would you be interested in something like that Jazlyn?'

'Nah, don't fancy it ... Prob'ly wouldn't survive anyhow ... Prob'ly won't even survive this.'

'Which brings me to the reason why I've summoned you here this morning for our little ... tête-à-tête.'

'What's that?'

'I've been authorised to put two propositions to you, Jazlyn.'

'Oh?'

'You've just rejected the first, so I must caution you that my second offer will be the last.'

'What? ... That was an offer? ... What kind of an offer was that? ... Having teeth implanted in my ovaries?'

'Before I go any further, I want you to consider your position. As one of this week's three nominees, you're in a precarious situation, and no doubt you understand that your immediate future is teetering on the whims of the viewing public.'

'A one in three chance.'

'It's a one in three chance if you believe that not participating in kitchen activities for the last four days is what our followers want to see; or if you can think of any reason why the viewing millions would vote for Stephanie or Taj rather than someone who appears to have dropped out. After all, the viewers didn't vote for them last week.'

'I'm feelin' much better after our chat, Head Chef, an' I'm ready go out there an' get stuck in again, an' give tomorrow's challenge everythin' I've got, whatever it is.'

'Will you also help with this evening's meal preparations? It's toad in the hole.'

'I'll have to.'

'That means making sausages.'

'I'm OK with that.'

'And will you be willing to sample everything on the menu – not just the vegetables?'

'I dunno ... I s'pose so ... I could have a big hole with a little toad inside ... As long as I have some, that'd be participatin', wouldn't it? ... Surely that'd be OK ... 's long as the cameras don't zoom in too much ... an' even if they do, I'll have plenty of sauce on it, so it doesn't look obvious ... an' I'll smile, like I'm enjoyin' it.'

'That's positive thinking, Jazlyn. Dressing the meal up to disguise the ingredients is exactly how the food industry operates – skilfully presenting and marketing dishes in such a way as to distract the consumer from the reality of what they're eating. The meals look and taste so good that whatever happened to the primary product is irrelevant.'

'Flick that switch, like you said.'

'The trouble is, Jazlyn, while that pretence might help you personally through the next few days, it's unlikely to win over a voting public who'll have already formed an impression based on your attitude since Saturday's announcement. Besides that, the audience will continue to be influenced by your fellow kitchenmates, who feel that the odds are very much stacked against you, judging by some of their comments.'

'What've they been sayin'?'

'They've only been stating the obvious – what we've all seen and what the viewers will base their votes on three days from now. If you're this week's award winner, not only will you go no further, but whoever you were going to share your free meals with for life will no longer have that chance.'

'You said you had another offer.'

'Who would you be most likely to share your free meals with, if you should be the eventual winner? You don't have a partner at the moment, do you?'

'My little sister.'

'What's your sister's name?'
'Dazlyn.'
'Dazlyn. And how old is Dazlyn?'
'Ten.'
'And who's looking after Dazlyn at the moment?'
'My friend, Siân.'
'Can your friend afford to look after Dazlyn indefinitely?'
'Prob'ly not.'
'So how would it be if you receive the award and Dazlyn ends up with nothing?'
'That was always the deal anyway, an' Siân knew that.'
'Here's what I propose, Jazlyn. You agree that, if you're this weekend's award winner, Sunday's processing will be postponed until Thursday, so that you can be the living centrepiece of three days of games. In return, Dazlyn will receive free meals for one at any participating restaurant in the world for life, or meals for two at half price.'
'What's everyone gonna eat for four days if I'm not processed till Thursday?'
'There's enough in the freezer to enable us to reschedule – even more since you haven't been partaking this week.'
'So, what games exactly?'
'You know the games are always a surprise.'
'But I'll be the centrepiece, you say ... an' alive.'
'That's the deal, Jazlyn. Consider the options. If you decline the offer and you're this week's award winner, all Dazlyn will get will be whatever souvenir the rest of the kitchenmates come up with next Friday, depending on what the challenge is. It's sure to be quite special if Stephanie's at her creative best, but

you have an opportunity now to do something wonderful for your little sister.'

'You're not gonna put me in with a bull or a lion, are you?'

'You know I can't reveal anything about the week's games in advance.'

'I dunno, Head Chef. Can I have some time to think about it?'

'You can have two minutes, Jazlyn, after which the offer will be withdrawn. Your thinking time starts now.'

CREDIT WHERE CREDIT'S DUE

'Cat! You know better than to just start eating!'
'Sorry, Dog.'
'You're always sorry, yet never sorry. Nonetheless, for what we are about to receive may we be, first and foremost, truly grateful to early human civilisations for the invention of the wheel, which has enabled subsequent generations to devise increasingly efficient means of transportation, without which we would not have the meal that has been placed before us today. May we also be thankful to Denis Papin, Nikolaus Otto and Rudolf Diesel, among others, for their ingenuity in developing their respective engines, which have made it possible for humans to transport larger quantities of dog and cat food more quickly than if they had to push it in carts or have it pulled by horses or oxen. And let us not forget the endeavours of Richard Trevithick and George Stephenson, who introduced the concept of rail travel to further expedite the passage of our provisions.'
'Don't forget Sir Frank.'
'Have I ever forgotten Sir Frank? Would you like to say a few words about Sir Frank yourself?'
'No, thanks, Dog. You express everything so much more eloquently than I do.'
'Merely naming the great man seems sufficient. His contribution to modern air travel and the transportation of dog and cat food sales representatives at unprecedented speeds hardly needs further mention.'
'It's a pity that some of the others don't need further

mention.'

'What's that, Cat?'

'Uh, nothing, Dog, only don't you think it's ironic that, while so much has been done during the course of history to expedite the delivery of our meals, once they're served we're compelled to reflect for such an awfully long time on those achievements before actually eating?'

'Nevertheless, Cat, it would be inappropriate to start without once again acknowledging the talents of Nicholas Appert and Peter Durand, who deserve full credit for beginning the process that has culminated in our being able to enjoy, without fear of contamination, the flavour, albeit not as if fresh, of many of our meals which are preserved in cans. Just think of all those poor humans in bygone times who, on happening upon a recently-deceased animal, had to either cool it, dry it, smoke it, salt it, eat it or sell it straight away for immediate consumption. These days, carved-up carrion can be safely preserved by one method or another until a human or a preferred member of a preferred variety of one of their preferred species is ready to eat it.'

'Now that's something to be really thankful for – being a preferred member of a preferred variety of one of their preferred species. I'm glad I'm not a rat.'

'If you were a rat, not only would you probably not be fed, I doubt that you'd even be refrigerated.'

'Not even valued as victuals, except maybe to feed lower-ranked species less preferred by humans, such as snakes.'

'And there's another point not to be overlooked, Cat – refrigeration. William Cullen! What a legend! How often do you hear that name uttered in the gutters at night? Let's give special thanks today to all of those pioneers of refrigeration: Cullen, Oliver Evans, Jacob Perkins, John Gorrie, James Harrison, Thaddeus Lowe …'

'Fair point, Dog. Imagine the inconvenience endured by humans throughout history before refrigeration – having to stalk an ageing creature for an unpredictable length of time while waiting for it to die of natural causes; or relying on the good fortune to be in the right place at the very moment when a passing animal died of some unfortunate circumstance so that it could be eaten fresh straight away. And how much would have been shared with their cats and dogs? Life would be so inconvenient without refrigeration. It doesn't bear thinking about, does it, Dog? A hearty thanks from me to all the creators of the fridge.'

'Heroes, indeed. And allied to food preservation – and no, Cat, I see you're about to interject, but let's not downplay the significance of this – we must express our gratitude to all those humans who pioneered the use of the camera obscura, and those who later perfected photography. Without the contributions of Joseph Nicéphore Niépce – a personal hero of mine, as you know – and the great Louis Daguerre, humans would have no way of knowing what was in the tins that are delivered to them. Thanks to Niépce and Daguerre, we can all see pictures of what is inside. Humans can confidently choose between potato salad, apricots or tuna for themselves, while easily deciding on what breed of dog or cat to feed us. If it were not for such human ingenuity, we might be eating asparagus spears or mushrooms right now.'

'I'm not eating anything right now, in case you hadn't noticed, Dog; although I'd very much like to.'

'Plastic, too. Mind-blowing stuff! Yes, you may well stare in incredulity with those excessively expressive feline eyes that turn humans to putty in your paws. Imagine eating off the ground, like cows do. And how bare would your corner look without those two bowls?'

'And my tray.'

'Yes, the tray. Incidentally, I think that's such a peculiar thing that you do over there in the corner when you think no-one's looking.'

'So you keep saying, but it's not half as weird as what I've seen you doing in the garden. Bordering on disgusting, whatever it is.'

'Polymerising the monomer.'

'Is that what you call it?'

'What? No, it's the basis of plastic production. We've talked about that before.'

'I'm well aware of polymerisation, Dog. I watched the moving pictures of Karl Ziegler and Giulio Natta. They certainly received the recognition they deserved. Have we thanked them today?'

'No, we usually do that at breakfast time, but we overlooked them this morning.'

'It's good that we just happened to think of our bowls, then.'

'Not forgetting our milk and cream, either, Cat, let us pause to reflect upon the work of Louis Pasteur. Who but Pasteur would have thought of warming up and cooling down cows' milk to prevent cats from becoming sick from the bacteria?'

'And dogs, Dog.'

'You say that every time, but you don't personally know any dogs that drink cows' milk, do you?'

'Let's move on to the water, then.'

'Yes, of course. May we also be sincerely thankful to the farmers of ancient civilisations, who learned and passed on the knowledge of how to channel water from where it was not needed by humans to where they wanted it. And we are equally indebted to all of today's architects and plumbers for adapting those primitive techniques to meet the needs of the human race in the 21st century, thus enabling this humble bowl of transparent liquid to be obtained by our humans without their having to carry buckets to and from the river like their ancestors did for their dogs.'

'And cats.'

'Dams!'

'What?'

'I almost forgot the dams. Not only are they a simple but effective method of diverting vast supplies of water from those creatures and plants that don't need much water to those that do, but they are also an ingenious way of producing electricity. Where would you and I be without electricity? We'd be eating raw dogs, or charcoal-grilled cats – in the dark! So I would like to pay tribute to everyone from the ancient Egyptians to the innumerable designers and builders of dams that have followed.'

'I still think beavers deserve some credit for the invention of dams. You can't give all the credit to humans when they probably got the idea from watching beavers.'

'Well, in that case, we might as well give credit to the birds for the invention of the jet engine, rather than Sir Frank Whittle! Yes, let's thank the spoonbill for the prompt delivery of our tins of chopped chihuahua and mashed Manx!'

'Now you're being silly, Dog.'

'It's no sillier than thanking beavers – as if beavers designed and built hydro-electric dams!'

'I'm not suggesting that we should be thanking beavers for our meals. I just think that the fact that they built dams first shouldn't be ignored. We don't need to discuss it every day. I just wish you'd acknowledge it once.'

'All right. I acknowledge it. May I continue?'

'Did you hear that?'

'What?'

'My stomach.'

'Cat, we cannot eat without giving thanks for our good fortune. The sooner we finish giving thanks, the sooner we can eat.'

'OK. Carry on. But hurry up. If I flatten my fur, you can see my ribs. Look, whenever I breathe out.'

'Further, let us be thankful for alternative sources of electricity that are used to power the industrial and household machinery that produces and preserves our food. Edmond Becquerel be praised!'

'Watt!'

'What?'

'What about Watt?'

'What about what?'

'Watt.'

'What?'

'James Watt.'

'Nothing to do with electricity. He improved the steam engine.'

'You didn't mention him earlier.'

'He mostly took earlier ideas and developed them further. Still, you have a point. We owe him our gratitude for that. And as for our biscuit snacks …'

'Your biscuit snacks.'

'As for my biscuit snacks, we ... I should express my appreciation to the humans throughout history who developed farming methods that enabled the efficient cultivation of wheat and other crops and the eradication of pests and diseases that, if unchecked, would jeopardise production and surely lead to biscuit rationing. From the hand-held plough through to biotechnology, we have a great deal to be thankful for.'

'And finally ...'

'And finally, for what we are about to enjoy may we be truly grateful to the two nice gentlemen who prepare and serve our meals, snacks and drinks – not geniuses likely to transform our world as others have; just simple humans adept at obtaining and opening cans and cartons and knowing how to present the contents to us in a pleasing manner twice a day.'

'Ah, men!'

Printed in Great Britain
by Amazon